ASTEROID: DIVERSION

The Asteroid Series
Book Two

A novel by

Bobby Akart

Other Works by Amazon Top 50 Author, Bobby Akart

The Asteroid Series
Discovery

Diversion

Destruction

The Doomsday Series
Apocalypse

Haven

Anarchy

Minutemen

Civil War

The Yellowstone Series
Hellfire

Inferno

Fallout

Survival

The Lone Star Series
Axis of Evil

Beyond Borders

Lines in the Sand

Texas Strong

Fifth Column

Suicide Six

The Pandemic Series
Beginnings

The Innocents

Level 6

Quietus

The Blackout Series

36 Hours

Zero Hour

Turning Point

Shiloh Ranch

Hornet's Nest

Devil's Homecoming

The Boston Brahmin Series

The Loyal Nine

Cyber Attack

Martial Law

False Flag

The Mechanics

Choose Freedom

Patriot's Farewell

Seeds of Liberty (Companion Guide)

The Prepping for Tomorrow Series

Cyber Warfare

EMP: Electromagnetic Pulse

Economic Collapse

DEDICATIONS

For many years, I have lived by the following premise:

*Because you never know when the day before
is the day before, prepare for tomorrow.*

My friends, I study and write about the threats we face, not only to both entertain and inform you, but because I am constantly learning how to prepare for the benefit of my family as well. There is nothing more important on this planet than my darling wife, Dani, and our two girls, Bullie and Boom. One day the apocalypse will be upon us, and I'll be damned if I'm gonna let it stand in the way of our life together.

The Asteroid series is dedicated to the love and support of my family. I will always protect you from anything that threatens us.

Acknowledgements

Writing a book that is both informative and entertaining requires a tremendous team effort. Writing is the easy part. For their efforts in making the Asteroid series a reality, I would like to thank Hristo Argirov Kovatliev for his incredible cover art, Pauline Nolet for her editorial prowess, Stef Mcdaid for making this manuscript decipherable in so many formats, Chris Abernathy for his memorable performance in narrating this novel, and the Team—Denise, Joe, Jim, Shirley, and Kenda—whose advice, friendship and attention to detail is priceless.

You'll be introduced to two characters in this story who, through their generous donations to charities my family supports, won the right to have a character named after them. One is a gentleman named Sparky Newsome in Washington, Georgia who bid at a local Rotary Club auction. As it happened, Sparky is the editor and owner of the local newspaper, *The News-Reporter*. This changed the trajectory of my story's outline considerably, and for the better.

The use of Mr. Newsome in the Asteroid trilogy, led to incorporating Washington, Georgia as a location, which then led me to the Deerlick Astronomy Village in nearby Crawfordville. Founded by two astronomers in 2005, the DAV is considered one of the darkest locations in the Eastern United States by DarkSiteFinder.com.

Jackie Holcombe, who donated to a special program at Village Veterinary Medical Center in Farragut, Tennessee that supports people who can't afford extraordinary medical procedures for their pets, was also a named character in the series. She earned a prominent role in the story, alongside Mr. Newsome, as you will see. A huge thank you to both of them for their generosity and allowing me to include them in this series.

The research associated with this project surpassed that of the Yellowstone series. In fact, the premise for this story resulted from my conversations with the team of scientists at NASA's Jet Propulsion Laboratory at CalTech over a year ago.

As I dug into the science, once again, source material and research papers were heaped upon my shoulders. My email inbox was put into circuit overload as so many folks from around the globe contributed to my research. One thing is certain—astrophysicists are uniform in their desire to inform the public as to the threats we face from near-Earth objects, especially those that are recently discovered, or remain undiscovered.

There are so many people and organizations to thank, so let me name a few.

I was fortunate enough to be introduced to some brilliant members of our military at Wright-Patterson Air Force Base in Ohio. The USAF's Aeronautical Systems Division, the ASD, provided me invaluable insight into America's future fighting aircraft. They told me what are capabilities are today, and where they'd likely be ten years from now, and beyond. Literally, the sky's the limit for these folks. Don't be surprised that one day, we'll be flying fighter jets in space.

Also, a great source for the technical descriptions of the aircraft of our adversaries was provided by the US Naval Institute's Military Database in Arlington, Virginia. A big thank you to Melissa Cartwright for helping me navigate through a sea of information. Let me add, anyone who thinks we should be cutting our defense budget is short-sighted, or uninformed. The military capabilities of Russia and China will astound you.

As I've already mentioned, my research regarding the Yellowstone Caldera started with the work of Dr. Brian H. Wilcox, an aerospace engineer at the Jet Propulsion Laboratory in Pasadena, California. Although his proposition that our greatest threat to humankind may not necessarily come from above, in the form of a near-Earth object, but rather, from below, as an eruption from the Yellowstone Supervolcano, he has cautioned that it's the newly discovered asteroids that have the potential to be planet killers. Frankly, I don't know how Dr. Wilcox sleeps at night.

Lastly, I must make mention of the team at NASA's Planetary Defense Coordination Office. The PDCO employs a variety of ground and space-based telescopes to search for near-Earth objects, determines their orbits, and measures their physical characteristics in order to accurately assess the threat to our planet. Their functions including warning our government of the threats, suggesting mitigation techniques to alter the course of an incoming object, and acts to coordinate with multiple agencies as an emergency response is formulated. Thank you to Linda Billings and others in the Public Communications office at the PDCO; Patricia Talbert in the Professional Outreach department; and of course, Lindley Johnson, the Program Executive of the PDCO.

Without their efforts, this story could not be told.

Thank you all!

About the Author

Bobby Akart

Author Bobby Akart has been ranked by Amazon as #50 on the Amazon Charts list of most popular, bestselling authors. He has achieved recognition as the #1 bestselling Horror Author, #2 bestselling Science Fiction Author, #3 bestselling Religion & Spirituality Author, #6 bestselling Action & Adventure Author, #7 bestselling Historical Author and #10 bestselling Thriller Author.

He has written over thirty international bestsellers, in nearly fifty fiction and nonfiction genres, including the chart-busting Yellowstone series, the thought-provoking Doomsday series, the reader-favorite Lone Star series, the critically acclaimed Boston Brahmin series, the bestselling Blackout series, the frighteningly realistic Pandemic series, his highly cited nonfiction Prepping for Tomorrow series, and his latest project—the Asteroid series, a scientific thriller that will remind us all that life on Earth may have begun, and might well end, with something from space.

His novel *Yellowstone: Fallout* reached the Top 50 on the Amazon bestsellers list and earned him two Kindle All-Star awards for most pages read in a month and most pages read as an author. The Yellowstone series vaulted him to the #1 bestselling horror author on Amazon, and the #2 bestselling science fiction author.

Bobby has provided his readers a diverse range of topics that are both informative and entertaining. His attention to detail and impeccable research has allowed him to capture the imaginations of his readers through his fictional works and bring them valuable knowledge through his nonfiction books.

SIGN UP for Bobby Akart's mailing list to receive special offers, bonus content, and you'll be the first to receive news about new releases in the Asteroid series:

Visit Bobby Akart's website for informative blog entries on preparedness, writing, and a behind-the-scenes look into his novels.

BobbyAkart.com

VISIT Amazon.com/BobbyAkart, a dedicated feature page created by Amazon for his work, to view more information on his thriller fiction novels and post-apocalyptic book series, as well as his nonfiction Prepping for Tomorrow series.

AUTHOR'S INTRODUCTION TO THE ASTEROID SERIES

June 13, 2019
I want you to imagine how vast our solar system is …

For those of us stuck on Earth, we might gaze up into the night sky and marvel at the size of our solar system, but we'll never get the opportunity to get a closer look. We take for granted the Sun that brightens our day, or the mysterious Moon that appears at night. The trained eye can pick out constellations and even other planets, if one knows where to look.

But just how big is our solar system? Before you can appreciate its vastness, let's consider the units of measurement that give it a sense of scale. Distances are so large that measurements like feet and miles are irrelevant. Most distances are defined in astronomical units, or AUs. One AU, based upon the distance from the Earth to the Sun, is roughly equal to ninety-three-million-miles.

To put that into perspective, if you flew around our planet, you'd cover twenty-five thousand miles. If you traveled to the moon, you'd cover about ten times that, or two-hundred-forty-thousand-miles. To reach the sun, we're looking at almost forty times the distance to the moon. And finally, to reach the outer limits of our solar system, where the Oort Cloud is located, is over one-hundred-thousand AUs, or nearly two light years away.

Now, that's a lot of space, pardon the pun. It would take our fastest spacecraft thirty-seven thousand years to get there.

That said, however, space objects travel the vast openness of our solar system with regularity. Over many millions of years, these objects, both large and small, wander the solar system. Some remain within the gravitational orbit of larger bodies, or within the asteroid belt that exists between Mars and Jupiter.

Others, the wayward nomads who are looking for a larger object's gravity to become attached to, float aimlessly, and mostly harmlessly, through space for years and years and years. Until …

They collide with other objects.

Asteroids are typically material left over from the period of planetary formation four-and-a-half billion years ago. They're the remains of what didn't form into planets in the inner solar system, or often the result of collisions in the past.

They vary in size from only a few feet to the big daddy of them all—*Ceres*, which measures about one-fourth the size of our moon. At almost six-hundred-miles wide, Ceres is about the size of Texas.

This story focuses on the threats our planet faces from a collision with a near-Earth object, or NEO. If you consider an asteroid can be as small as a few feet across, there are an estimated five-hundred-million of them considered to be near-Earth—between us and the Sun. If you limit the number to potentially hazardous asteroids, those within four-and-a-half million miles, then the number is reduced to around twenty-thousand.

That's a lot of traffic in our neighborhood, and yet only ninety percent are accounted for. While NASA and other space agencies around the globe do an admirable job of identifying and tracking these NEOs, the fact of the matter is that they only have identified ninety percent of the threats. That leaves a one-in-ten-chance that an object remains undiscovered.

The big uncertainty is that we haven't discovered many near-Earth asteroids, so we don't know if they are on a collision course with Earth. Now, there is comfort in knowing that the vastness of space might make the odds in our favor that one of these wandering nomads doesn't hit us.

However, because of the size of our planet, and the gravity associated with Earth, asteroids can be pulled toward us. It's happened before, on many occasions.

NEO impact events have played a significant role in the evolution of our solar system since its formation. Major impact events have significantly shaped Earth's history, have been implicated in the formation of the Earth–Moon system, the evolutionary history of life, the origin of water on Earth and several mass extinctions. The famous prehistoric Chicxulub (cheek-sha-loob) impact, sixty-six million years ago, is believed to be the cause of the Cretaceous–Paleogene extinction event that resulted in the demise of the dinosaurs.

Could it happen again? Absolutely. When? Nobody knows. At present, there are only a few potentially close-shaves in our future, at least, that we know of. It's the ones that we haven't discovered that keep astrophysicists and amateur astronomers up at night, watching the skies.

Thank you for reading and I know you'll enjoy the Asteroid series, a Gunner Fox trilogy.

Real-World News Excerpts

The Asteroid Peril Isn't Science Fiction ~ *The Wall Street Journal, July 5, 2019*

International scientists assembled near Washington, D.C. to tackle an alarming problem—what to do about an asteroid hurtling toward Earth.

Astronomers at a mountaintop observatory in Hawaii had spotted 800-foot-wide asteroid, initially dubbed 2019 PDC ... smaller by comparison to the asteroid that wiped out the dinosaurs 65 million years ago.

Still, this asteroid, approaching at 31,000 miles an hour would have an impact upon the planet larger than any nuclear bomb detonated in history.

An asteroid hit Earth right after being spotted by telescope this week ~ *Eric Mack, C-Net, June 25, 2019*

What's most concerning about 2019 MO was the fact that it was spotted by telescopes just before impact. The impact was recorded at the equivalent explosive power of five-thousand-tons of TNT.

The same-day notice provided in the case of 2019 MO illustrates the weakness in preparing for a much bigger asteroid smacking into the Earth's atmosphere.

Massive asteroid to pass Earth with second closest approach in over 120 years ~ *Aristos Georgiou, Newsweek, June 18, 2019*

The space rock, known as 441987 (NY65), is estimated to measure nearly one-thousand feet in diameter according to NASA's Center for Near Earth Object Studies.

Because of its close proximity to Earth, it is classified as potentially hazardous. What makes this asteroid particularly interesting for study is that with each pass around the Sun, it grows increasingly closer to the Earth due to our planet's gravitational pull.

A space rock of this size would cause devastation across localized regions in the event of a land impact, or a tsunami that could badly damage low-lying areas if hit the ocean. In addition, the collision of NY65 would have wider-reaching effects and could result in global climactic changes that could last for years.

Such an impact would produce an explosive force containing 65,000 times more energy than the Hiroshima atomic bomb.

NASA estimates that two-thirds of NEOs larger than 460 feet remain to be discovered, so there are likely many potentially hazardous objects which are unaccounted for.

EPIGRAPH

"I despise the lottery. There's less chance of you becoming a millionaire
than there is of getting hit on the head
by a passing asteroid."
~ Brian May, English astrophysicist and lead guitarist
for the rock band Queen
*****

"When you have an asteroid threatening Earth, it's uncertain
where it will hit until the last minute."
~ Rusty Schweickart, former U.S. Air Force
fighter pilot and astronaut
*****

"Immediately after the tribulation of those days shall the sun be darkened,
and the moon shall not give her light, and the stars shall fall from heaven,
and the powers of the heavens shaken."
~ Matthew 24:29
*****

"The great mountain encompasses seven stadia
After peace, war, famine, flooding
Shall spread far, sinking many countries
Even the ancient landscapes to their foundations."
~ Nostradamus, Centuries I, Quatrain 69
*****

"Sooner or later, we will face a catastrophic threat from space. Of all the
possible threats, only a gigantic asteroid hit can destroy the entire planet. If
we prepare now, we better our odds of survival. The dinosaurs never knew
what hit them."
~ Michio Kaku, American Physicist

ASTEROID: DIVERSION

The Asteroid Series
Book Two

PROLOGUE

Command and Control Deck
The *Dmitriy Donskoy*
Off the Continental Shelf near Bermuda
Atlantic Ocean

The old Soviet Union was a master at propaganda, and despite the fact that the world witnessed the collapse of the U.S.S.R. in 1991 into fifteen separate countries, the tools of media manipulation were still maintained in the *Land of Rus*.

Longtime Russian president Vladimir Putin had been trained as a foreign intelligence officer in the KGB and focused his efforts on the weaknesses of the United States, beginning with its gullible media—news, entertainment, and social.

In 2017, Moscow announced, in a show of détente to the new American president, that it would be destroying two of the largest strategic nuclear submarines in the world. The *Dmitriy Donskoy* and the *Severstal* were holdovers from the old Soviet Union and slated to be decommissioned.

However, unbeknownst to Washington, as other Akula-class submarines were being mothballed, these two warhorses of the seas were being retrofitted with RSM-56 Bulava ballistic nuclear missiles. Like the newly designed Borei class of subs, these last two Akula class were designed to be an integral part of the Russian nuclear triad of submarine-based, aircraft-launched, and space-based weaponry.

The Americans took the Russians at their word, but due to the secrecy surrounding all Russian military activity, they were unable to verify the continued existence of these two nuclear submarines until recently.

The *Donskoy*, bearing hull number TK-208, lurked along the cold, dark waters just off the continental shelf, sailing as far south as the Blake Ridge off the coast of Savannah and upward along the shelf toward Norfolk Canyon before circling back into the Atlantic Ocean, ostensibly to return to the Russians' Northern Fleet.

Instead, the *Donskoy* was deployed in a circular pattern, making a wide sweep east of the island of Bermuda before approaching U.S. territorial waters again. Like a shark circling its prey, the *Donskoy* waited for that moment when it was time to strike.

Captain Third Rank Gorky, the submarine's first officer, strolled through the central command deck of the *Donskoy*, looking over the shoulders of the ship's crew as they intently studied the Americans' activities at Cape Canaveral.

On the surface, it appeared to be a routine rocket launch of the newest technology deployed by the NASA space agency—the Falcon Heavy rocket system, on a mission to divert 2029 IM86. However, their intelligence reminded them that the Americans were not to be trusted, and Moscow had a vested interest in landing on the asteroid first.

The crew had been ordered to combat stations the day before, tracking the activity at the Kennedy Space Center using the American news media's camera feeds, as well as their own Kosmos reconnaissance satellites.

It was quiet on the command deck as Captain Second Rank Stepanov, the submarine's commander, walked briskly toward his first officer. He nodded to his subordinate and leaned in to whisper his directives.

"It has not been confirmed. Intelligence believes the Americans have deployed a nuclear payload on Falcon Heavy, but without further evidence, we're told to stand down."

Gorky, whose surname ironically meant *extremely bitter*, grimaced. He'd been steeling for a fight. Like his father before him, he'd been passed over for advancement during his career. He was anxious to show his superiors what his capabilities were, but found himself hamstrung by Moscow's unwillingness to take the fight to the Americans before their adversaries gained the upper hand.

"Our nuclear-detection systems will provide us the evidence, no?"

The commander nodded, taking a stroll through the command deck with Gorky. "*Da.* The Chinese upgrades to our system will alert us within thirty seconds of a nuclear launch. Our advanced missile launch systems can react quicker than any nation on the planet."

Gorky patted one of the Russian sailors on the shoulder. "Place the communications feed from NASA on the overhead speakers."

The young man quickly complied, and the first words the crew heard were *T minus thirty-one seconds and counting.*

"We will know soon enough about the Americans' intentions," said Gorky as he stood back and rotated his body three hundred sixty degrees. He nodded his head and smiled inwardly. He wasn't formally in command of the *Donskoy,* but this was his ship nonetheless.

T minus ten seconds. Nine. Eight. Seven.

Stepanov was stoic as he gladly allowed his subordinate to take the helm. He was close to retirement and a relaxing future on his farm in Russia's southern Rostov region. Stepanov remained out of the way, standing near one of the two lowered periscopes, occasionally glancing up at the monitors that encircled the command deck.

Gorky stood behind the two fire-control computer displays, peering between the heads of the two michmanny, the rank equivalent of a seaman in the U.S. Navy.

Solid rocket booster ignition and we have liftoff of Orbital Slingshot One!

Gorky could hear the cheers from the Launch Control facility in Florida and sneered at the video screen depicting flag-waving Americans cheering the launch.

"We'll see how long you will be cheering in a moment," he snarled, but barely above a whisper.

Power and telemetry are nominal.

The rocket was forty-five seconds into flight. Frustrated, Gorky slammed the back of the padded swivel chairs of the michmanny. Stepanov had a different reaction.

"This is for the better," he said, breaking the tense silence on the command deck. "The fate of the asteroid and the mission to land is no longer up—"

WARNING! Nuclear launch detected. WARNING! Nuclear launch detected.

The sub's onboard computer system screamed into Gorky's ears, causing him to jump slightly. Beads of sweat immediately poured off his forehead, and his hands began to shake. He'd been waiting for this moment his entire career. An opportunity to show the arrogant Americans they were not superior to anyone.

Vehicle is supersonic.

"It's getting away!" he shouted as Commander Stepanov joined his side to study the monitors. "Arm countermeasures and prepare to fire."

"You will not fire unless on my command," ordered Stepanov, slightly shoving Gorky away from the two nervous michmanny.

"But, sir!"

"You heard me. Stand down until I order otherwise!"

Gorky studied the computer screens and shook his head in disbelief. The artificial intelligence calculated that the Falcon Heavy rocket would be directly over Bermuda in a matter of seconds. Once it cleared the island, it would be in a perfect position to be intercepted and destroyed by the submarine's Bulava nuclear missiles.

Maximum dynamic pressure achieved.

Gorky stomped his right foot and swung away from the console, visibly upset, and pounded his way toward the other end of the command deck.

He couldn't contain himself. "How long since liftoff?"

BECO.

He understood rocket launch procedures, having been enamored with the space race as a child. He knew that the booster engines were being cut off, and soon the Americans and their nuclear payload would be out of reach.

"Sir, we are running out of time. We cannot be responsible for allow—" Gorky was interrupted by the submarine's voice warning system.

WARNING! Nuclear launch detected. WARNING! Nuclear launch detected.

"We will wait for our authorization!" Stepanov was angry now. "You will stand down, Gorky, until the proper orders have been received."

MECO.

"Sir, the American orbiter will be under its own power now. We've lost our opportunity." Gorky dropped his chin to his chest and shook his head in disgust. He gave up the fight, suddenly realizing that the insubordination shown to his commander in front of the fully staffed command deck would likely end his career.

Stepanov, who remained calm throughout, turned to the monitors. He read the launch time aloud. "Three minutes, forty-five seconds."

Separation ignition.

Captain Second Rank Stepanov stood and exhaled. He understood that their mission was over. The decision to have the *Donskoy* stand down was made for reasons he'd never know. He shoved his hands in his pockets and watched the American crew of eleven soar into space.

Until they weren't.

6

PART ONE

Friday, April 13

ASTROMETRY

Identification Number: 2029 IM86

Right Ascension: 08 hours 42 minutes 13.3 seconds

Declination: -21 degrees 01 minute 39 seconds

Greatest Elongation: 20.0 degrees

Nominal Distance from Earth: 0.30 astronomical units

Relative Velocity: 27,992 meters per second

CHAPTER 1

Friday, April 13
National Control Defense Center
Russian Ministry of Defense
Moscow, Russia

"You cannot fight in here. This is the war room, and now we may be at war with the United States!"

Sergei Mikalov had lost his composure as his subordinates argued with one another over the tactics used against the American rocket. The longtime Minister of Defense—who'd shepherded the Russian Federation through the annexation of Crimea, the protection of Syria's president Bashar al-Assad, and the installation of a puppet government in Venezuela—was uncharacteristically perturbed.

He kept glancing nervously at the double doors leading to President Putin's private office suite at the Russian Ministry of Defense building. Then his attention was focused on the video of the Americans' space orbiter being destroyed.

The three-tier, multibillion-dollar control center might have been fortified against nuclear armaments dropped from above, but nothing could protect the occupants staring at the movie-theater-size screens from the wrath of President Vladimir Putin.

The facility's legendary nerve center was designed to coordinate Russian military activity around the world and beyond. Knowingly violating every treaty in existence, even those proposed regarding the strategic nuclear deployments in space, the top brass under Mikalov's command watched in dismay as the artificial intelligence of the Astra Linux computer operating system, developed to meet the need of the

Russian armed forces and intelligence agencies, refused to respond to its human operators' demands to stand down.

The result was not only catastrophic for the Americans' space mission, but might also result in the commencement of World War III. In a single mishap, Russia's nuclear space program was exposed, eleven American astronauts were killed, and the world would be bracing for nuclear Armageddon.

Mikalov knew who would be held accountable. His fate would rival those of his counterparts in North Korea, he surmised.

Except, he was wrong.

The double doors swung open and the sound of the heavy leather boots donned by President Putin's security team marched along the tile floor with the loud claps of a quarter horse. The small-statured Putin, somewhat frail after decades of restoring Mother Russia to its greatness, walked into the room with his head held high and a smile on his face.

The entirety of the staff turned to observe his entry, averting their eyes from the diplomatic train wreck that had unfolded thirty minutes ago. Every man and woman in the National Control Defense Center prepared themselves for a tongue-lashing. What they got astonished them all.

President Putin stopped and began clapping. "Bravo! Bravo! *Otlichno!*" He was commending the team on their excellent work. In fact, he could hardly contain himself.

He strutted over to Mikalov and stuck out his hand to shake. Mikalov, slightly older and much more obese, was still sweating, but made a quick attempt to dry his right hand on his uniform. President Putin shook it heartily, causing sweat to spray off the Defense Minister's forehead.

"But, sir, the Americans will be, um, are—" Mikalov stuttered as he tried to remind his president of the ramifications of the nuclear strike.

"Oh, who cares about the Americans," Putin said, waving his hand as if to erase the thought from the air. "They won't do anything. They never do. Be happy, Sergei. Your nuclear defense system is a success. We just sent a message to the world that not only do we have superior offensive strike capabilities, but no nation dares test our defenses, or their rockets will suffer the same fate as the American orbiter."

Mikalov furrowed his brow and nodded. "Yes, Mr. President, I suppose you are correct. Our fail-safe system performed as expected, only the artificial intelligence did not respond to our direct counter-commands."

President Putin wasn't interested in putting a damper on his nation's success. Once again, he waved his hand through the air with the intent of dismissing his Defense Minister's concerns. "A minor glitch I am sure your technicians will correct. Better to make a mistake and live than succeed, only to die, *da*?"

Mikalov shrugged, somewhat confused by Putin's meaning. "Yes, Mr. President."

"Good. Now, Sergei, advise your staff to continue monitoring the skies, and I will attend to the diplomatic issues."

President Putin looked around the room and beamed with pride. This was his baby, built during a period of a massive decade-long modernization of Russia's military capabilities.

The hundreds of billions of dollars needed to create the facility had been made through a combination of oil sales and extortion from despots like Venezuela's Maduro and Syria's al-Assad. President Putin's modus operandi was a simple one: We will provide you protection and ensure your reign. You provide us unfettered access to your natural resources or geographical points of significance.

During times of military conflict, or heightened cold-war tensions, President Putin often came here to observe missions in real time. To be sure, their surveillance capabilities had some holes, as evidenced by the American operatives' advancement to their Cosmodrome in Far East Russia, but overall, Russia's military capabilities were now second to none, and with China as a strong ally, the Americans' influence in the world had been greatly diminished.

The downing of the orbiter was just more egg on Washington's face, and it delighted President Putin immensely.

An aide rushed through the doors and scurried to President Putin's side.

"What is it?"

"I have an update on our mission to the asteroid, sir. And, well, the Americans are, um, shall I say—*apopleksicheskiy*?"

President Putin roared with laughter, once again drawing the attention of everyone in the massive trilevel war room. "They are? Apoplectic? Good! Let's go pretend to apologize!"

He began laughing again, something that didn't happen often unless he was truly pleased with himself.

"Yes, Mr. President. Exactly so. They have already demanded a United Nations' inquiry."

"Who cares? Another waste of time."

"Um, yes, sir. Also, they are demanding our envoy's presence at the White House immediately."

President Putin began to march away from the aide and back toward his office suite. "Has Minister Lavrov arrived?"

The aide scurried to keep up with the president, who was marching with a purpose. "Yes, sir. The Minister of Foreign Affairs has just arrived. Ambassador Antonov is awaiting his instructions."

Still beaming, President Putin slowed to take one last look around before exiting. In his mind, he'd already prepared a statement to give the Americans, one that would confound them and provide his cosmonauts time to land on the asteroid.

CHAPTER 2

Friday, April 13
Presidential Emergency Operations Center
The White House
Washington, DC

In the White House, the mood was anything but celebratory, and President Mack Watson's demeanor was far from jovial. Unlike his Russian counterpart, who was shaking hands and patting backs for a job well done, the U.S. president had a panicked look on his face as he was rushed into the bowels of the East Wing toward the Presidential Emergency Operations Center, commonly referred to by its acronym, PEOC.

In the early years of the Cold War, beginning in the 1950s and continuing through the Reagan administration of the '80s, America's defense warning system evolved from duck-and-cover protocols to advanced computerized responses being initiated to defend the nation's citizens and prepare the military for an attack.

The PEOC, initially constructed during the Roosevelt administration, had undergone substantial changes over many decades so that it was impenetrable to any form of nuclear missile threat.

President Watson glanced up at the low-hanging ceilings and the elaborate network of pipes that contained hardened wiring designed to protect the facility's electronics from an electromagnetic pulse attack. In the event of a nuclear-delivered EMP, the PEOC's communications and mechanical equipment wouldn't be destroyed by the massive burst of energy.

The president was escorted through the final stretch of tile-covered hallway into a reception area. Several members of his cabinet had gathered in the small conference room near the entryway. He nodded his head toward them, but was abruptly pulled away by his security team toward a large conference room that adjoined the main command and control center of the PEOC.

White House Chief of Staff Maggie Fielding was huddled around the conference table with several aides and uniformed members of the military. She was the first to notice the president enter the room.

"Mr. President!"

Everyone came to attention and stood to the side so the president could make direct contact with Fielding.

"Maggie, what the hell happened?"

She gestured toward a chair at the head of the conference room table, but the president didn't move. He glanced through the large one-way mirror that overlooked the PEOC's nerve center, the equivalent of the Situation Room that was located below the Oval Office in the West Wing.

He began to pace the floor, which was his nature, causing the other occupants of the conference room to make way. He strutted back and forth along the wall of mirrored windows, periodically stopping to observe the frantic activity going on below them, and turned to Fielding as she spoke.

"Mr. President, we are still awaiting details from our recon satellites. We've analyzed video obtained from the news networks, as well as footage provided to us by India. It's apparent that shortly after the main-engine cut-off phase of the launch, at which time the orbiter came under its own power, a tactical ballistic missile of unknown origin and throw-weight struck the spacecraft, completely obliterating it." The throw-weight of a ballistic missile refers to its nuclear payload.

"Come on, Maggie, we know it came from Russia!" The president was incensed, losing concern for his safety after entering the PEOC.

"That's just it, Mr. President. We have no indication, nor do any of our allies, that the missile was launched from Russia or any other land-based battery."

"Air-launched?"

"Possibly, sir. Again, based upon our best suppositions, the Russian Kh-47M2 Kinzhai air-launched ballistic missile certainly has sufficient range to down our orbiter. If they were tracking Falcon Heavy's launch and had intentions of shooting it down, then this ordnance could easily make that happen."

"Then drag their asses over here and demand some answers!"

Chief of Staff Fielding once again gestured for the president to take a seat. "Sir, please, would you like to sit down?"

"No, Maggie. Out with it! What else is there?"

Fielding inhaled and continued. "Sir, there is a real possibility that the origin of the missile was space based."

The president turned toward the glass and raised his arms over his head, pressing his palms against the window frame. He was eerily calm as he asked, "Are you saying Moscow has ballistic weapons deployed in space?"

Fielding, whose military point of view was invaluable during a crisis like this one, quickly responded, "Russia's Aerospace Defense Forces successfully created a hypersonic interceptor missile that is certainly capable of destroying our orbiter. It has never been deployed to space, as far as our intelligence has been able to confirm."

"Do they have other means of bringing down the orbiter?" the president asked.

"Sir, this might have been done via laser technology. Both of our Defense Departments have been working on putting interceptors in space. The difference is that we've abided by the treaties and, based upon the initial analysis of the explosion, they have not."

President Watson turned to Fielding, who was now joined by the chairman of the Joint Chiefs. "How am I supposed to give direction and formulate a response without information? Right now, three hundred million plus Americans think I'm a fool. I promised them we'd keep them safe. Now our means of doing so, not to mention the lives of eleven damn fine astronauts, is scattered all over Greenland."

The president wasn't a military veteran, but he certainly respected the work they'd done in protecting the nation from attack. He felt the need to rush out of the conference room and get away from the eyes that were awaiting him to take leadership, or ownership, of what had happened.

He had been stupid to include a nuclear payload in the Falcon Heavy launch. The Russians were always one step ahead of the U.S. For all he knew, Putin had a man in the room at that very moment.

"I need to walk, and think. Give me ten minutes, and when I return, I want to know when I'll be face-to-face with the Russian ambassador, and more importantly, I need to discuss our next move against the asteroid."

"But, Mr. President, there isn't—"

"Maggie, I'm not going to sit in here and commiserate or wring my hands. You folks get your game plan together and brief me in ten minutes." The president walked out of the conference room and turned toward the carpeted stairwell that led to the multilevel PEOC operations center. Then he shouted, "And get me that damned Russian ambassador!"

CHAPTER 3

Friday, April 13
Presidential Emergency Operations Center
The White House
Washington, DC

President Watson paced along the upper level of the theater-style operations center. He tried his best to appear presidential, commander-in-chief-like, but his emotions came through. Putin had gotten the better of him, and it would make him look weak in the eyes of world leaders and especially the American citizens.

Politically, he'd be in a much stronger position if he hadn't insisted on including a last-resort nuclear payload on board the orbiter. NASA had gone along with his directive reluctantly because they were fully aware of the threat IM86 posed to humanity. The president didn't have the time to go to the United Nations to debate the matter, only to be vetoed by the UN Security Council. He had to be bold, and his go-it-alone approach might have cost the lives of eleven American astronauts.

He stopped to rub his temples as a headache began to set in. His doctor had counseled him about his stress levels, and since he'd learned that he had a forty-seven percent blockage in his carotid artery, he'd heeded the warnings. He cut out the alcohol, changed his eating habits, and incorporated some moderate exercise into his routine. However, the nation's chief adversary, President Vladimir Putin, a pain in the neck of every administration for decades, remained one for President Watson.

The two prior administrations had placed a heavy emphasis on creating a space force and colonizing the Moon. Many believed the

Space Force, designed to be an independent branch of the military, was absolutely essential to promote U.S. dominance in space and necessary to protect national security. Others argued that weaponizing space would militarize a domain where peaceful cooperation should prevail.

Then the Chinese landed a rover on the far side of the Moon, and the stakes were raised. His predecessor intended to focus his administration's limited budget on establishing a lunar outpost, and the successful mining operation was applauded around the globe.

Putin, however, had other plans for his budget. While Americans were digging up dirt and rocks on the Moon, he'd beat the Americans into space with a weapons defense system, and now they'd effectively destroyed a nuclear-laden space orbiter.

President Watson recalled a campaign speech he'd made just a year prior at a rally in Brevard County, Florida. The words rang in his head as he stared at the monitors below him, many of which were replaying the point of impact in slow motion.

"In a way, space is already a competitive and a militarized domain. The task now is to protect U.S. and allied military interests in space and to guard against catastrophe resulting from overreaction. That means both strengthening U.S. capabilities to deter and defend against strikes on its satellites and working with other nations to establish accepted rules of engagement.

"The most important norms are against attacks on so-called strategic-warning satellites, which underpin nuclear deterrence by detecting missile launches in real time. The reasoning is obvious. Such attacks could be interpreted as a prelude to a nuclear strike and result in unintended nuclear war."

Russia was notorious for using cyber warfare as a prelude to invading another nation. Their cyber attacks had caused instability in Georgia, Estonia, Lithuania, Ukraine, and Venezuela before the Russian military gained a foothold. President Watson envisioned a similar military tact in which Russia would disable America's reconnaissance satellites prior to a nuclear attack.

He began to process the events surrounding the orbiter's

destruction. The Russians had made no statement, and they hadn't made any additional overt militaristic moves. Although the ramifications of these events for both countries were monumental, there was no time to debate geopolitical brinkmanship. He still had to deal with the incoming asteroid.

His chief of staff interrupted his thoughts. "Mr. President, the Russian ambassador has arrived."

"Good, Maggie, let's hear what he has to say. Am I meeting him in the conference room or upstairs?"

"Sir, under the circumstances, because of the uncertainty in all of this, we've set up a video conference with him from the Diplomatic Reception Room."

The Diplomatic Reception Room served as an entrance to the White House from the South Grounds for arriving ambassadors. Oftentimes, the president would meet his guest there for a more formal gathering. Sometimes, depending on the nation, the ambassador was shown directly into the Oval Office. The Russian ambassador hadn't made it past the Diplomatic Reception Room in a dozen years.

As Chief of Staff Fielding led the president back to the conference room, she provided him a quick update. "Sir, we have an additional complication."

"Wonderful," he responded sarcastically.

"The nuclear detonation, caused by what appears to be a ballistic missile striking the orbiter, sent an electromagnetic pulse through the atmosphere, resulting in power outages from Eastern Quebec Province into Greenland and Iceland."

"Okay, what else?" At the moment, the president was unconcerned with the collateral damage of this debacle.

"Moscow has fired a preemptive diplomatic shot across our bow, sir."

"Let me guess, they've filed a complaint with the United Nations over our sending a nuke into space."

"Yes, sir. They're taking the moral high ground, sort of."

"Putin's a crafty devil. I'll give him that. Well, this certainly changes our approach to what happens next."

"I don't know that we can trust any of this, Mr. President. We always have to work under the assumption that further hostilities are imminent."

"Maggie, do you think Moscow wants a nuclear war with us? The timing doesn't make—" The president paused his own thought. Actually, the timing was perfect. His administration was preoccupied with the impending threat. His mind entered an inner debate.

Should I order the Pentagon to retaliate, or defend? Do I abandon our efforts to deal with the asteroid, trusting the Russians to successfully divert or destroy it?

"Mr. President? Sir? Do you need a moment before we return to the conference room? The Joint Chiefs are present, as well as the directors of our intelligence agencies. Maybe I should get you a glass of water or something?"

He stopped and smiled. "No, Maggie. I'm all right. When they knock you down, you just get back up again. You know, back in the saddle. I can't wait to hear the horseshit spewed by the ambassador. Let's listen to him and send him on his way. Afterwards, I want to focus on saving our planet from the asteroid. I'll deal with Moscow later."

CHAPTER 4

Friday, April 13
Presidential Emergency Operations Center
The White House
Washington, DC

The Russian ambassador played it perfectly, and exactly as he was instructed by President Putin. He apologized on behalf of the Russian Federation for the lives wasted by the Americans' poor choices. He pointed out that their use of a superior missile defense system proved necessary because the Americans' nuclear payload was launched into space without notice to the nation-states of the UN Security Council, and they had no idea what the Americans' intentions were. Finally, the ambassador pledged to work in full cooperation with the Americans in whatever way possible to face the real threat posed by 2029 IM86.

The video conversation lasted just over five minutes. The president was in no position to force the issue because he'd knowingly violated treaties himself. He too pledged a spirit of cooperation, although he wasn't certain what that entailed. The conversation was beginning to wind up with mutual promises to dispel any thoughts of retaliation, or escalation, in the interest of saving mankind from the real threat.

Then the president, a former judge and Chicago Cubs fan, threw a curveball at the ambassador. "Mr. Ambassador, there's just one more thing."

"Yes, Mr. President, of course."

"When was the Russian Federation aware of this asteroid that has been designated IM86?"

"Well, of course, that would've been three years, ag—" The ambassador caught himself and feigned a coughing fit. He began to hack and choke so much that a White House staffer rushed to his side with a bottle of water, which he quickly consumed.

The president squinted his eyes, recognizing the ambassador's deflection immediately. "Mr. Ambassador, are you all right?"

The Russian grimaced and nodded his head, taking the opportunity to gather his thoughts as he took another gulp of water. "Yes, of course, Mr. President. I am. It has been a difficult morning for us all. I will relay your sentiments to President Putin. Thank you."

The ambassador stormed away from the camera and could be heard speaking to his aides in Russian.

"Mr. President, shall I stop him at the door?" asked Fielding.

"No, he gave us the answer. The Russians have known about IM86 for three years, and based upon our intelligence gathered from the Cosmodrome, their intentions are clear. They intend to stake their claim on the asteroid and, apparently, will stop at nothing to do so."

"Sir, do you think they shot down our orbiter on purpose? To delay our attempts to place our own team on the surface of the asteroid?"

The president stood and began his nervous pacing again. "Maggie, I think it's a distinct possibility. Many questions have now entered my mind, from when did they discover IM86, to whether they deliberately shot down our people."

"Mr. President," interrupted the chairman of the Joint Chiefs, "treaties aside, they've committed an act of war, for which we should retaliate."

"Very true, General, but this is why Putin's move with the UN was brilliant. He preempted our accusations by claiming self-defense. He was one step ahead of us, leaving us playing catch-up, as always."

Fielding tried to bring the conversation back to the president's primary concern—the asteroid. "Whether it was their hypersonic interceptor, or laser technology obtained from the Chinese, we're back at square one on dealing with the threat to us all. We simply cannot wait to see if the Russians can successfully land on the surface, much less execute a diversionary maneuver."

"I agree," said the president. "Have we heard from NASA?"

"Yes, sir," replied the Secretary of Defense. "I hope I haven't overstepped, but as soon as I observed mission failure, I contacted Acting Administrator Frederick and told him to take a moment to mourn the dead, then consider how many more lives are at stake if he doesn't come up with a solution." Jim Frederick was a former congressman who had been nominated by the president to head up the space agency.

President Watson leaned against the back of a leather chair and twirled it on its base. He did not sit the entire time during the briefing. "I realize the projected impact date is two weeks off, but it was my understanding that our window of opportunity to employ the orbital slingshot method ended today. Am I wrong? What did Jim say?"

"No, sir, you are not wrong," replied the Secretary of Defense. "Frederick is a pragmatist and he laid out the situation in very simple terms. Our eleven best astronauts are dead. The remainder of active-duty astronauts are primarily academics, you know, scientists, astronomers, etcetera."

"What's the point?" asked the president.

"Well, sir, the point is Frederick thinks our best option, no, maybe our only option, is to nuke it."

The president sighed. "Okay, that opens up a huge can of worms in light of what happened this morning—diplomatically and legally. I mean, we'd have to go hat in hand to the UN and ask for the member states to approve our mission, or agree to participate." The president paused and then slapped the back of the chair. "Damn. Is there nothing else? Are we too late for other options?"

"Yes, sir, apparently so, unless we want to pin our hopes on the Russians. A nuclear detonation or, actually, multiple pinpointed detonations, as Frederick told me, would be required."

The president didn't respond. He simply stared at the empty chair in front of him.

His chief of staff picked up the conversation. "Mr. Secretary, when will NASA have a detailed plan, a proposal, as to what we should do, other than nothing?"

"Naturally, they're working out the details as we speak. He made no promises, but he clearly understands the need for urgency here."

A light tapping on the door caused everyone to pause. Fielding motioned to her assistant to answer it. It was an aide to the Secretary of Defense.

"Mr. Secretary, I have an urgent message for you, sir." The young woman approached and handed him a white nine-by-twelve envelope. The defense secretary dismissed the aide, and when the door was closed, he began to speak.

"Our recon satellites report that the Russians are deploying their RS-24 and Topol-M mobile intercontinental missile launchers to their borders, especially along their eastern and northern perimeters."

"The shortest paths to our mainland," muttered the president.

The defense secretary pulled out a satellite photograph and handed it to the president. "Sir, this was taken one hour ago. It's a Borei-class nuclear-powered ballistic submarine."

The president studied the image and pointed to a small island. "Where is this island?"

"Sir, that is Isla de la Juventud. It is the second largest island in Cuba."

"A hundred miles from Key West," added the president, studying his Defense Secretary.

"Yes, sir."

The president stood from his hunched-over position and stated with conviction, "I'm beginning to question the veracity of the Russian ambassador. I am not going to be lulled into a false sense of security. I believe we need to get on a war footing, *posthaste.*"

CHAPTER 5

Friday, April 13
NASA Headquarters
Two Independence Square
Washington, DC

"Well, for better or worse, he's on board," announced Jim Frederick, the former astronaut who'd been nominated to be NASA's first African-American administrator by the president. Like the other members of his team in the large conference room, his face was gaunt and his eyes reflected the solemn mood in the room. Despite the tragedy that had struck the space agency, as Frederick put it: *It's time to pull on our big-boy pants and do our jobs.*

Nola Taylor, head of the Space Technology Directorate, frowned. "This whole thing sickens me. The loss of American lives is bad enough. But, from a scientific perspective, I feel an opportunity of a lifetime will pass us by."

During many of these briefings, there was always a lone voice of dissent. A voice that was pragmatic, no-nonsense, and oftentimes resented by the others who had an idealistic vision of space exploration.

Hal Rawlings, the chief of NASA's Flight Director Office, was that voice of reason, or truth, as he chose to view it. A native of Borden County, Texas, population six hundred forty-two, Chief Rawlings, as he was known by everyone, shunned the cowboy lifestyle of others growing up in West Texas. He rebelled at the thought of working the oil fields or on a ranch like his friends.

Instead, while his buddies were staring at the sky at night, dreaming of rodeos and buckle-bunnies, Chief Rawlings imagined being up there, looking back at Earth.

His family saved for his college from the day he was born. After graduation, he enrolled at Texas A&M and earned his bachelor's degree in mechanical engineering. He immediately applied for a job at NASA as a flight controller in the thermal operations group directly responsible for the multiple subsystems that powered the International Space Station.

However, being tethered to a desk was not what Chief Rawlings had in mind for his future. He gathered friends within the halls of the Johnson Space Center, took graduate classes at night, and got the requisite three years of professional experience that qualified him to be an astronaut.

Then he threw his cowboy hat into the ring along with eighteen thousand other AsCans, the nickname given to astronaut candidates. It took Hal Rawlings eight applications in eight years, but he was eventually accepted into the program.

Those eight years weren't wasted. During that time, he worked in all aspects of NASA operations, even taking a demotion one time just so he could work directly with AsCans in training.

When Chief Rawlings's career as an active astronaut ended, he'd logged more hours in space than any other. He'd spent more hours tethered to the ISS conducting space walks. And he'd been afforded the honor of being in the first lunar lander during the Artemis Two mission three years ago.

His opinion was respected because he had no agenda other than the application of common sense. For that reason, Chief Hal Rawlings often won every argument.

That morning, following the tragedy, when he made an off-the-wall suggestion coupled with the perfect mix of personnel to bring his plan to fruition, a consensus was immediately reached.

NASA was going to attack IM86 with a heretofore untested spacecraft, a new array of technologically advanced nuclear missiles, and an Air Force pilot who'd never been into space and was borderline suicidal—Gunner Fox.

"Nola, I understand and we all wish that we weren't faced with this dilemma," added Frederick. "However, our backs are against the wall. By all calculations, our window of opportunity lies between oh seven hundred hours on the twenty-fourth and nineteen hundred hours on the twenty-fifth. That's a thirty-six-hour time span that will move at the speed of light as far as my nerves are concerned."

Chief Rawlings continued to remain quiet during the conversation, periodically looking down at his watch. He'd learned that there was very little sense of urgency within the halls of government. Pencil-pushin' and paper-shufflin' were only surpassed by meetings as the top wastes of human resources, in his opinion.

The director of Human Exploration and Operations addressed Chief Rawlings. "I don't know where to start in training this man. The only thing he knows about NASA is what his wife may have relayed to him."

Chief Rawlings reached down for his spit cup. For most of his life, he'd kept a chaw of Levi Garrett chewing tobacco in his mouth. When he applied to be an AsCan, he was told by medical that he'd have to give up the habit.

He did. Until he returned from the Moon and was placed on inactive status. He immediately sought his old friend Levi and, much to the disgust of his fellow directors seated around the conference room table, never left home without it.

He spit out the excess moisture and casually wiped the corner of his mouth with his tobacco-stained, grizzly hand. "I'll train 'im myself."

The room erupted in chatter as nearly everyone shook their head from side to side. Everyone except Frederick, the decision maker.

Nola Taylor was the loudest voice of dissent. "Chief, with all due respect, we have professionals who handle training. You know that. Our protocols are regimented and specifically designed to weed out AsCans who are incapable of dealing with space travel. As you know, this is an intense process that's not for everyone."

Chief Rawlings nodded, acknowledging Taylor's honest opinion. Under most circumstances, he'd agree wholeheartedly. Every mission required a team, and the astronauts had to be able to trust each other implicitly. Their lives depended upon it. There are no do-overs in space.

"Ma'am, respectfully, you don't need an astronaut for this mission. There are no experiments to conduct. No far away galaxies to observe. What you need is a stone-cold killer and a damn good pilot. Gunner Fox is your man."

"He's never been in space!" protested one of the attendees.

"Neither have you," countered Chief Rawlings calmly.

"You know what I mean, Chief. There are two years of classes. You have to go through survival training, mental evals ..." Her voice trailed off. "We're putting the fate of the planet on the shoulders of a man who has been proven to be mentally unstable. The dossier provided to us this morning revealed that he tried to fly an experimental aircraft halfway to the Moon before it disintegrated."

Chief Rawlings was undeterred. "That's exactly what this mission needs. Major Fox is a thrill seeker but not suicidal, according to the psychologist at Eglin. He understands how to deal with threats, emergencies, contingencies, and then come up with solutions."

"He tore up a hundred-billion-dollar aircraft and then dropped out of the damn stratosphere! Chief, that's not stable!"

"Maybe, maybe not. Listen, in space, you're on your own. You don't have anyone else to ask except Mission Control. You do realize that we may lose communications with the spacecraft based upon the proposed intercept point, right? He's not gonna be able to call in or Google the problem. He's got to apply his own common sense and experience to any complications, if they arise."

Taylor spoke up. "We can beef up his knowledge database. He can lean on artificial intelligence for answers."

"Okay, that's fine. But know this, in space, you only get one breath to save your ass. What I can teach him in the week I've got is a crash course in the necessary knowledge it takes to pull off this mission—not all the extra stuff thrown in by the shrinks and the phys-ed team."

"Chief," began acting director Frederick. He thumbed through a copy of Dr. Brian Dowling's file on Gunner. "What about his mental condition? Frankly, I haven't had time to look at this extensive psychological profile on Major Fox, but the mere fact that it exists is a red flag to me. Shouldn't we at least interview other combat pilots, candidates who are, as we've pointed out, more stable?"

"I've been assured that he's mentally ready," said Chief Rawlings. "I've known his commander from his Special Forces training days for a long time. I got on the phone with him minutes after the mission fail because I knew this discussion would be taking place. This guy is as cool as a cucumber. Calm, ready, competent. And capable."

"But—" the director of Human Explorations and Operations began to argue, but Chief Rawlings shook his head, causing her to stop.

"Ma'am, back in the glory days of Mercury 7, we sought out fighter pilots with nerves of steel, men who lived on the edge, just like Major Fox. As our technology advanced, missions changed. We needed scientists in space in order to study ways to get farther into our solar system. I get that.

"Today is different. We need a space cowboy. You know, like in the movies. We need a guy who is fearless, and yes, due to circumstances, perhaps with nothing to live for. I guarantee you that if you lined up fifty candidates who qualify, only one will honestly say that he'd give his life to save our planet. That's Gunner Fox."

Frederick leaned forward and looked Chief Rawlings in the eye. "Chief, I spoke directly with the contact who recruited your man this morning. Major Fox didn't even ask what he was being asked to do."

Chief Rawlings calmly spit more of his tobacco juice in the cup and smiled. "Exactly. Because it didn't matter."

CHAPTER 6

Friday, April 13
The Doomsday Plane
Forty Thousand Feet
Somewhere over Missouri

The U.S. Air Force's E-4B was a militarized version of the 747-200 commercial airliner. Known as the *doomsday plane,* it acts as the principal airborne command and control operations center during times of war or catastrophic events.

It was capable of withstanding the force of a nuclear detonation. Unlike its technologically advanced counterparts, the doomsday plane was equipped with analog flight instruments that were less likely to be fried by the electromagnetic pulse released after a nuclear detonation. It's also shielded to protect the crew, and its most important passenger, the President of the United States, from the nuclear and thermal effects during an attack. With its giant fuel tanks and ability to refuel in the air via the Boeing KC-135 Stratotanker, the doomsday plane can stay airborne for weeks.

In addition to the president, the six-story aircraft—complete with eighteen beds, six bathrooms, and room for one hundred twelve crew members—carried the Secretary of Defense and the Joint Chiefs of Staff. In preparation for all contingencies, there were six of the E-4B doomsday planes stationed throughout the world.

President Watson strolled through the command and control work area, periodically sticking his head into the operations team center to see if there was any activity. He was bored and somewhat fussy that his security team insisted that he be whisked away from the White House. To be sure, the Russians couldn't be trusted, and most

30

likely, their blatant, highly visible maneuvers were intended to be an act of deterrence against a U.S. counterstrike. Nonetheless, he had a wife and grown children to protect, and the doomsday plane would certainly do that.

"Mr. President, sir?" His chief of staff interrupted his thoughts.

"Yes, Maggie."

"Sir, NASA is prepared to give you a briefing via video linkup in the command center conference room on the fourth floor. They assure me they're prepared to move forward with a viable alternative."

The president gestured for Fielding to lead the way to the carpeted spiral staircase. He didn't want to bother with the elevator to travel down one level. He chatted along the way.

"Do we have the Secretary of State ready to begin making phone calls? She needs to garner the support of our allies, and they, in turn, need to be prepared to pressure the Russians and Chinese if necessary."

Maggie reached the next level and paused to allow the president to catch up. His increased exercise regimen had taken a toll on his knees. His doctors had suggested knee replacement surgery, but his political advisors said that would generate bad optics during his first term, so he dealt with the discomfort.

"Sir, I don't want to preempt NASA's presentation, but I suspect you're correct. Unless they were overstating the time frames in our earlier briefings, the so-called orbital slingshot method is off the table at this point."

"We gotta nuke it," the president said bluntly.

"Yes, sir. That will require everyone to sign on, not just our allies. Otherwise, we run the risk of our launch suffering a similar fate as the one this morning."

They reached the conference room door, and the president glanced in to find the Joint Chiefs seated, patiently waiting his arrival.

Fielding continued. "Mr. President, I'm coming directly from a military perspective, as you know. My background in the Navy did not train me for the political world that you clearly understand."

"Maggie, if something is on your mind, say it."

She nodded and swallowed before speaking. "Sir, the Russians kept us in the dark regarding IM86 for a substantial amount of time because, in my opinion, Putin wants to gloat about being the first to land on, and mine, an asteroid. While it's true that may afford him a period where he can claim a political victory over us, the setback we suffered is minimal compared to the losses we face if this asteroid strikes the planet."

"I understand all of this, Maggie. That's why if going nuclear is our only option, then I'll approve the mission."

Fielding rolled her neck on her shoulders. "Sir, the Russians, and their friends in Beijing, may not sign off on the U.S. nuking the asteroid. Maybe the destruction of our orbiter today was a mistake by their AI. Or perhaps it was intentional to prevent us from reaching the asteroid's surface before they do. But, Mr. President, one thing is certain. The Russians will never let you detonate nuclear weapons on the surface of IM86 if their people are present or in the vicinity."

"Well, they need to get their people out of the way. I mean, according to NASA, we have no confirmation that their lander has managed to reach the surface of the asteroid. I'm sure President Putin would be beating his chest in delight if they had."

The president began to walk inside, and Fielding touched his arm to stop him for a moment. "Sir, all I'm saying is that you might have to concede the Russians the opportunity to fulfill their mission, with some type of deadline to, as you say, get their people out of the way."

The president smiled and nodded as he broke off the conversation. He entered the room and everyone immediately stood at attention. Acting NASA administrator Frederick also stood from behind his desk at NASA headquarters. His position didn't afford him the protection against a nuclear attack like others within the government.

"Thank you, everyone. Let's give Jim Frederick all the time he needs to lay out NASA's proposal, and then we'll open up the floor for comments and questions. Understood?"

A chorus of *yessirs* filled the room, and everyone took their seats after the president got settled in. President Watson began by telling Frederick to get started.

"Mr. President, I'll be completely honest with you. The agency only has one option on the table, and it has become far more complicated by the passage of time."

"Nuclear?" asked the president.

"Yes, sir. Only, it can't simply be an impact strike as envisioned in the past. Because of the size of IM86 at just over one-point-two miles at its maximum length, and its irregular shape, it will take more than a single kinetic impact to divert it."

Envisioned decades ago by scientists from the world's five major space agencies, the kinetic impactor approach was intended to move the asteroid off its trajectory enough to avoid striking Earth.

"Are you talking about DART?" asked the Defense Secretary.

"Yes," replied Frederick. "As a congressman, I co-sponsored the Double Asteroid Redirection Test bill that created the mission. Designed by scientists at Johns Hopkins Applied Physics Laboratory, it uses a kinetic impactor technique whereby a fast-moving spacecraft would smash into a NEO, causing it to gradually shift its orbit."

"Plan B," the president muttered. Only his chief of staff heard the utterance, and she imperceptibly nodded her head.

Frederick continued. "Several years ago, we successfully tested the asteroid-deflection technique by smashing a refrigerator-sized spacecraft into a nonthreatening asteroid. It moved the asteroid ever so slightly from its original orbital path.

"Then we became more ambitious. With the cooperation of the other space agencies, we identified a binary pairing of asteroids, Didymos A and Didymos B, which was only five hundred thirty feet wide. Using a slightly larger spacecraft with a nominal nuclear payload, we successfully moved Didymos B away from the gravitational pull of A. Technically speaking, so we understand, B, also known as Didymoon, is significantly smaller than Didymos.

"We never got the opportunity to test a nuclear weapon on the larger asteroid, as the cooperation between our nation and Russia ceased. Nonetheless, we learned a lot from the DART missions.

These objects are quite rocky, not necessarily a smooth, rounded object. With each pass by the sun, their compositions change somewhat, which is a benefit to our mission because it creates points of weakness that can be exploited."

The president was growing anxious for Frederick to get to the point. "How does the DART mission help us today?"

Frederick, who had been a big supporter of the president while on the campaign trail, knew his boss well. "Sir, the DART mission allowed scientists the ability to analyze the effects of these impacts, especially as it relates to how many kinetic impacts are required to sufficiently move a single target."

"Do you have any data on the composition of IM86?" asked Fielding.

"We don't, but we suspect the Russians do," replied Frederick. "At this time, they haven't given any indication as to whether they've landed. However, they possess the same technology we do, which enables them to assess the composition of the asteroid while orbiting it. If they would share this data with us, we could better formulate a plan of attack."

"That's an interesting choice of words, Jim," said the president.

"Well, sir, that's basically what we propose. We need to attack IM86 with nuclear missiles that strike strategic points of weakness on the surface. The more information we can have in advance, the better we can prepare our pilot for this complicated endeavor."

The president appeared puzzled. "Jim, you have to help me out here. Do we even possess a spacecraft capable of conducting an air raid on an asteroid? One that is equipped to launch nuclear missiles?"

Frederick took a deep breath and averted his eyes from the camera momentarily. It was a sign that his confidence in the mission was not one hundred percent. "Yes, sir, we do. It's experimental. In fact, it's never been flown into space."

"That's comforting," said the president sarcastically. Then he asked, "If you've never flown said spacecraft, do you even have a pilot to command this mission?"

The chairman of the Joint Chiefs, an Air Force general, squirmed uncomfortably in his chair.

Frederick's answer was curt. "Yes, sir. There were several candidates, but we believe we have the right one for this particular mission."

"Good," said the president, seemingly reassured.

The chairman of the Joint Chiefs closed his eyes, as if in prayer.

CHAPTER 7

Friday, April 13
Gunner's Residence
Dog Island
Florida Panhandle

"Long time no see," Cam said casually as she exited the elevator. The mood was subdued, and she was the last to arrive at Gunner's home on Dog Island. Ordinarily, the trio of best friends would be celebrating one thing or another, but not on this day. Certainly, they'd mourned the loss of loved ones before, but this time, decisions would have to be made concerning their future.

"Hi, Cam," Pop greeted her with a smile. He rubbed his hands off on his blue chambray apron with his name stitched on it and met her at the elevator. She dropped her duffle bag, packing lighter than normal because she only expected to be there for a couple of nights.

"Hi, Pop." She leaned in and planted a kiss on his cheek. He was covered in flour and she wasn't quite ready to dive into his baking activities.

"Cam, do you wanna beer? The guys are out on the deck with Howard."

"Not just yet, Pop. I'd better hear what's up, first."

He reached for a plate of butter crescents and offered her one. Surprisingly, she passed for now. She wasn't in the mood for cookies or beer.

Gunner had the wall of windows fully open. The four large sliding windows moved on tracks until they were hidden behind the exterior walls, lending the appearance that the home was completely open to the outdoors. With the cooling temperatures, Gunner and Pop had opened up the beach house, allowing the Gulf breezes to flow throughout. On any other day, Kenny Chesney would be blasting through the Sonos wireless speakers, the Oyster City beer would be flowing, and the smell of cigars mixed with burgers on the grill would permeate her senses.

Not today. The failure of the launch from Cape Canaveral had damaged the psyche of the entire nation, and especially the Fox family, of which she considered herself to be a part. When Pop had sent her the text after Gunner had been approached at The Tap Room in Apalachicola, she called Bear, and the two of them agreed to head for Dog Island to lend the guys some moral support.

"You know, the Merlin engines have an insane amount of power," Bear said as she walked onto the deck. "I watched those static fire tests at the SpaceX facility in McGregor, Texas. It was awesome, man."

Cam used the pause as her opportunity to interrupt. "Hey, guys."

Bear stood up and snapped a salute to the new major in the Air Force.

"Sit down, Sergeant King. That's an order."

"With pleasure, Madam Major."

Gunner stood and gave his best friend a hug. "Cam, you guys didn't need to come over here. Seriously, it's all good. Besides, I'm not sure what to tell you at this point."

She held him for another moment and then allowed him to take his seat on the Adirondack chair. Cam leaned against the rail and pushed her way up until she was seated on top of it.

"Um, Cam, you do know it's almost twenty feet to the ground, right?"

Cam, a tomboy at heart and generally fearless, laughed. "I do. But, hey, we've done worse, remember?"

"Don't you know it!" exclaimed Bear. "I'll never forget how you two suckered me onto that ledge. You swore you'd keep me between the two of you in case these size thirteens slipped." Bear held his feet up. Bigfoot had nothing on Staff Sergeant Barrett King.

Cam laughed. She remembered the operation well. The three of them had almost died that day. "Yeah, well, it was either that or you'd be indoctrinated by the Taliban by now, like that guy on *Homeland*."

"Yeah, well, then I could've hooked up with Claire-what's-her-name. You know, the crazy blonde chick."

"Dude, the last thing you need is a crazy blonde girlfriend," said Cam. "How's it going now that you're back with your main squeeze?"

"Not bad," he began in reply. "She's all apocalyptic, you know. She goes online and reads all of these reports of how we're gonna be extinct and stuff."

"It's a shame they frighten people that way," added Cam.

"Well, it's great for my sex life. Don't get me wrong, I'm not ready to be cancelled by some asteroid, but I really dig the sextacular bedroom activity."

"TMI, Bear," grumbled Gunner, who'd remained quiet during the back-and-forth. He rotated his beer in his right hand, periodically following seagulls that flew across the horizon.

"Sorry, man. Anyway, about the Merlin engines."

Gunner shook his head, so Bear stopped explaining his theory. "No, I know what I saw. There was a flash bang preceded by a streak of white light. I know what a missile impacting an aircraft looks like, even from a distance."

Cam dangled her feet and studied Gunner. He was troubled by the cause of the accident, perhaps more than the loss of life.

"Gunner, the logical culprit for such a bold move would be the Russians. China has the capability, but they'd have no incentive to shoot down a NASA space mission, especially one that was intended to save the planet."

"Why would the Russians shoot it down?" asked Bear.

"I don't know," replied Gunner. "However, I agree with Cam that the Chinese probably didn't do it. And, hopefully, but nothing is certain in this world, we didn't shoot it down ourselves."

Cam twisted her back to stretch. "Guys, do you think there's a correlation between our mission to the Cosmodrome and what happened this morning? I mean, it's pretty damn coincidental."

"I do," said Gunner bluntly. "Our intelligence agencies must've suspected that the Russians were up to something, perhaps a launch to get to the asteroid. They needed us to shed light on their activities."

"So what's with the mining equipment?" asked Bear.

Gunner applied his expertise garnered from his education in Earth sciences. "It's twofold, Bear. For one thing, there might be minerals and resources that man has never been exposed to. You guys may not know this, but the periodic table is constantly being adjusted based upon newly discovered elements with unknown chemical properties. Imagine what a space rock originating from the other end of our solar system might contain."

"Weapons-grade plutonium or something like that," speculated Cam.

Gunner nodded. "Exactly. A find of that nature could change the balance of power on our planet in a significant way."

Bear chuckled. "Yeah, so when the asteroid misses us, we can either let the Russians blast us off the face of the planet, or pack our shit and head for the Siberian salt mines."

Gunner shook his head and laughed at his somewhat negative friend. "The other thing is purely scientific. An asteroid of this size could provide insight into the origins of the solar system."

"And what good will that do us?" asked Bear.

"So we'll know, you dope," Cam shot back.

Gunner smiled for the first time. He enjoyed the playful, albeit hostile at times, banter between Cam and Bear.

The group grew quiet for a moment, during which time Pop came outside and told them he'd made lasagna for dinner. He told the trio to let him know when they were an hour away from being hungry.

Bear roared uproariously at that statement as he asked Pop how he was supposed to predict the future, to which Pop replied, "Just guess, then."

Cam turned the conversation back to Gunner. "So, this mysterious no-name guy who showed up at the bar earlier, did he give you any idea what the mission is? I take it we're not involved."

Gunner shrugged. "He didn't say anything about you guys, and

I'm gonna let 'em know, as I always do, that we're a team. All he said was, quote, *your country needs you.*"

Bear laughed. "You could've told him to go pound sand or that you gave at the office."

"I pretty much did, at first. But then, I don't know, I saw the video on the TV behind the bar, and something struck a nerve, I guess. I think that spaceship was shot down, guys, and it could be the DOD needs me to look into it."

"Without us?" asked Cam with a slight pout.

"Like I said, I'll let them know how I feel about working without you guys."

Bear speculated that it might be a solo flight, a run-and-gun type assault in retaliation for the Russians shooting down the orbiter.

Cam agreed. "I think Bear may be right. It's the only thing I can think of that wouldn't involve us."

Their conversation was interrupted by a text message coming into Gunner's phone.

"It's from Ghost."

GHOST: *Pickup at 0800 tomorrow. Pack light.*

Gunner passed his phone to Bear, who then tossed it up to Cam.

"That's all you get?" she asked.

"It appears so. Just like the Russian mission. I've got no clue where I'm headed, or why."

CHAPTER 8

Friday, April 13
Gunner's Residence
Dog Island
Florida Panhandle

Gunner couldn't sleep that night. He was not one to suffer from anxiety, as most people define it. Anxiety was an expected part of life. It could be partially from excitement of what the new day might bring, or it could be intense, persistent worry that consumes someone's mind. For Gunner, his sleepless night was a combination of old memories invading the present, coupled with an overwhelming sense of unease that he'd volunteered for a one-way mission.

Howard, like many dogs, was able to read human emotions. He and Gunner had been best pals since Howard had been weaned off his mother. Over the years, Howard had studied Gunner's and Heather's voices. When he heard positive sounds, he would study their faces, and he'd do the same when something negative was being communicated.

Over time, the lovable basset hound had integrated the two sources of sensory perception of emotion and internally categorized them. He'd developed a cognitive ability to read Gunner's emotional state, and used those emotional cues to make his human companion feel better.

So when Howard began licking his face at three o'clock that morning, coupled with emitting several dog-talk sounds, a smile came across Gunner's face. Gunner reached for his phone, checked the time, and realized it was way too early to wake up. He glanced outside into the darkness, where a new moon allowed the stars to shine brightly.

"You know what, buddy," Gunner whispered, disregarding the early hour, "let's go for a walk on the beach. Whadya think?"

Howard loved the beach, and it was one of the few words that set his tail on fire, so to speak. He immediately began to put out the fire by pounding it against the bed.

"Shhh," Gunner admonished his faithful friend. "You'll wake Cam. Come on, we'll take the stairs. I'll carry you so you don't make a lot of noise."

Howard crawled out of bed and stood patiently by the elevator. He didn't quite grasp the carry-down-the-stairs thing until Gunner knelt down and hoisted him into his arms.

"Damn, you big old sixty-pounder. Has Pop been feeding you cookies again? Or is it that Nummy Tum Tum stuff?"

Howard licked Gunner's face and passed gas in response.

Gunner laughed and the two headed downstairs, attempting to be all stealth-like. Once they reached the concrete pad underneath the house, he put Howard down, who immediately hustled off toward the beach as fast as his stubby legs could carry him. His elongated body swayed side to side, opposite to the motion of his long wagging tail.

Thirty seconds later the two of them stood side by side, staring off toward the water that was gently lapping on shore. It was deathly quiet except for the occasional trills and squeaks emanating from the dolphin pod, which had grown in size in the Gulf waters surrounding Dog Island.

"Which way, pal?"

Howard looked back and forth before moseying westward toward St. George Island. Gunner's property was on the western end of the barrier island, fronting the beach and stretching across two sandy roads to a private dock on St. George Sound. Following a series of hurricanes, three of the four houses farther west had been destroyed in part, and later demolished. The owners, who had no insurance, couldn't afford to rebuild, so Gunner's home became somewhat secluded.

This suited Howard just fine because he wasn't a social pup. Unlike other dogs who couldn't wait to encounter another dog, going through the customary ritual of wagging tails and sniffing butt, Howard preferred human companionship. In a way, his basset hound was more people than pup.

As they walked, Gunner talked it out. "Howard, I've got a bad feeling about this mission, especially since I have no idea what it is they want from me. Don't get me wrong, I'm not afraid. There's a difference between danger and fear. I don't walk tightropes without a net because I don't get enough benefit from walking along a rope where I could die for no reason.

"Danger is different. You overcome fear of being killed in a dangerous situation by being competent. That's why I push these aircraft to their limits. That's why I train at the range and role-play using live rounds with other operators."

Howard pressed forward into the darkness, periodically stopping to inspect the turtle nests that were staked off by local volunteers. He was listening, Gunner was sure of it. So he continued. "Once I make a decision, I'm optimistic about the outcome. I work it through in my head, and when I attack a problem, I know I'll succeed."

Gunner managed a laugh as Howard stopped to urinate on a discarded beer cooler with the New Orleans Saints logo on it.

"The thing is, I've heard that people call me arrogant. Egotistical. I prefer to look at it as confidence. There was an old baseball pitcher named Dizzy Dean who said it ain't braggin' if you can do it."

Gunner looked down at Howard, who was losing interest in the conversation and now turned his attention to a scent that caused him to pick up the pace.

"Heather used to say that God blessed us both with these talents. I've given up on thinking like that. I've experienced too many things to believe that God could possibly have a hand in them. Do you think I'm wrong for thinking that way?"

Howard ignored the question and raced ahead, if you could call a basset hound's waddle racing. Gunner jogged behind him in the pitch dark, stumbling over a piece of driftwood on one occasion and avoiding a dead jellyfish on another.

When he caught up to Howard, his old pup was sprawled on the beach in front of several dead red drum fish, also known as redfish, piled near some debris that had washed ashore. The smell was overwhelming, which was probably what drew Howard to this point, but it also stopped him in sheer disappointment when he arrived.

Gunner walked hesitantly toward the debris when something caught his eye. The stars provided just enough illumination to cause a reflection on a shiny brass object. He pulled his tee shirt over his mouth and nose and approached the glistening object.

He reached down and picked up a twelve-inch desk globe. He stretched his arm away from his body and held it high before turning the miniature version of Earth on its axis so that the remnants of seaweed could fall off. He continued spinning it, faster and faster, until it broke loose from its base and landed in the water near his feet.

"Well, we can't have that, can we?"

Howard gruffed in response.

"Come on, boy. Let's get this home and fix it up."

CHAPTER 9

Saturday, April 14
Gunner's Residence
Dog Island
Florida Panhandle

Gunner never went back to sleep after his middle-of-the-night stroll with Howard, who was so exhausted that he had to be carried to bed. The sheets were covered in sand, but Gunner didn't care. He'd just pile them up and throw them in the wash before he left.

Pop rolled in just after sunrise with a Tupperware container full of cinnamon-pecan buns, one of his many *specialties*.

"Ghost said pack light," said Gunner as he chomped into the sugary delight. With his mouth full, he explained to Pop what packing light meant to him. "I don't have a bag. There's not a change of clothes. I don't need stuff like a toothbrush, deodorant, and the like. What you see is what you get." Gunner held his arms out as if to put himself on display. He wore khaki pants, a black polo shirt, and black sneakers.

"Shouldn't you at least put on your fatigues, son? Last time you went in to see your superiors, you were a little disrespectful."

Gunner finished off the first of two breakfast treats. He nodded his head to indicate he understood and agreed. "I know, Pop. I admit that I went to Eglin that day with a bit of an attitude. It wasn't fair to them and was certainly out of line. Dr. Dowling and I hashed it out; plus I apologized to the colonel the next time I saw her."

"What about today? Shouldn't you—?"

Gunner cut him off. "Pop, are you seriously nagging me about my attire? I'm likely to be put on a C-130 to who knows where, for who

45

knows how long. They'll dress me out for the mission."

"Okay, I'm just, you know. Son, I've always believed you were destined to do great things."

Gunner wrapped his right arm around his father's shoulder and led him toward the deck. Bear and Cam had just left and said they'd be back to say their goodbyes. "That's what every pop says."

His father laughed and wrapped his arm around Gunner's waist. "Well, this Pop means it. Listen, you've experienced highs and lows in your life, and I'm not just talking about Heather. Do you remember when you didn't make the varsity basketball team?"

Gunner chuckled. "Yeah, best thing that ever happened to me."

"True, in hindsight. But, at the time, you were devastated. There were other things, minor instances, that have shaped your life. You're a survivor, like your mother. You've always bounced back from adversity and attacked life with a vigor I never had."

"Until now," said Gunner, turning to face his father. He finished the second cinnamon-pecan bun. "Look at you. You fly airplanes for a living. You bake like Betty Crocker. You take care of me."

A tear came to Pop's eye with the last statement. He was proud of the role he'd played in his son's life, and appreciated it when Gunner noticed. "Son, you've made me proud in so many ways. But no more so than the way you have managed the past few years. It's what you do after you've lost everything that defines who you are. I'm very proud of the man you've become."

Gunner hugged his father again, and the two shared a moment.

"Pop, don't worry about me. I don't know what they've got in store for me, but it isn't anything that I can't handle. You know that."

Pop wiped the tears off his face and squeezed his son around the waist. "I know that, but then again, I can't help being concerned. Since your mom died, I've put on a good front, but I miss her terribly. I know she'd be very proud of you and—"

Gunner let out a hearty laugh. "Get real, Pop. If Mom knew what I did for a living, and especially if she knew you were flying an airplane full-time, plus baking cookies with a bunch of biddies, hellfire would rain upon us both."

Pop laughed with his son and glanced out toward the beach. "Hey, what's that?"

"What?"

"There's writing in the sand. See?"

Gunner shielded his eyes from the rising sun and looked down toward the beach. The letters were somewhat disproportionate, but it was clear what they read.

Day by day.

Minute by minute.

Ride or die.

We stick together.

And after the last word, Cam and Bear stood arm in arm, both holding sticks high over their heads, waving them triumphantly.

CHAPTER 10

Five Years Prior
Dog Island
Florida Panhandle

"Sometimes an unpleasant ending is nothing more than a new beginning."

Heather was feeling philosophical that morning as she and Gunner observed the armada of barges delivering building materials and equipment to their job site on Dog Island. The night before, the two of them, and Howard, had made camp on their beach.

They'd built a bonfire, which was especially helpful in fighting off the bugs that had descended upon the island that spring, and cooked hot dogs for dinner. Beers were consumed, laughter was had, and love was made under the stars.

Their excitement was building as the distant sound of the diesel engines churning their propellers through the water approached the island from nearby Carrabelle. Building on an island that didn't have vehicular access was complicated and expensive. The money they saved by purchasing the unusual piece of beachfront property was easily offset by the additional cost of construction.

But the couple didn't care. They had a stranded-alone-on-a-deserted-island mindset. They enjoyed each other's company more than anything, with Howard, of course, being their only child.

They'd discussed having kids on occasion but agreed their lives were so great together that they didn't want to introduce another human being into the mix. Plus, there was always the risks associated with their careers. Heather had not yet been into space, but she would be within two years. Gunner was a combat pilot who, at that early stage in his career, had already been shot down several times. He often said that he couldn't bear the thought of leaving his child fatherless, and by the same token, he couldn't go into a firefight worried about the consequences of his death.

So, the two, plus Howard, lived happily together in DeFuniak Springs until this property came available. Because they lived modestly but were generally savers, they could easily pay cash for the parcel, and their credit enabled them to secure a bank loan in Apalachicola. That day, their dreams were coming to fruition.

"I hate what happened during the Artemis launch," added Gunner. "But you and I wouldn't be standing here if it hadn't. That day had an effect on us like 9/11 had on our parents. Something like that, an emotional event, has the ability to transform your way of thinking."

"Life's too short," said Heather.

"It is, and that's why we took the plunge to become homeowners. And there it is, our home, or at least pieces of it."

Heather laughed and pulled out her phone to take some pictures of the momentous occasion. "This is incredible. Look, I've got chills."

Gunner rubbed his wife's arms and held her tight, taking a moment to steal a kiss. He let the breeze muss his hair before getting philosophical. "Before the invasion of Normandy, as early as 1942, Army infantry divisions rode onto this beach on barges not that different from the ones we're looking at. Over time, a quarter of a million soldiers prepared for amphibious landings in both Japan and France. Standing here, I can feel the excitement and energy of those brave guys who knew they were going to leave for battle overseas and possibly not come back."

Heather looked up to her husband. "Do you ever feel like that? I mean, you know, that you might not come back."

"No, darling, not once. I have too much to live for. I hate being apart from you for a second, but it's my duty. Just like you have to get ready to leave the planet, for Pete's sake. Let me turn the question back on you. Do you lie awake at night thinking that I might rocket off into space, never to return?"

Heather hesitated and kicked at the sand. "I'm not going to say that being an astronaut is different from what you do. At least in space, nobody's trying to kill me. There's just no margin for error. If you make a mistake, you can die. Simple ones, like not putting your suit on correctly before a space walk or flipping the wrong switch on the spaceship's console."

"I get it. In our respective professions, mistakes can be deadly. That said, do you think we should consider another line of work?"

Heather laughed. "Not on your life, buster. I'm going into space, come hell or high water."

Gunner then teasingly began singing the lyrics to Elton John's "Rocket Man." Heather quickly joined in, yelling the lyrics so loud that Howard began to howl.

"And I think it's gonna be a long, long time!"

CHAPTER 11

Present Day
Saturday, April 14
Defense Threat Reduction Agency
Fort Belvoir, Virginia

With a hint of apprehension, Gunner gazed through the windows of the helicopter that had whisked him away from Tate's Hell State Forest hours earlier to the sprawling complex that made up Fort Belvoir. The U.S. Army complex, located largely on a peninsula extending into the Potomac River in Virginia, was developed on the site of the former Belvoir Plantation, home of the prominent Fairfax family for whom Fairfax County, Virginia, had been named.

The base was headquarters for a number of military units, including Army Intelligence and Security Command, the Missile Defense Agency, the National Geospatial-Intelligence Agency and the Defense Threat Reduction Agency.

Gunner's last visit to the DTRA had reunited him with his old mentor and friend Colonel Gregory Smith, who was now working within the U.S. intelligence apparatus, coordinating dark ops for the government. Code-named Ghost, Colonel Smith had the highest regard for Gunner, which was why he'd picked his team to be inserted into Russia to investigate the Cosmodrome.

The chopper took a circular sweep across the front of Fort Belvoir, where Gunner could see a heavily armed sentry detail searching vehicles before entry. The line of vehicles was a clear indication of the enhanced security measures put into place since the president had increased the terror level threat to its highest point since 9/11.

Scattered throughout the complex was an army of satellite dishes, antennas, and microwave transmission devices, which had been upgraded to be used in cyber warfare. The bright sun glistened off the various devices, causing them to twinkle and at times blind him. The mesmerizing effect caused Gunner's mind to wander—back to his flight aboard the F/A XX, high into the stratosphere, where he'd soaked in a view of the universe.

The chopper landed abruptly on the concrete pad, jarring Gunner back into the present. Two armed soldiers hustled toward his ride and immediately took up positions flanking the Sikorsky's exit. Gunner waited for the copilot to give him clearance, and he opened the door, enjoying the warm sun on his face.

"This way, sir," instructed one of the guards. Gunner's mind raced as he began to question why it was necessary for an armed escort. Seconds later, he was escorted through two security doors that were also monitored by armed personnel. Once inside the tiled hallway, he sensed the faint echoes of whispered conversations emanating from each office. It was a Saturday, and ordinarily this facility would be operating with essential personnel only. Clearly, it was all hands on deck in light of yesterday's failed mission launch.

Gunner was led down a different hallway than the one the other day when he and his team had met with Ghost. Through another set of doors, the sterile white walls and shiny tiles were replaced with plush carpet, high-gloss white trim, and walls adorned with massive photographs of rocket launches, battleship christenings, and experimental aircraft. The kinds of towering achievements that made the military proud and provided for the defense of the nation.

Another set of doors appeared before Gunner, except these were not the glass and aluminum entries that had preceded them. Large, ornately carved wooden doors were slightly ajar as an Army captain stood to greet Gunner.

"Major Fox, welcome to Fort Belvoir and the DTRA. Follow me, please."

He led Gunner into a room where a nurse stood behind a medical table. Off to her right was a series of computers and a LabCompare

DNA analysis device. The elderly nurse stood without expression, holding a hermetically packaged cotton swab.

"Well, this is a first," muttered Gunner.

"Yes, sir," said the captain. "Advanced security protocols dictate these measures. I apologize for the inconvenience."

The nurse removed the plastic covering and Gunner assisted by opening wide. She placed the swab under Gunner's tongue, who obliged by closing his mouth briefly before she began to pull it out.

The nurse quickly went about her business, and within ten seconds, she nodded to the captain that Gunner was, in fact, Gunner.

The captain nodded to the armed escorts. "Thank you, gentlemen. I'll take it from here."

"Captain, I've been around a while and that's the first time I've been DNA tested to enter a building. I know there's a terrorist alert, although I suppose there was an ulterior motive for raising the threat level, but this is a little over the top, don't you think?" When Gunner had first heard about the alert, he'd speculated that the action was a precursor to declaring martial law.

The captain nodded and didn't answer for a moment. He gestured for Gunner to follow him down another hallway. Unlike the other parts of the building, where office doors were open and voices could be heard, this area was silent, as if devoid of life.

The DTRA was a highly secretive agency known for its covert activities. It was especially active in the war on terror, but also played a pivotal role in the newly revived cold war with the Russians.

The captain reached a bank of elevators and retrieved a key from his pocket. He inserted it and led Gunner inside. The first thing Gunner noticed was that the cab did not have the customary control panel indicating floor numbers, the open and close option, or an emergency button. There was only a place to insert the key again.

Wondering what the hell was going on, Gunner shrugged and shoved his hands in his pockets. He was going into the belly of the beast, and he hoped that he came out alive.

When the elevator doors opened, the serene impression left by the floor he'd just left was replaced with a cacophony of sounds ranging from commands being issued to computer printers spitting out reports. Satellite images flashed across ten-foot-wide television monitors that surrounded a half-oval wall. Some screens featured military personnel providing a briefing, but one that could only be heard by the officers who were patched through on their terminals.

The hustle and bustle jarred Gunner's nerves at first, and then he settled down somewhat when he was approached by a familiar face.

Ghost greeted Gunner and extended his hand to shake it. Reluctantly, Gunner, who'd already begun a salute, changed his motion and shook his old commander's hand.

"Seems odd not to salute, doesn't it?" asked Ghost.

"It does take some getting used to, sir." The military salute was a long-honored tradition dating back to the Roman Empire. In today's military, it was customary to salute a uniformed officer and was considered a courteous exchange of greetings, as well as a show of respect. Veterans and out-of-uniform personnel restricted their salutes to the raising and lowering of the flag, or during the national anthem.

"Come on, I'd like you to meet somebody."

Gunner followed Ghost through the operations center, turning sideways at times to make his way through the large numbers of personnel on hand.

A man wearing dark slacks, a short-sleeve white shirt and a navy-blue tie stood alone, studying the monitors. To describe him as a stereotypical accountant would be appropriate, right down to the balding head, black-framed glasses, pens in his shirt pocket, and slightly protruding belly that hung over his belt.

Branson Ford, the director of the Defense Threat Reduction Agency, was anything but plain or ordinary, despite his outward appearance. This gentleman spent every waking moment with his eyes on the nation's deepest, darkest secrets. His short stature was not indicative of his importance to the U.S.

"Director Ford," announced Ghost as he approached his boss. "I'd like you to meet Major Gunner Fox."

Without taking his eyes off the monitor, Director Ford reached around and shook hands with Gunner. "Nice to meet you, son. Good job the other day."

"Um, yes, sir. Thank you. It was a team—"

"Excuse me a moment," the director interrupted and scampered down two levels to a bank of computer terminal operators dressed in Army fatigues.

He patted a young man on the shoulder, who slid his chair out of the way, allowing Ford to take over his keyboard. Shortly thereafter, one of the monitors revealed a satellite feed that began to zoom in on a snow-covered location near a large body of water. The director spoke to the young man and patted him on the back. The soldier nodded and resumed his work.

Ghost leaned into Gunner and whispered, "He's very hands-on. I didn't tell you this before, but he was present for almost the entirety of your operation. Director Ford broke protocol and scrambled the 176th at Elmendorf to ward off the pursuing Russian fighter jets as you hustled home. As he put it, 'We protect our assets, especially the ones with that kind of talent.'"

Gunner chuckled. "I've been called a lot of things, especially asshole. Talented is not one I've heard very often."

Ghost smiled. "Let's just say talented asshole and leave it at that, shall we?"

Director Ford returned to them and apologized. "Sorry for the interruption. It's been a busy twenty-four hours. Corporal!" he shouted to his aide, who was standing off to the side. It was a heavy-handed approach to someone who was only ten feet away.

"Yes, sir."

"Fetch the NASA liaison from the DOD and bring him to my office. He needs to meet this young man, and we can brief him, albeit briefly." Director Ford laughed at his word repetition.

"Yes, sir." The corporal excused himself and headed for the elevator.

Director Ford led Ghost and Gunner to the back of the massive operations center into a room that stretched along the entire back wall. In addition to his desk, which was flanked by the U.S. flag and the Army's flag, a round conference table set in the middle of the room was surrounded by fabric-covered barrel chairs, and a large conference table made up of touch-screen computer monitors filled the last third of the space.

"Gentlemen, take a seat here," the director said brusquely, pointing at the round table. Folders were set neatly in a stack at the center of the table. "There's a folder for each of you, but I'd prefer you wait until the DOD man arrives. I need to keep an eye on the floor."

Like the head of a casino's security team, Director Ford adjusted his headset and began to slowly pace the length of his office along the window, adjusting his earpiece from time to time and pressing a button that changed its channels.

Ghost and Gunner exchanged glances and sat patiently while they awaited the fourth member to attend the briefing. Moments later, a gentle tapping at the door preceded the corporal, who brought with him Colonel Maxwell Robinson of the Department of Defense, and the military liaison to NASA's Johnson Space Center.

Gunner immediately noticed the colonel's face when they made eye contact. He looked like he'd seen a ghost, and it wasn't in reference to Gunner's former commander sitting to his right. The man's demeanor struck Gunner as odd and immediately put him on edge that the DOD representative was already familiar with him.

Introductions were made, and Director Ford instructed the three attendees to open their folders. The trio thumbed through the combination of reports and satellite images of yesterday's Falcon Heavy launch, together with the subsequent explosion of the space orbiter.

Director Ford was known for getting to the point, and he didn't change his approach today. "Russian artificial intelligence aboard one of their orbiting defense satellites ordered the destruction of our orbiter shortly after the main engine cut off yesterday. According to their ambassador, once the orbiter was under its own power, their computer technology determined that it was hostile. Seconds later, the orbiter was obliterated by a ballistic missile."

"Nukes? In space?" asked Ghost.

"Better to ask forgiveness than permission," mumbled Director Ford as he changed channels on his headset again.

Gunner noticed that Colonel Robinson was studying him, but he resisted the urge to look at him. *Let the DOD man play his game.* He addressed the director. "Sir, if the Russians deemed the orbiter to be a threat, then is it safe to conclude their AI mistook our launch as a nuclear provocation?"

"Yes, and no, Major. Our orbiter was carrying a nuclear payload; it just wasn't destined for a Russian target."

Ghost dropped his folder on the table with a thud. "What?"

Director Ford, without turning around, responded, "Colonel, would you like to explain?"

Colonel Robinson cleared his throat and answered Ghost. "The orbiter's primary mission was to initiate a diversionary tactic known as the orbital slingshot method. If this tactic failed, then the commander and his crew were prepared to give their lives by instituting a contingency plan ordered by the president."

"A nuclear payload," Gunner surmised.

"That's correct, Major," continued Robinson. "NASA's testing with kinetic impactors has been successful in the past, but not on this magnitude, obviously. In the event the orbital slingshot method was unsuccessful, then, quite simply, the commander of the orbiter would fly it into the asteroid at a high rate of speed. The resulting explosion would hopefully knock IM86 off its current trajectory in time to divert it away from Earth."

"Hopefully?" asked Gunner. He was incredulous. In his mind, this had been an ill-conceived plan from the beginning. "Eleven people were destined to die whether by the Russian missile or by crashing into an asteroid."

"Not necessarily, Major," countered Colonel Robinson. "The orbital slingshot method was a viable alternative to—"

Director Ford cut off the debate. "It's water under the bridge, gentlemen. The debate is not ours to have. We have new orders, and it's our duty to carry them out."

"I agree," interjected Ghost. "Let's get into the details so that I can get Major Fox on his way."

"To where?" asked Gunner.

"Your new ride."

CHAPTER 12

Saturday, April 14
Wallops Flight Facility
Wallops Island, Virginia

Gunner was lost in his thoughts as the newly commissioned MV-22C Osprey tiltrotor transport tore across the late afternoon sky toward the Wallops Flight Facility a hundred forty miles to their east. The bizarre developments weighed heavily on his mind as the Osprey pilot made a wide sweep across the Wallops Island National Wildlife Refuge, skirting Watts Bay as he began to adjust his tiltrotors and dropped down to a smooth landing adjacent to the NASA building on Stubbs Boulevard.

He and Ghost, together with the mysterious Colonel Robinson, sat in silence during the quick flight. That was fine with Gunner. He had a lot of questions for Ghost, including gaining background information on the colonel. Gunner had an uneasy feeling about the NASA liaison and was anxious to quiz Ghost about him when he had the opportunity.

For now, he had to grapple with the prospect of not only flying into space, but also that his mission was to pilot an unproven spacecraft loaded with nuclear armaments. It caused him to pause and wonder if he wouldn't be better served to exit the Osprey and run for his life.

Wallops Island was one of NASA's oldest launch sites. With the expansion of Cape Canaveral and the onset of private contractors like SpaceX using locations in Texas, the NASA facility here had been diminished in importance.

Today, it was still used for intelligence satellite launches and the

59

testing of experimental aircraft, similar to what Gunner did for the Air Force at Eglin. Gunner had never been to the facility, but knew Wallops Island to be NASA's base of operations hidden from the media spotlight.

Once they landed, Gunner's eyes were blinded by a mammoth shape glistening in the distance. His heart almost stopped as he shielded his eyes from the shiny silver object rising into the sky.

"What the hell is that?" asked Gunner.

"*That* is your new ride, or at the least the first leg of your mission, the SpaceX Starship," replied Ghost. "It's designed to carry us to the Moon and even to Mars once the Merlin engines are fine-tuned. For now, it is part of your mission to destroy IM86."

"You're joking, right? I'm supposed to fly that shiny-lookin'—" Gunner caught himself before he made reference to a phallic symbol, in deference to his all-female crew, who could hear him over the comms.

"Actually, this is only part of your mission, Major," replied Colonel Robinson, who'd remained mostly quiet during the briefing with Director Ford and during the flight to Wallops Island. "The Starship will carry you to the lunar outpost. From there, a different hypersonic aircraft will be within your command."

The Osprey's rotors began to slow, and the ground personnel on the tarmac prepared for their exit. Gunner couldn't take his eyes off the Starship, and the moment the doors opened, he shot out of the Osprey and began to walk briskly at first, and then broke out into a fast trot to get a closer look at *Liquid Silver*, the nickname applied to the Starship by SpaceX founder Elon Musk.

Ghost tried to contain his high-spirited fighter pilot. "Gunner! Wait. We have to go inside for a briefing first!"

Ignoring his former mentor's commands, something the two of them had come to expect from the protégé, Gunner continued until he met up with several NASA engineers dressed in white coveralls adorned with the NASA meatball-design logo featuring a planet, the stars of space, and a red chevron wing representing the aeronautics missions associated with the agency.

A white circular streak was indicative of an orbiting spacecraft. Gunner found this aspect of the logo ironic. It implied that the spacecraft left and then returned to its point of origin, something that was not always the case. It was a sobering reminder of the task at hand, yet it didn't damper his excitement.

One of the NASA ground personnel saw his approach and immediately held both hands in the air, indicating that Gunner should stop. "Sir, this is a restricted area. You should not be on the tarmac or anywhere near this spacecraft."

Gunner heeded the man's warning to an extent, stopping just short of the Starship and looking skyward. Liquid Silver resembled a stainless-steel Airstream trailer that was designed to perform like a space shuttle, only it was shaped like a glycerin suppository.

The diameter of the spacecraft was roughly thirty feet, and it was easily a hundred feet tall. The Merlin engine assembly was enormous. The three men surrounding Gunner could easily fit within one of its cones.

"Gunner! We need to go inside!" Ghost had caught up with him and was now insistent. Gunner understood his tone, having differentiated between Ghost's subtle suggestions and direct orders in the past.

"Roger that, sir," said Gunner, who tore himself away from the spacecraft but managed one last, long look before joining his commander.

The three men ducked inside the Wallops Flight Facility building adjacent to the tarmac. They were greeted by several NASA personnel, all carrying computer tablets and casually dressed, the norm for governmental agencies outside the military.

After introductions were made, the trio were escorted into a video-conferencing room, which included scale models of the Starship as well as two other aircraft.

Gunner couldn't contain his excitement. "I've already seen this bad boy," he began, pointing at the Starship. "What are these other two?"

One of the NASA engineers replied, "This is the new Boeing x-59 QueSST experimental aircraft. It's designed for quiet supersonic travel, eliminating the disruptive sonic booms that prevented commercial supersonic flights in the past."

The engineer casually walked to the other corner of the room in front of a scale model of a spaceship similar in design to the one located outside. It, however, more closely resembled the recently decommissioned space shuttles, which had been replaced by a bus-style transport that ferried astronauts and supplies to and from the lunar outpost.

"This beauty is known as the Starhopper. It's the same technology and basic design as the Starship you observed outside, only it's smaller and has the maneuvering capability of an Earth-based aircraft."

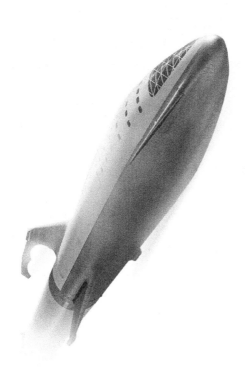

Gunner was intrigued and couldn't resist approaching the model to run his hands along the top as if he were petting Howard. He turned to the NASA engineers and began peppering them with questions. "Does it have the horsepower to get to the Moon, or is it simply an Earth orbiter?"

"It can reach the Moon, but then it requires refueling," one of them replied. "Depending on the mission, the Starhopper would be coupled with a Falcon 9 rocket to propel it into space, where it would then reach deeper points of destination, like Mars. Otherwise, it's powered by the Raptors."

Gunner persisted in his questioning. "Do you fly it to the Moon?"

The engineer was hesitant for a moment. "Well, this spacecraft wasn't initially designed for that purpose, so thus far, it hasn't undergone a trip to the lunar outpost. We've been utilizing the combination of the Starship together with our Falcon 9s instead."

A puzzled look came over Gunner's face. The engineer was skating around the question.

"However," interjected another NASA engineer, "the Starhopper is capable of deep-space exploration if it launches from the lunar surface. You see, because of Earth's atmosphere and tremendous gravitational pull, it takes a very large amount of thrust to get a spacecraft to even the lowest Earth orbit. In space, with the lesser gravity of the Moon, Newton's third law of physics works to our benefit."

Gunner interrupted. "For every action, there is an equal and opposite reaction."

"That's correct, Major. Consider a balloon. When you blow it full of air and then let it go without tying a knot, the air rushes out and propels the balloon in an opposite direction. It's Newton's third law that governs the launch of a heavy rocket into space. Fighting the immense gravitational pull and atmosphere of Earth, we need a lot of propellant.

"Now, consider this. If we're able to use a similar amount of propellant in a rocket that's launched in a weightless atmosphere, with far less gravity, like the Moon, we can push ourselves deeper through the vacuum of space. Once in flight, unlike planes that require air to lift them up, we can use only slight amounts of force to maneuver and move forward. The more force, the faster we travel. Using only a slight amount of propellant, we'll still get to our destination, just in a longer period of time."

Gunner studied the two spacecraft. "Do you have the capability of launching the Starhopper from the lunar surface?"

Again, a slight hesitation took place before one of them responded, "Capability, yes. Have we done it in practice? Not yet. Um, you'll be the first."

Most of the people in attendance received a response from Gunner they did not expect.

"Great! Let's get started!"

PART TWO

ASTROMETRY

Identification Number: Unknown

Right Ascension: 16 hours 44 minutes 35 seconds

Declination: -19 degrees 22 minutes 55 seconds

Greatest Elongation: 66.0 degrees

Nominal Distance from Earth: 0.25 astronomical units

Relative Velocity: 30,056 meters per second

CHAPTER 13

Sunday, April 15
Publix Super Market
Tallahassee, Florida

Pop first sensed that something was amiss as he approached the Publix Super Market at Forest Village in Tallahassee, Florida, when the traffic was backed up on the highway at least a mile before he reached Lake Munson. It was a Sunday morning, his favorite day to travel into the *big city*.

Tallahassee, despite being the state's capital, ranked well down the list of population centers in Florida, at fourteenth behind towns that aren't familiar to most people around the country, like Bonita Springs, Lakeland, and Melbourne. The Florida Panhandle was sparsely populated, with large swaths of land being designated as state or national parks, or owned by the large U.S. Air Force bases at Pensacola, Tyndall, and Eglin.

Nonetheless, Tallahassee offered Pop the big-city amenities such as Walmart, a shopping mall, and his favorite supermarket—Publix. So every Sunday morning, he loaded up a couple of coolers and made the sixty-mile trip into Tallahassee for provisions.

He'd spoken with Gunner briefly that morning. His son had explained they wouldn't have very many opportunities to talk over the next several days, and sadly, he couldn't provide Pop the details of what the government was asking him to do.

Pop said he understood and he simply asked Gunner to try to be safe in whatever mission he'd been tasked. Gunner's response was stated confidently. *"I'll try* means I might fail. For me, there's only *do."*

It was that confidence that Pop had instilled in his son when he was a young boy and, much to his chagrin, Gunner lived life on the edge as a result. After the conversation, Pop was reassured, and with a lighter step, he decided to drive his Ford Mustang convertible on the back roads leading into the city.

The *Chiclet blue pony*, as Gunner referred to it, was part of Pop's self-awarded retirement package. It was way too fast, but it seemed to fit the lifestyle he'd adopted after his days in the Air Force. At least, as his wife said, the wheels stayed on the ground. She silently cursed him the day he purchased the Cessna seaplane. At first she'd acquiesced, never thinking he'd go through with it. When he did, a chill came over the Fox family dinners for several nights.

With Gunner gone for an indeterminate amount of time, Pop would be shopping light and chose to put his Mustang through the paces. The highway was generally free from traffic on Sunday mornings, and the county deputies didn't bother with speed traps as a result.

Pop entered the final S curve before Lake Munson a little too fast and found himself standing on the brakes as a long line of cars entering the city was stopped ahead. Cursing and questioning what was going on, he inched along the final mile to Publix, barely approaching ten miles per hour. Stop and go, brake lights as far as the eye could see.

Crawfordville Road widened, and Pop noticed that virtually all the vehicles were making their way into a jam-packed Publix parking lot. He shook his head in dismay, wondering if perhaps he'd been transported into September on the morning of a Florida State Seminoles football game. His next thought was the fact he hadn't paid attention to the weather.

Did I miss a hurricane forecast? Wait a minute, it's only April. What the hell?

For ten minutes he traversed the parking lot in search of an open space, along with dozens of other cars. Finally, like several pickup trucks, Pop opted to pull his pony onto the grassy median between the shopping center and the highway. He grabbed his Publix shopping totes and headed toward the store. What he found astonished him.

People were pushing and shoving to get inside. There were no shopping carts to be found. Pop followed a large heavyset man, using him like a running back might follow his fullback, to force his way through the glass doors, where the chaos roared.

The cashiers were overwhelmed. There were no baggers as people shoved their purchases into pockets, suitcases, and beach totes. He made his way to the right, toward the bakery, produce and deli counter, only to find the refrigerated shelves empty. A young man was trying to unload boxes of Chiquita bananas, only to be knocked to the side by the crowd. Shoppers, rather than grabbing a bunch, were attempting to tote whole cases in their arms. That was because there was nothing else to buy.

Pop approached the disheveled young man and asked, "Are you okay?"

"Yes, sir. To be honest, I wanted to quit after yesterday, but my folks told me I needed to work because the store manager promised first dibs on meat that came in today's delivery. Only, the delivery never showed up."

An argument broke out behind them, and Pop pushed the young man to the side where organic vegetables were usually on full display, except for today.

"This started yesterday?" asked Pop.

"Well, really Friday night right at closing time. I guess the reality of the rocket ship blowing up frightened people. The next thing you know, they came to the store and began buying up all the bottled water and batteries. You know, the usual stuff we run out of when a hurricane is on the way."

"I've seen it before, but ..." Pop hesitated as another scuffle broke out as one of the women in the bakery brought out a tray of baked bread and several men fought over it. "This is ridiculous."

"Yes, sir. There was a line of a hundred people standing at the door when we opened yesterday morning. By early afternoon, virtually everything edible in the store had been cleared out. It was totally insane. Late yesterday afternoon, when the truck arrived from our Lakeland distribution center, people rushed through our stockroom and tried to grab case packs of canned goods. They got angry when our managers told them the products weren't for sale until they'd been scanned into the inventory system. It almost caused a riot."

The sound of breaking glass and two women cursing one another could be heard over the uproar concerning the bananas. Pop subconsciously pulled his grocery totes and opened them, confirming they were empty, and imagined they would likely stay that way. He wasn't prepared to do battle with the crazed shoppers.

Just the day before, he'd gone into Apalach to pick up a few things from the Gulfside IGA. Nothing had appeared out of the ordinary as he made his purchases of primarily baking-related items.

"Good luck, sir," the young man said as he began to walk away. Then he added, "You'll be able to catch it on the news tonight, probably. ABC 27 sent a crew over a little while ago, and the mob didn't disappoint them. A fight broke out in the parking lot over a shopping cart full of soda. Can you believe it?"

Pop shook his head, but not in disbelief. He'd heard the stories of economic and societal collapse coming out of Venezuela for the past decade. As the socialist regime tried to hold on to power, propped up by the Russians and the Chinese, the people suffered. Empty grocery shelves and emaciated children were the norm in a nation that was once the wealthiest in South America. Pop just never imagined it could happen in America, albeit for different reasons.

He didn't hesitate, immediately turning and bulling his way through the throngs of would-be shoppers trying to force themselves into the store. If this melee was about to hit the news, then he only had one chance to stock up before the quiet little town of Apalachicola would react.

CHAPTER 14

Sunday, April 15
CBS Broadcast Studios
New York, NY

"Jackie, don't be nervous." Sparky Newsome tried to encourage his friend to relax. "I mean, I know how you feel, but once you start talking, it's easy. Just tell the truth about what happened and, most importantly, keep your answers short. If you go on and on, then Jack will have to interrupt you, and it throws you off track. You know?"

Jackie Holcombe had experienced the worst side of the way the American government was capable of treating innocent citizens when, in the name of *national security*, they cast aside the Constitution and civil liberties. Sadly, over the last half century in America, national security had been used as an excuse to operate in the shadows, allowing actions to be taken that were hidden from public view. Jackie was a victim of this trend, but now she was bravely going to tell her story.

Jack Young, the CNN national correspondent whom Sparky had contacted first the day Jackie was abducted, entered the green room to speak with his interview subjects. "Okay, it's almost go-time. Let me reiterate, there's a reason we don't like to rehearse these types of interviews. Our viewers aren't interested in staged Q and A's. They want to hear the truth and will smell a ruse in a heartbeat."

Jackie grimaced and then managed a smile. She appeared embarrassed. "Jack, I'm afraid I'll start crying as I retell what happened."

Young nodded reassuringly. "Then, by all means, cry. Let out the raw emotions that naturally resulted from the ordeal you've been through. People need to know you were being diligent, concerned you'd be labeled a fearmonger if you were wrong. You were never given the chance to share your findings, you know, that started with a hunch by that deceased young man."

"Okay," said Jackie with a slight sniffle.

Sparky patted his old friend on the shoulder and reminded her of a day from their childhood. Do you remember when you had to quit Briarwood Academy because your dad lost his job? You thought that was the end of the world."

Jackie chuckled. "Yeah, I felt like such a jerk because I made fun of you for going to public school, and here I was, the new kid, slummin' it at Washington-Wilkes High School just like you."

"And we came out just fine, didn't we? You became interested in the stars, met the love of your life, and now you're famous. You just never know what will come out of a seemingly crappy turn in life."

Jackie smiled and turned her attention to one of the production assistants entering the green room.

"Mr. Young, they're ready for all of you now."

"Okay, guys, it's showtime. Remember, Jackie, keep it real. Sparky, you're an old hand at this now. How many interviews have you given in the last week? Seven?"

"This will make eleven," he replied. "They say I'm a natural, but my wife says that I ham it up too much for the camera. Honestly, I just keep saying the same thing over and over again, so it's become kinda routine."

"The truth can be mundane at times," said Young. "But in a story like this, it never gets boring. Come on."

Young followed the PA, with his two guests in tow. Following a brief stop at hair and make-up, the two ordinary citizens, now famous because of the discovery of IM86, settled into director's chairs across from Young.

Minutes later, the interview was in full swing.

"Now, Miz Holcombe, you had taken the time to check and recheck your findings. Do you regret not coming forward sooner?"

Jackie hesitated because she had second-guessed herself repeatedly since the night she found Nate Phillips's computer and the video recording. "Jack, I wasn't sure. Maybe it was just fate that I happened to see the obscure streak of light in the background of Comet Oort's long tail. I don't know. But I had to make sure before I went public. You know, the media." She paused and smiled at Sparky, then to her host. "The media doesn't always treat someone respectfully when they make a claim like this one. You know, tinfoil-hat-wearing conspiracist and all that."

Young furrowed his brow. "What happened the next day?"

"Well, Sparky was pretty insistent that we contact the appropriate authorities, which, for me, was the Minor Planet Center at Cambridge. I insisted on speaking with someone in charge and got the head of the MPC, which really shocked me. After I provided her everything I knew, and sent the email with all of my findings, it was like a huge burden had been lifted off my shoulders."

"Then what happened?" asked Young.

"To be honest, it frightened me so bad that I thought I'd been swatted," replied Jackie. Swatting was a harassment tactic whereby someone would deceive 911 emergency operators that a hostage situation or bomb threat or active-shooter scenario existed at an individual's address, resulting in a heavily armed SWAT team descending upon the premises. At times, the homeowner had been fatally injured as a result of the heinous practice.

"Did they announce who they were?" asked Young.

"No. No knock. No warning. Only the kicking in of my front door. Within seconds, I was pulled off my sofa and thrown to the floor. I was handcuffed and threatened to stay quiet. The entire ordeal took less than a minute. They jerked me off the floor and threw me in the back of a van. It was just like you might see in the movies."

"Then what?"

"I was blindfolded and gagged. I couldn't stop crying and began to hyperventilate. I kicked and tried to beg them to let me breathe, but the driver and the passenger ignored me. I kinda lost track of time, but I'm guessin' it was an hour later when the van came to a stop and I was dragged into a helicopter."

Young shook his head and provided the camera an appropriate look of disgust. "At some point, you were allowed to speak, correct?"

"Yes, only for a moment, while on the helicopter. They didn't ask me about the comet or the asteroid. They didn't seem to care about any of that."

"What did they want to know?" asked Young.

"Who I'd told about the asteroid. At first, I lied because, um, I'd only talked to two people, Sparky and my husband. I was worried for them both, so I told them nobody. I was still blindfolded and really scared, especially when a man with a deep voice began screaming at me. He said he had my phone and saw that I'd placed two phone calls. He read the numbers off and confirmed they were Sparky and my husband from the address book. That's when I fessed up."

Young studied his notes and looked toward Sparky. First, he turned back to Jackie. "What happened to your husband?"

"Well, my husband is a truck driver, and he'd come back from being on the road," she began. She glanced over at Sparky, and tears welled up in her eyes. "He, um, I'm sorry."

"That's okay, Miz Holcombe." Young waved to a production assistant, who already had a box of Kleenex at the ready to provide to Jackie in case she broke down.

Jackie lost all sense of decorum and blew her nose, a common human act that was rarely seen on live television. She regained her composure somewhat and continued. "Anyway, he came home and found our place torn apart by the same people who took me away. He was concerned and called Sparky after trying several other friends of ours. During their conversation, Sparky's phone went dead, and James freaked out. He drove down to the Taliaferro County Sheriff's Office and started to get suspicious because they wouldn't take his missing person report. When they really stonewalled him, well, he has a bit of a temper and, um, kinda lost it on 'em. They locked him up and refused to allow him a phone call for a day and a half. Then, out of nowhere, in the middle of the night, they let him go. He had to walk home from Crawfordville in the dark, not having any more answers than he did when they locked him up."

Young allowed a dramatic pause and turned to the camera. "When we return, we'll show you what happened when *60 Minutes* correspondents attempted to get an on-camera interview with the sheriff in this rural Georgia county, as well as the response I got when I confronted the head of the FBI field office in Atlanta about the treatment of Miz Holcombe and Mr. Newsome."

Sparky reached over and patted Jackie on the arm, who'd begun to cry again. "Hey, hey, you did great. It's all over now."

"No, it's not over. Other networks want to talk to me, too. Sparky, I don't know if I can. I break down every time. I was so scared."

"Listen, Jackie. I don't know what's gonna happen with this asteroid. I do know our stories need to be told so people are aware of what's happening. The most important thing for you and me to do now is get back home to the people who love us, and plan on how we're going to prepare for what's headed our way."

Young had walked away, and the production assistant allowed the two guests to linger a little longer on the famous set. "Sparky, you do understand that if the Russians don't succeed, and whatever NASA has planned as backup doesn't, we're all toast."

Sparky laughed. "Yeah, I know. Mary and I have reconciled ourselves to that. I'll be honest, I was never into that whole preparedness thing. Beans, Band-Aids, bullets, you know, the doomsday prepper stuff. I've really changed my opinion. As soon as I cashed the check CBS gave me last Monday, Mary and I scooted around town buying up supplies. Heck, we made more trips to Walmart in Thomson than I care to admit. We decided to fight like hell to survive."

Jackie dropped her chin to her chest. "I wish I could get James on board with something like that. He's like *c'est la vie*. You know, whatever happens, happens. I didn't want to fight with him because he was like an ostrich sticking his head in the sand."

"So do it anyway. I mean, buy some food, bottled water, and

maybe a bunch of medical supplies. Do you guys have a gun?"

Jackie laughed. "Come on, Sparky. Everybody back home has at least one gun."

Sparky smiled and shrugged. He hadn't until all of this came about.

Jackie continued. "You know, James is kinda in denial. Would you believe he took a trip to the West Coast this morning? He's gonna be gone a week."

Sparky stood as he sensed the production team needed them to wrap up their conversation. "Okay, maybe that's a good thing. You know, you'll miss him and everything, but while he's gone, you can get ready. On our flight back to Augusta, I'll tell you what I learned from a fella in town who's into that stuff."

CHAPTER 15

Sunday, April 15
Johnson Space Center
Houston, Texas

The usually unflappable Gunner Fox arrived at the Johnson Space Center mentally exhausted. He prided himself upon being unmoved by excitement, always possessing a stoical approach to the cards dealt him in life. After Heather, some said he'd become jaded. Others wondered if he'd ever return to his amiable self. Today, his mind was a ball of mush following his whirlwind trip to Fort Belvoir and, later, Wallops Island. He was ready to hit the sack and start fresh in the morning.

A car met him at the gate, and two friendly members of the NASA security team drove him to Building 9, the home of the astronaut training center and the technologically advanced Space Vehicle Mockup Facility.

He recalled Heather telling him about the famed building that had become such an important part of NASA's operations. Since 1980, every astronaut had walked the floors of Building 9, where astronauts trained and engineers developed the next generation of space-exploration vehicles.

Within Building 9, located in the heart of the NASA Johnson Space Center, the astronauts studied in full-size classrooms that resembled a variety of space vehicles, from the original shuttles to the latest in experimental spacecraft like the Starhopper.

For the moment, all normal operations within Building 9—involving training for future missions, or the construction of space vehicle mockups—had been halted. The facility had been cleared for just one purpose—training Gunner and the team of astronauts who'd make the second attempt to protect Earth from the planet-killing asteroid, IM86.

"Major, you've been assigned one of six housing units within Building 9 at the request of your assigned training officer. Most likely, you'll spend ninety percent of your time here, I'm told."

Gunner nodded as he exited the car and followed the two security personnel into the building. "Can you tell me the name of this training officer?"

"I'm sorry, sir. That's not up to us. Once you get settled in, take a shower, and have a meal, an orientation officer will reach out to you and give you an idea of your schedule."

Gunner shrugged and walked through the desolate building. It was late on Sunday night, and he suspected any last-minute arrangements for tomorrow's training sessions had already been made.

"What about clothes? As you can tell, I packed light." Gunner held his hands out to his sides, reminding his escorts that he didn't have any luggage. He waited for an answer as they approached a security desk guarding a set of steel doors.

"Sir, we're going to hand you off now. This gentleman will be able to assist you further. Good luck, sir."

Good luck? I'll need more than luck, but I won't turn it down if it comes my way.

"Sir," began the desk guard, "welcome to Building 9."

"Thanks. Um, where is everybody?" Gunner looked around again at the dimly lit complex of offices and classrooms.

"It's been a busy forty-eight hours, sir, in preparation for tomorrow. You're the last to arrive."

Gunner appeared confused. "I am? I mean, there are others?"

"Yes, sir. You are one of six bunking at Building 9. Two senior officers are located at other residential housing units here at the JSC."

"Okay." Gunner stretched out the word as he glanced around again. "Say, do you have any clothes hanging around here? You know, maybe one of those cool white jumpsuits with the NASA logo on it?"

The security guard laughed. "No, sir. There are khakis and white polo shirts in a variety of sizes inside your quarters. Also, your superior officer had this package delivered for you. It contains some clothing and other personal effects."

He pointed toward an Air Force blue duffle bag with his name imprinted on it. Also, the guard reached to the side of his desk and handed Gunner a box that had been sent via courier. There was no return address.

Gunner accepted the deliveries and then asked, genuinely confused, "Which superior officer?"

"I wasn't told, sir. All I know that is that the package was cleared upon arrival. Anything else at this moment? You can expect a phone call from one of the training coordinators within the hour to let you know when and where to be tomorrow morning. Obviously, it will be within Building 9."

"Yeah, Building 9, like the other guys said. Well, I'm ready for a hot shower and a bunk, but I can manage to stay up long enough for that phone call. Lead the way."

Gunner followed the security guard down a long hallway until they reached the last room on the right. Once he entered the sparsely furnished efficiency-style apartment, he recalled that Heather had stayed here for a brief period of time in preparation for the first failed Artemis One mission. He walked inside, dropped the package on the kitchen bar, and foolishly looked into the refrigerator, hoping that a six-pack of Oyster City beer awaited him. Even a Shiner would do.

He shook his head in disappointment at the dozen bottles of water and cans of 7 Up. He shut the refrigerator and wandered around the one-room efficiency. There was no television, no radio, and no phone. Gunner scowled and moved the sheers out of the way to see if iron bars prevented him from leaving.

A solid plate-glass window overlooking a long span of concrete pavement was all that separated him from stepping out on the town. He'd come into Houston once to visit Heather while she was training. During a weekend furlough she was given, they'd spent their time at nearby Kemah Boardwalk, an entertainment and restaurant venue on Galveston Bay.

Bored, he checked his watch, glanced at the package that came for him, and headed for an armoire that looked like it came straight out of an IKEA catalog. As he was told, the shelves were full of khaki slacks and white polo shirts. After finding his size, he was headed toward the bathroom to shower when something in his gut stopped him.

He set the clothes on the bath vanity and returned to the deliveries. He emptied the contents of the duffle bag on the kitchen island. Then, his curiosity getting the best of him, he ripped off the clear tape and viewed the contents. He pulled out a CIA-issue Globalstar satellite phone and a note. There were several Air Force tee shirts and a long-sleeve tee adorned with the NASA logo and an image of the space shuttle on the back.

He read the note aloud. "We thought you'd like a few things from home, and Ghost wanted to make sure you had comms with GPS in case you get lost and need directions. *Ride or die*. Major Mills."

Gunner smiled and looked at the shirts on the counter. The Air Force logo tees were similar to the ones he wore around Dog Island or when he was training at Tyndall. The NASA shirt was new and a design he'd never seen before. He held it up and studied the logo on the back depicting the space shuttle. It brought a tear to his eye as he thought of Heather.

Then he noticed something. Words were written behind the logo with a black sharpie. Gunner quickly turned the long-sleeve tee inside out. He fumbled with the fabric and held it up to the light. It read ... *Watch your back – G.*

CHAPTER 16

Monday, April 16
Building 9
Johnson Space Center
Houston, Texas

The packages sent from Cam and Ghost made for a sleepless night. Despite his exhaustion, thoughts swirled through his mind as he tried to decipher Ghost's cryptic message. The words were simple, often used, but had a distinctive meaning. *Watch your back* meant someone was out to get you.

And why would Ghost have Cam send him a satellite phone? Unless Gunner missed something somewhere, the range on the Globalstar didn't extend to the Moon, much less to where the asteroid was coming from. *Is he suggesting that I might need to contact him from Building 9? Is the threat within this facility? Or somewhere else?* Gunner glanced upward. *Like, up there.*

He fumbled with the unique device specifically designed for CIA operatives to withstand the scrutiny of X-ray security checkpoints. Ghost had to know that the package would be scanned, so it was a risk to send it to Gunner. Yet Cam had made a joke about it in case it was confiscated.

He flexed his fingers and was about to power the device on when a hard knock on the door startled him.

"Major Fox, they're assembling in the briefing room."

Gunner quickly stowed the phone deep in the middle of his mattress and replied, "Wait up. I'll need directions."

He checked himself in the mirror. He looked like a college student at a preparatory school up East. He'd really hoped for a uniform of some sort.

Gunner entered the hallway, where a young man waited for him with an arm full of three-ring binders. "Sir, you won't be using all of these today, but the chief said to bring them with you."

"The chief?" asked Gunner.

"Yes, sir," the young man replied, shoving the binders into Gunner's chest. "You'll have the honor of being trained by a legend. You're very lucky, Major."

Gunner chuckled. "Yeah, everybody keeps telling me how lucky I am, and others wish me good luck. I sure hope that there's more to this than luck and a prayer."

The young man escorted Gunner down the hallway toward the front reception desk where he'd arrived last night, and opened the door for him. "Sir, in my opinion, I'd rather have prayer on my side. Godspeed."

Gunner furrowed his brow and looked inside. His eyes grew wide as he walked into a miniature version of an IMAX theater. The orbiting rocket of the NASA logo was circling around the room, periodically displaced by images of the International Space Station flying in orbit around the Earth.

"Major Fox, please join us."

Gunner recognized the crusty old codger that stood in the center of the theater-like classroom. He'd seen him before but couldn't quite place him. He suddenly realized that a dozen sets of eyes were intently studying him, and each of those sets of eyes were from astronauts in uniform. In fact, everyone in the room, except for the man who greeted him, was fully dressed in NASA fatigues.

From the glares he was receiving, he suddenly understood two things. One, he was not one of them, hence the reason he was outfitted in mundane khakis and a white shirt. Second, Ghost was giving him a heads-up that the daggers might be out for him.

He was prepared for the naysayers, those who would ridicule him, criticizing the world's premier space agency for going outside their own ranks of seasoned astronauts for this mission. Gunner knew how Heather would feel about that.

But then, if challenged, he'd look any one of them in the eyes and ask if they'd ever flown a combat jet at Mach 3? Or had they ever made a precision missile strike? Gunner was not discounting their expertise and importance to this mission. However, he also knew that he was the only one in the room with the expertise to do what they needed, and succeed. *With a little luck.*

"Ladies and gentlemen, we're gonna get right to it because there is no time to waste. Everyone in this room knows who I am, except for maybe Major Fox. Am I correct, Major?"

Gunner set down the set of binders on a desk with a thud and slid into a padded swivel chair in the front row. "Well, sir, all I know is that you're a legend. At least that's what the fella who handed me this stack of stuff said."

Laughter spread throughout the room as Chief Rawlings managed a smile. He reached over for his NASA coffee mug, not to take a sip, but to spit out some of his tobacco juice.

"Major Fox, some folks around here might say that. Others think I'm a complete prick. It'll be up to you to render your own judgment. One thing is certain, I'm the best chance you have of coming home from this mission alive."

The room quieted down and the astronauts fidgeted nervously in their seats. Not Gunner. He'd faced death more than once. It never crossed his mind that death was a possibility, unless it affected someone he loved.

Chief Rawlings had full command of the room. He wandered about as he spoke, standing next to each astronaut, somehow gauging their interest and comfort level with this mission. As he briefed them, he clicked the remote device in his hand.

"Let me say this from the git-go, what we're about to attempt has never been done on this scale. Oh, sure, there are a bunch of computer whiz kids, who are a helluva lot smarter than we are, running simulations and applying different scenarios and coming up with probabilities about the success of this mission. As we all know, this has never been attempted. But hey, there's a first time for everything, right?"

Nobody laughed, although it was said more in a sarcastic tone than a jovial one.

Chief Rawlings continued. "Here's our boogeyman. 2029 IM86. The first asteroid of its size, or even close, for that matter, to be on track to cross orbital trajectories with our planet in sixty-six million years. Make no mistake, people, this is a planet killer." He emphasized the last five words by speaking them with a different cadence, intentionally slowing down and separating each word. His intentional drama worked, and the astronauts glanced over at one another. Thus far, Gunner was unfazed as he continued to soak in the information.

"Now, I want to show you something that will put some minds at ease and infuriate others. Or, frankly, all of you."

The screen changed from IM86 streaking through space to the orbiter that had just been detached from the Falcon Heavy rocket boosters. The video played in slow motion, showing the exact moment the ballistic missile struck the orbiter, causing it to explode.

Gunner felt the room fill with fury and despair. Several of the astronauts fought back tears, as they'd likely lost friends on the first mission to attack the asteroid. Some of the astronauts balled their fists and scowled, the rage building inside them as they were prepared to punch the assholes who were responsible. Gunner remained stoic, partly because he'd seen the video yesterday at Fort Belvoir, allowing him the opportunity to let his anger build and then subside.

"I didn't show you this to get your dander up or cause you any more distress than you've already suffered at this senseless loss," continued Chief Rawlings. "I'm showing you this for the sole reason to inform you that what happened on Friday was not a mission failure on the part of NASA. Our space program is the safest and most advanced of any in the world, despite what that moron in Moscow might believe. And I intend to prove it once again."

Heads nodded throughout the room as high fives and fist bumps were exchanged. Thus far, nobody acknowledged Gunner, so he didn't feel the same sense of camaraderie.

"Now, let me tell you how we're gonna attack this booger."

CHAPTER 17

Monday, April 16
Building 9
Johnson Space Center
Houston, Texas

"Hypervelocity Asteroid Mitigation Mission for Emergency Response—HAMMER." Chief Rawlings paused to laugh to himself, and then he relieved his mouth of some tobacco juice. Over several decades, he'd seen many technological advances come and go. The visions of scientists came to fruition. The fictional imaginations of authors became realities.

"HAMMER," he continued, "came out of the Apophis sighting back in '04. Initial observations indicated a two-point-seven percent chance of an impact event with Earth. It was an oh shit moment for everyone."

He changed the image to show a model of Apophis, a quarter-mile-wide asteroid that didn't pack near the punch that IM86 potentially possessed, but the impact of which would have been devastating on a regional scale.

"Apophis was named after a Greek god who was often referred to as the *Uncreator*, an evil serpent that dwelled in eternal darkness." Chief Rawlings paused and changed the image on the IMAX-style monitors to provide the astronauts a visual of Apophis and IM86 side by side. There was no comparison.

"If Apophis was the Uncreator, as they say, then what the hell are they gonna call this booger? Here's the thing, no two asteroids are alike. They vary by size, mass, density, speed, geologic makeup—I could go on.

"When NASA and the Energy Department developed the HAMMER project, they designed it for Apophis, which was scheduled to zip dangerously close to us on April 13, last Friday. This possibility kept Apophis as a Level 4 on the Torino scale until further study reduced the risk. As of now, 2036 is the revised date on which it could impact Earth. But Apophis won't matter if we don't deal with IM86 first."

He switched the screen to a spacecraft that resembled a satellite. "This eight-point-eight-ton craft was designed to alter the orbital trajectory of Apophis, either by crashing into it or detonating a nuclear device on its surface. This kinetic impactor, based upon NASA's projections, would've effectively saved Earth from a damaging collision with Apophis. Great concept, but totally worthless as it relates to IM86."

The screen switched back to IM86. "This booger is simply too big for a little old satellite-sized spacecraft. That's why we've been forced to take it up a notch, to a level never before attempted. I call it Project JACKHAMMER."

The next image he revealed showed an artist's rendering of the Starhopper flying toward IM86. He continued. "When I was a kid, I'd take any job I could find. Growing up in tiny Gail, Texas, there wasn't such a thing as bagging groceries for the summer to make a little spare change. You either worked on a ranch or twiddled your thumbs. But one summer I got a job helping the Reinecke Company expand one of their oil drillin' units by leaning on a jackhammer for eight hours a day.

"Here's what I learned from that. You can hit a big old rock with a big old sledgehammer with all you've got one time, and ain't nothin' gonna change. Oh, you might flick off a shard or two, but that's it. Give me that jackhammer, and let me pound away at cracks, crevices, and indentations, and in no time, I'll bust her up. That's what we're gonna do to IM86—break that booger into pieces."

Chief Rawlings was a storyteller, and he had the room full of highly educated adults captivated as he related his childhood experiences to saving humanity from a planet killer. He spit out a little tobacco, and then he walked next to Gunner. His hands were rough and somewhat wrinkled from years of West Texas dirt and sun. He placed them on Gunner's shoulders.

"This man is not an astronaut. In fact, I suspect that flying a mission for NASA is the last thing he wants to do. However, he is likely one of the best combat pilots in the Air Force, and he knows how to drop a missile so that it finds and destroys its target.

"IM86 will have to be destroyed with more than a single kinetic impact. It's gonna need multiple precisely placed nukes to break it apart. Major Fox is the guy who can do that, and every one of us, if called upon, will make sure that he gets that opportunity."

Gunner smiled and mumbled, but loud enough for the others in the room to hear, "Sounds easy enough." This drew a few laughs and several eye rolls from the group of astronauts.

Chief Rawlings slapped Gunner on the back and walked away. He found his remote control and changed the screen to the original NASA logo. A tall swivel chair had been pushed against the wall, and Chief Rawlings retrieved it, sliding onto the seat to take a load off his feet. He'd barely slept in preparation for the monumental task of training someone to not only travel into space for the first time but to operate a nuclear-armed spaceship that was designed for ferrying humans to and from the Moon.

"Questions?" he barked as he reached for his spit cup.

A female astronaut, a senior member of the group, spoke first. "Chief, with all due respect to the capabilities of Major Fox, there's a huge difference between the aerodynamics of an aircraft and a space vehicle like the Starhopper. As Major Fox can attest, his combat jet relies upon air to generate lift, thrust, and maintain stability. A spacecraft, on the other hand, is wholly dependent on the thrust generated by its rocket engines and, in the case of the Starhopper, the cold gas thrusters. The vacuum of space is a completely different environment."

Chief Rawlings began to respond to her point when Gunner interrupted him. "May I?"

"By all means."

Gunner stood and addressed the group. He felt confident, as always. "It's true that I've never flown into space, well, except for the stratosphere, you know, just to get a better look of what you guys have experienced. Anyway, flying a combat jet is actually more difficult because of the air, wind and other atmospheric conditions. It's not a vacuum-like environment, so the pilot must always make adjustments as the conditions dictate. In space, once you get the feel of the controls, it would seem to me that the tiny thrusters could provide more control over the maneuverability of the craft."

The female astronaut continued to be the voice of her comrades. "My concern, Major, is that it takes years of training to get *the feel*, if you will. Too much thrust, or too little, can result in your spacecraft crashing into its docking partner, or a hard landing on the lunar surface that compromises the structural integrity."

"Well, there's another issue," interjected another astronaut. "Speed. Major, your fighter jets can travel up to, say, Mach 3, in most cases. That's just over two thousand miles per hour. Even hypersonic travel doesn't compare to what's required to keep up with an asteroid."

"How fast is IM86 moving?" asked Gunner.

"TBD, but estimates place it at just under sixty thousand miles per hour," responded the astronaut.

Gunner turned to Chief Rawlings. "And how fast will my spacecraft travel?" Gunner intentionally referred to the Starhopper as *his spacecraft*. It was time to remind everyone in the room who was necessary to pull off this mission. Something Cam and Bear always understood was that there could only be one person driving the bus.

"It can push seventy K if need be," he replied.

"Well, there you have it," said Gunner. "Speed's relative. As long as the spacecraft can keep up with the target, and it maneuvers as I need it to, then we can take care of business. Am I right?"

The female astronaut was persistent. "But, again with all due respect, Major, you've never done it."

Gunner shut down the conversation. "And neither have you. Nor anyone else, for that matter. Pinpoint bombing isn't like playing video games on your sofa. It takes more than training. It takes an eye for the target, a steady hand, and perfect timing.

"Even with advanced technology that can be used on *seekers*, those missiles that use heat or GPS to latch on to a target, without that touch—the innate ability to transmit commands from your brain to your fingertips—you'll miss. A miss means failure. Failure means everybody dies."

Chief Rawlings stood and shoved his hands in his pockets as he surveyed the room. He gave Gunner a nod of approval. He turned around and addressed the room.

"No pressure."

CHAPTER 18

Colonel Maxwell Robinson had a storied history with the Department of Defense, one that would never be told. The U.S. government, like others like it around the globe, had its secrets. Matters of state, as they're known, that never see the light of day.

To be sure, every government has its whistleblowers—those who pull back the curtain to give the rest of us a look, except in the communist regimes, which use fear, intimidation, and executions, if necessary, to keep the curtain closed. Names like Edward Snowden, Bradley Manning, and Julian Assange dominated the headlines for decades as America's secrets were exposed.

Did that open up the halls of government so that the American people could see how things work? Not hardly. If anything, it forced the deep state farther underground. The shadows grew darker. Lips remained shut. The curtains were pulled tighter together.

Colonel Robinson was one of those individuals who'd take his knowledge of shadowy dealings to his grave. He considered himself a red-blooded, patriotic American, who, when called upon, did the deeds that nobody else had the intestinal fortitude to do.

In a way, he was not that different from someone like Gunner Fox. Gunner's missions were always *off the books*, *dark ops* kind of stuff that the American people suspected were going on, but didn't care to know about. Envelopes were pushed. Laws were ignored. Morals and values were cast aside at times. All for the greater good.

Colonel Robinson could sleep at night without remorse or regret. He always justified carrying out his orders, even if he overstepped his bounds at times. Those who gave them, longtime officials of the State Department and the Pentagon, took orders from the administrations they served. Make no mistake, regardless of political affiliation, presidents and their teams have relied upon the Colonel Maxwell Robinsons and Gunner Foxes to do their deeds. They were considered indispensable in the defense of the nation.

Colonel Robinson rubbed his temples as eyestrain began to overtake the rest of his head, causing a migraine to emerge. A combination of sleepless nights and stress were taking their toll on the sixty-four-year-old, who should've retired many years ago. He didn't continue working for the money, as his pay and *bonuses for a job well done* made for a comfortable lifestyle. He did it out of a sense of duty.

The astronauts' dossiers were spread around his desk, some neatly stacked into piles, others laid open with Post-it notes marking pages of interest. Robinson had several legal pads on his desk, each containing his thoughts on the different candidates.

While Chief Rawlings was preparing Gunner for his mission, Colonel Robinson was actively seeking his replacement. It was a vetting process that only a handful of people knew about. Officials of the government at the Pentagon and within the West Wing. People who wanted to find a way to keep Gunner Fox on Earth.

In his chosen line of work, Colonel Robinson operated under one basic principle—*gossip kills three people. The one who speaks it, the one who listens, and the one about whom it was spoken.*

The director of Flight Control One in the Mission Control Center, Mark Foster, did not give orders to Colonel Robinson. He just happened to be in the wrong place at the wrong time during a sad time in NASA's history.

In fact, there was a point when Colonel Robinson had performed this same exercise to find a replacement for Foster, but was told to stand down. He tried to argue his point with his superiors, without appearing to question their directives. He knew Foster to be weak and therefore vulnerable to pressure. But, as the events of three years ago unfolded, and the details of the tragedy were hidden within the dark recesses of government, Foster acknowledged that he had a vested interest in keeping his mouth shut. Nonetheless, Colonel Robinson would've preferred to eliminate Foster, one of the *gossips* in his axiom.

A light tapping on the door brought him to attention, and he quickly scrambled to cover up his project. "Who is it?"

"Mark."

Robinson rolled his eyes and sighed. "Sure, come on in." He really didn't want to be interrupted, but Foster could provide valuable insight on the three candidates he'd identified to replace Gunner on the mission.

Foster entered and headed for the chair, immediately annoying the colonel.

"Foster, my door was shut for a reason. Please close it behind you."

After closing the door, Foster plopped into the chair across the desk. "What have you come up with?"

Robinson organized the notepads in front of him, revealing four names arranged in columns, with a series of notes labeled pros and cons underneath.

"Basically, it was a process of elimination. Some of these astronauts are totally worthless. Strictly eggheads who fill up beakers or stare through microscopes. These four have the aptitude to pull off the mission because they've flown the Starhopper, both to the lunar outpost and to dock with the ISS."

"That's a far cry from what Major Fox is tasked with," interrupted Foster.

"No shit. But at least they can pull it off. It might be a suicide mission for them, but that's not my problem. They all know what they've signed up for."

Foster leaned forward and scanned the desk. "Can I see?"

Colonel Robinson handed him the two legal pads. "On this one, I've got two options with military experience. Both of them are equal, but this one worked at Creech Air Force Base for a period of time, piloting MQ-9 Reaper drones."

"I know Hector well," said Foster. "She's got a level head. But she's also married with a kid. She may sign on for the first leg to the Moon, but I seriously doubt she'd agree to head to IM86."

"She would if her president asked her to!" Colonel Robinson couldn't understand why anyone would turn down a mission as critical as this one, much less refuse to answer the call to duty.

Foster studied the other notepad. "Crawford is a good candidate. He's single and has a reputation as a space cowboy. He's an attention seeker who always seems to find the cameras when the media comes around."

Robinson grabbed his dossier. "He's got a pedigree. His dad was one of the early ISS crew members. No military experience, but he's flown the Starhopper more than once. He might be our guy."

"Honestly, I would've pointed to him from the beginning if anybody had asked me."

Robinson dropped Crawford's file back on the desk and rubbed his head again. "Rawlings has been driving this mission from the beginning. He had the benefit of sitting in the conference room with the chief of staff when the whole thing started. It's hard to overturn his plan without something drastic."

"Do you wanna change the mission?" asked Foster, appearing puzzled by the colonel's statement.

"No, his proposal is solid. I'm just not comfortable with whom he recruited to carry it out, for obvious reasons."

Foster nodded in agreement. He looked at the legal pads again and then returned them to Robinson. "Max, I can subtly approach Crawford and see if he's mentally up for the task. Everyone in that training program created by Chief Rawlings realizes that if they're tapped to ride along with Major Fox, they may not return."

"Yeah, do that," instructed Robinson.

"Max, have you thought about what I just said? That this is a one-way mission?"

"Yeah, and I know where you're headed with this. If Fox was

flying solo and had no contact with the other astronauts or the personnel on the Moon, I'd send his ass up there to die. The problem, the lunar outpost is crawling with Russians, many of whom were on the ISS that day. I can't risk him coming in contact with them and then causing a damn revolt."

"I get it," said Foster. "What about Fox? How will you keep him grounded?"

"Leave that to me."

CHAPTER 19

Tuesday, April 17
Building 9
Johnson Space Center
Houston, Texas

Gunner slept hard the night before. His exhaustion and wakefulness had finally caught up with him. He crashed soon after having dinner in the cafeteria with several of the astronauts who had been friendly to him during the day. Gunner sensed the hostility, but others went out of their way to make him feel comfortable, especially those who'd known Heather. Much of the conversation over dinner was devoted to her rather than the looming mission.

When he was awakened by the alarm on his watch, he jumped out of bed well rested, hit the showers, and hustled downstairs to the large conference room, where a light breakfast was served.

He was excited about today's schedule because the classroom work was mostly behind him now, and later that afternoon, it would be time for him to slip into the seat of the Starhopper simulator.

But first, he had to undergo the worst part of the entire week—the psychological evaluation. When he was told by Chief Rawlings that it was an absolute necessity, Gunner tried to argue that NASA was stuck with him, so the process was a waste of time. Besides, he had a three-inch-thick file to peruse from Dr. Dowling at Eglin if he wanted to see what made Gunner tick.

Chief Rawlings was not persuaded by Gunner's argument. While it was true that NASA's astronaut psychological examination was known to eliminate candidates at times, in Gunner's case, it was more to expose any mental weaknesses that he might have concerning space travel. Once identified, then the psych team, along with Chief Rawlings, could modify his training to address the potential scenarios and responses.

After some last-minute grumbling, Chief Rawlings led Gunner to the psychologist and said he'd be waiting outside to ensure the doctor got everything she needed.

"Major Fox, I'm Dr. Blasingame. I'm fully aware of the expedited process due to the circumstances we face, so I'll be dispensing with the preliminaries. Naturally, for most AsCans, this aspect of their application is just as important as their education, experience, and physicality.

"It is a rigorous process designed to separate the wheat from the chaff. Truthfully, it's an elimination process rather than an inclusion technique. AsCans don't get the benefits afforded to you in this particular case. If they don't have the right stuff, as the saying goes, they're removed as a candidate. In your case, we're looking for those attributes that will make you a great astronaut, albeit temporary, and any weaknesses that I believe warrant special attention as we move forward. Do you understand?"

"I have a question," said Gunner.

"Fire away."

"What do you mean by *albeit temporary*? I mean, I'm not temporary and fully intend to return to Earth after I blast this sucker."

"No. No. Major, that's not what I meant. I was referring to your length of time in this temporary career as an astronaut."

"What makes you think that I don't want to sign on to future missions? I mean, I feel like I'm ready for a career change and—"

Dr. Blasingame was furiously writing notes, and Gunner stopped mid-sentence. As she continued to write, he leaned onto her desk to catch a glimpse of her notepad. She quickly covered it up and peered at him over her glasses.

"What?" he asked, feigning innocence.

"Argumentative. Deflective. Delusional. Uses charm as a defensive mechanism. Strong will to live."

Gunner's eyes closed slightly. He didn't like to be psychoanalyzed.

"So? What's your point?"

Dr. Blasingame laughed. "Two things. Number one, I read your file from Dr. Dowling, who, by the way, happens to be an old colleague of mine and, therefore, shared his true opinion by telephone yesterday. You see, there's a patient's file, and then there's that unwritten file that a psychologist will only share with a close friend."

Gunner frowned. "Doesn't that break some kind of ethical rule or something?"

Dr. Blasingame leaned onto her elbows and studied Gunner. "The last thing that Brian said to me after our hour-long conversation was *please keep him alive.* That's what I intend to do, Major. So let's get started."

Gunner was stunned by her statement, but appreciative at the same time. He and Dr. Dowling had worked together for years, but it was only after he crashed the F/A XX that he realized the good doctor truly cared about his well-being. It had changed Gunner's approach to treatment.

"Major, I only have two hours with you. The first part of the testing usually involves an interview process. We're already underway, as you can see; plus I have the benefit of Dr. Dowling's clinical notes and appraisal of your mental state."

"What's the second part?"

"Ordinarily, we put our AsCans through a variety of field exercises to determine their fitness for space. The job that an AsCan is selected for is often determined by this process. For your purposes, we need to focus on keeping you mentally stable long enough for you to *blast that sucker*, as you put it, and then get you home safely."

"Sounds like a plan."

Dr. Blasingame removed her glasses and dropped them onto the desk. "The two most challenging aspects of spending an extensive amount of time in space is the close quarters and the isolation. You have the benefit of training as a combat pilot, where you're used to squeezing your body into the cockpit of an aircraft with little or no room to move other than to operate the controls. The Starhopper will seem like sitting in a cushy recliner compared to that.

"Secondly, the matter of isolation from friends and families. Major, I'm familiar with your situation. I evaluated your wife many years ago. I understand heartbreak. A concern of Dr. Dowling's is that you haven't been able to move on and, at times, you exhibit reckless behavior. You do realize that will get you killed in space, and any others who might be within your sphere of influence."

"I understand."

"Okay. We're going to spend time discussing sleep deprivation, something that's common in astronauts in the months leading up to launch, as well as in those initial days following arrival at the ISS or the lunar outpost, as the case may be. Again, your case is different because of the time limitations, but you're not going to have the benefit of the sleep aids ordinarily provided to the astronaut team. You must remain completely alert and be able to respond to emergency situations at all times. As you'll see once you arrive at the lunar outpost, the schedule could change based upon solar activity, updates on the trajectory of IM86, and any number of other unforeseen events."

"Got it."

"Before you and I finish up with this morning session, let me forewarn you that we'll be getting together at the end of what will be a very long day for you. That is by design. Days in space are like nothing you've ever experienced before. It takes a toll on your mind and body. There is a battery of stress tests that I'll be putting you through this evening, designed to be administered when you're at your weakest state."

"Sounds simple enough. I've got pretty good endurance."

Dr. Blasingame laughed and retrieved her glasses. She was getting ready to get down to business, but she added, "Major, it's less about endurance than it is hand-eye coordination. You'll be required to track targets on a computer screen and push buttons as prompted. We've learned that astronauts make tracking mistakes twice as often during a mission than prelaunch. Your reaction time is significantly less, and accuracy suffers as well.

"Frankly, there is nothing more important than the results we glean from the Test of Reaction and Adaptation Capabilities, or TRAC. You're our gunner, pardon the pun. You need to be a deadeye marksman for this mission to succeed."

Now it was Gunner's time to laugh uproariously. "Doc, if that's all we need to know, I can leave now. There isn't anybody better than me, under any conditions, in any aircraft, or spacecraft, for that matter."

Dr. Blasingame made another notation on her notepad.

Overconfident? Arrogant? Justifiably so?

CHAPTER 20

Tuesday, April 17
Building 9
Johnson Space Center
Houston, Texas

Chief Rawlings had just escorted Gunner back to his quarters when his phone rang. It was Dr. Blasingame, who requested to see him as soon as possible. Chief Rawlings had been present during the TRAC session with Dr. Blasingame, and the two of them discussed it as they walked back to Building 9.

Neither knew the actual results, but Gunner did express frustration that the test was unrealistic and, on several occasions, he made suggestions on how to make it better. Chief Rawlings tried to explain that the test was not of his abilities in the flight deck of a combat jet, but rather, how well he reacted under tired, stressful conditions.

It was just past eleven that evening when he arrived at the psychologist's office. Dr. Blasingame waved him in and reached into the bottom of her desk drawer to retrieve a bottle of Garrison Brothers Bourbon Whiskey. Unlike its Kentucky and Tennessee cousins, Garrison Brothers featured bolder flavors of black cherry, licorice, and cinnamon. By aging in barrels in Texas locales where the weather tends to fluctuate, the Garrison Brothers bourbon tends to be more flavorful with a big taste.

She poured a couple of straight shots into two glasses, and after they clinked them together, the two old friends downed their first round.

Dr. Blasingame reached for a report on her desk and sighed. She spun it around and shoved it toward Chief Rawlings.

"What's the verdict?" he asked.

"Below average, which surprised me," she replied. "But, that said, it was better than you on your first try."

Chief Rawlings laughed and slid his shot glass toward the half-full bottle.

She poured them both another shot and continued. "The problem was not a slow response time, but quite the opposite. It was as if he was predicting where the target would be in an attempt to game the system, so to speak. In other words, he tried to anticipate when the prompt to press the button was going to occur."

The former astronaut scowled. "He's used to shooting moving targets. It's kinda like bird hunting. You follow the target and sometimes you fire to a spot rather than at the bird."

"Okay. His brain was defaulting to his air-combat experience rather than performing the test as instructed. So I have to ask, did you have any similar issues with him in the simulator?"

"A couple of times. He wants to be a fast learner, and make no mistake, he is. I've never seen anyone grasp the concept of commanding a spacecraft so quickly. That said, he has a tendency to skip steps, and he expresses an understanding of a procedure I show him, but later he can't perform it."

Dr. Blasingame looked through the file provided by the medical team at Eglin. "Did you know he's had at least six concussions in the last few years? Maybe we should run a CT scan and some other cognitive tests."

Chief Rawlings shrugged. "I guess we could do that, but I think it might be something else. Gunner is feeling an inordinate sense of urgency."

Now it was Dr. Blasingame's turn to shrug. "Well, when he wakes up in the morning, he'll be forty-eight hours from launch. Here's what I think. This imperative to act quickly has resulted in his choosing to ignore or disregard certain critical steps. The TRAC results show that he's trying to anticipate rather than be patient and react. You're telling me that he claims to have a grasp of a concept, but later can't perform the task as required."

"I need to slow him down, is that what you're saying?" asked Chief Rawlings.

Dr. Blasingame leaned back in her chair and stared at the ceiling for a moment. While she did, Chief Rawlings poured them both another drink.

"The thing is," she began before pausing, "you can't slow him down. There's no time. You just have to make him think that there's no rush. Try to curtail his adrenaline."

"Oh, okay. I'm supposed to rein in a thoroughbred on the final stretch as he races to win the Triple Crown."

"No, let him race, just remind him to breathe, focus, and absorb. It'll make a difference."

CHAPTER 21

Wednesday, April 18
Defense Threat Reduction Agency
Fort Belvoir, Virginia

The DTRA complex within Fort Belvoir, where more than a dozen military and intelligence agencies were garrisoned, was open twenty-four hours a day, as the war on terror never paused, and the new threat from the Russian Bear began to rise to a boiling point.

The Sikorsky chopper that had gathered up Cam and Bear from Tyndall Air Force Base in the Florida Panhandle earlier that evening made a gentle landing on a helipad adjacent to the parking lot of the main headquarters building. Despite the late hour, lights were on in most of the offices, which were full of communications specialists, their support staff, and the handlers whom operators like Cam and Bear relied upon to keep them safe while in the field.

When Ghost contacted them, he simply indicated that they were on a personal mission for him, on behalf of a friend. Cam and Bear never questioned his motives for calling them rather than using other operatives at his disposal who were based at the DTRA. They were anxious to stay busy, although it felt strange undertaking an op without Gunner leading them.

As soon as they cleared security, Ghost was waiting in the hallway near the same conference room they'd used prior to their Russian mission. He motioned for them to join him, looking nervously about, something totally out of character for the steely ex-colonel.

"Good evening. My apologies for the short notice," he greeted them as he urged them inside the office.

Cam entered first and noticed Special Agent Theodora Cuccinelli sitting quietly behind a laptop on the far side of the conference room. The Jackal had earned the respect of Gunner's team during the Russian mission, and Cam regretted that she hadn't personally reached out to thank her.

Cam walked around the table and gave the young woman a hug. "Thank you for everything you did for us two weeks ago. After the debriefing, I wanted to call, but—"

"That's okay," interrupted the Jackal. "There was no need. Besides, you wouldn't know how to reach me anyway. Do you think Ghost is a ghost? I'm just as bad." She made this last statement with a devious grin that caused her eyes to glisten.

Cam studied her face for a moment and inwardly wondered if the Jackal had a little *badassery* deep down inside her.

"Hey, Agent Jackal," greeted Bear with his customary approach of using silliness to make a grand entrance.

"Hello, Staff Sergeant Barrett," she replied dryly, with a smirk. It was her way of toying with him.

Ghost shut the door and began. "Everyone, please sit down. As you can see, Agent Cuccinelli is still with me at the DTRA. After you gathered the intel from Russia, and in light of what happened on Friday, this small, informally created unit will continue to work together for the foreseeable future, such as it is."

"Sir, that had a hint of gloom to it," interrupted Cam. "I have every confidence in Gunner's ability to assist NASA in whatever they have in mind for him."

"As do I," said Ghost. "However, he is facing some headwinds, and that's part of the reason I've called all of you here. And that is also why I wanted that package delivered to him. Chief Rawlings contacted me for advice as to who could help his astronaut team destroy the asteroid. When he laid out his proposal, I gave him Gunner's name and nobody else's."

"Is Rawlings losing confidence in the choice?" asked the Jackal.

"No, not at all, although I haven't spoken with him since Monday night. It's just that he made it abundantly clear that Gunner was prohibited from outside contact, and he also got the sense that someone, or several someones, are hoping he'll flunk out of class early."

"Who would want that?" asked Bear. "If they need somebody to drop bombs and find their mark, Gunner's the guy."

"I have my suspicions," began Ghost, "but I believe the answers lie in the past."

"What do you mean, sir?" asked Cam.

"It relates back to his wife's days at NASA, and, um, how things ended. I knew Heather and was very fond of her. I took a special interest in Gunner's training while at Hurlburt Field, and I was instrumental in getting him into ancillary programs that put his career on the fast track. But before I made that commitment to my protégé, if you will, I had to make sure his family, in this case Heather, was on board. I made it a point to have informal gatherings that included their families for the occasional lunch or round of beers. I had to be one hundred percent certain that Heather would be okay with me pulling her husband away."

"She was," interjected Cam. "She never complained, and because her career kept her in Houston much of the time, it actually worked out for the two of them."

Ghost nodded. "Yes, I know. My vetting process of Heather resulted in a close bond that made what happened to their family all the more difficult. That's part of the reason I brought you here today. I have unanswered questions about those days three years ago, and the answers lie with a man in Crimea."

"What's his connection?" asked Cam.

The Jackal addressed her question. "He held a position as the project manager of the ISS while he worked within the RKA Mission Control Center. During his days with the Russian Federal Space Agency, he flew several ISS flights and eventually retired from space, only to take up a position overseeing their involvement with the space station."

"What does he know that our own people don't?" asked Bear.

Ghost wandered around the room to stand next to the Jackal. "I've had Agent Cuccinelli nose around a little bit, and we've learned that this project manager, Karlov, suddenly retired three years ago and was moved from Moscow to Crimea, where he took a job as a professor. He was only forty-three years old at the time, young as retirement age goes in Russia."

"Do you think he knows something about Heather?" asked Cam, who was showing an excited, genuine interest in pursuing this lead. She'd always had questions about that day.

"Listen, Major Mills, I know that you and Heather were close—" began Ghost before Cam interrupted him.

"We were best friends, sir. I introduced her to Gunner. Like you, I truly liked her, and I loved the two of them together. They had the kind of love that I wish I could find someday."

The room fell silent as Cam became emotional thinking about her friend. She regained her composure and apologized.

Bear was ready to get started, so he asked about the operation. "Do you want us to have a talk with this Karlov guy? What exactly are we expecting him to say?"

Ghost smiled and sat down next to the Jackal. "Agent Cuccinelli, since you have the clearest head regarding the players involved, why don't you explain what we're looking for, and then I'll discuss the logistics of their insertion into Crimea."

"Do I get to fly a Valor again?" Bear's voice was hopeful.

"No, this time you two will be entering the front door as respected scientific journalists."

Cam started laughing. "I can pull it off, but I don't think he can."

"Shut up, Cam. I can act smart, too."

CHAPTER 22

Wednesday, April 18
Building 9
Johnson Space Center
Houston, Texas

With less than forty-eight hours to liftoff, Gunner remained singularly focused on his training and his upcoming mission. However, his mind couldn't help but wander to Pop and his extended family, Cam and Bear. He'd been given the satellite phone for a reason, but he was certain it wasn't for the purpose of phoning home to chitchat. He'd resisted the urge to call them on several occasions, especially at night when he lay in bed, processing the day's activities and the monumental task before him.

Make no mistake. Gunner Fox fully understood what he'd signed on for. Outwardly, he played it nonchalant, rarely discussing the threat the asteroid posed to the planet. He was very workmanlike in his approach, gathering and absorbing the information by day, and digesting it in the privacy of his room at night.

Today was another important step in this greatly abbreviated training process. Spacecraft were very different from the combat jets and experimental airplanes that he flew. The technology was complicated and required a working knowledge of physics and engineering.

Gunner was used to going fast. He'd broken sound barriers and traveled to heights only experienced by a few aircraft pilots. The designs of spacecraft had taken a hyperjump in the last decade. Prompted by an administration that wanted to return America's space program to greatness, expert designs and innovative engineering made faster-than-speed-of-light spacecraft, solar electric propulsion, and composite cryogenic storage tanks a reality.

Chief Rawlings took Gunner on a brief tour of these new innovations as they sipped coffee that morning. He stopped at a scale model of the IXS *Enterprise*, a conceptual interstellar spacecraft designed by NASA scientist Harry White.

"*Star Trek* is alive and well," quipped Gunner as he walked around the twelve-foot-long model. The spaceship was centrally located and wrapped by two large rings.

"These warp bubbles are the key to interstellar travel," began Chief Rawlings, pointing to the rings. "Currently, we can travel as deep into space as we want using solar electric propulsion. The problem is that we'd travel so slow the astronauts wouldn't live long enough to reach their destination. With these warp bubbles, a spherical ring is created that, theoretically of course, causes space and time to move around the ship, pushing and pulling it forward at unimaginable speeds."

"I can only imagine," said Gunner. "I'm still trying to wrap my head around driving the Starhopper at sixty K an hour."

"Well, it's like you said, speed is all relative to the objects around you. The old saying *passed me like I was standing still* applies here. Once in your space, drawing a bead on your target, everything slows down because there isn't anything to indicate how fast you're going. The key is matching the velocity of this booger."

Gunner finished his coffee and stepped away from Chief Rawlings to throw the cup away. He caught a glimpse of himself in a shiny piece of spacecraft and noticed his beard. He recalled that he hadn't shaved in several days, and his typical five-o'clock shadow had become furry.

"Chief, I'm putting a lot of trust in you, and especially in the engineers at SpaceX. The Raptor engines designed to power the Super Heavy booster have not been tested in space. Listen, don't get me wrong, I have no problem being the first. That's my job here on Earth; why should space be any different?"

"Well, the biggest difference will be the amount of power at your disposal. The Super Heavy combo is capable of delivering two hundred twenty thousand pounds into low-Earth orbit. The Raptor engine combo was designed to send their stainless-steel Starship, the one you saw at Wallops, all the way to Mars. It's gonna be strapped onto your Starhopper. Trust me, you'll have the power to keep up with IM86."

Chief Rawlings led him out of the enormous hangar, which housed the experimental spacecraft, toward the simulation rooms attached to Building 9. As they approached, the seasoned NASA veteran began to address Gunner's progress.

"Gunner, yesterday you spent time in the simulator learning the basic operations of the Starhopper. Fortunately, certain aspects like landing and docking are being omitted because you'll have crewmates to handle those functions. I'm concerned as to whether you have a full grasp of the relationship between navigating the spacecraft and the use of artificial intelligence to map your targets."

"Chief, I understand that at times yesterday, it appeared to be a little rocky. Everybody learns differently. Some have to study, absorb, and then give it a try. I like to dive right in, especially during sim time. Trust me, I hear everything you're telling me, and it goes inside my brain for future reference. I can't explain how I do it, but everything gets stored for retrieval on an as-needed basis. I'll be ready."

Chief Rawlings slapped his new protégé on the back and gestured toward a nondescript steel door marked *no entry*. He swiped his NASA security badge, and a green light illuminated as the door popped open.

"I suspect today is the day you've been waiting for. You've learned to fly, and now, you'll learn to kill the killer."

"That's what I do best."

For the next several hours, Chief Rawlings and Gunner navigated the Starhopper within the virtual world of a flight simulator. The two made an excellent team, using one another's knowledge of spaceflight and air combat to systematically attack a simulated version of IM86. After the morning session, Chief Rawlings was feeling better about Gunner's progress.

"Well, you were clearly in your element this morning. I see why Ghost recommended you."

"Ghost? My Ghost?"

Chief Rawlings laughed. "Yeah, your Ghost. He and I have been old friends for years. When I asked him for candidates to undertake this mission, he didn't hesitate in giving me your name. And, by the way, you were the only one he suggested."

Gunner stood a little taller and nodded his head. "I have a lot of respect for my former commander. Chief, um, I haven't always toed the line, if you know what I mean. Ghost has bailed me out of a few, um, predicaments."

"I've been there, young man. Trust me. Let's grab a bite to eat, and I'll explain why blasting this rock is much more difficult than the morning session revealed."

While they were eating, Chief Rawlings relayed the concerns the scientists had. "Gunner, I'll be honest. Many of the scientists who've proposed various methods of diverting an incoming asteroid have chosen options other than nuclear weapons. I believe that they're against the use of nukes in general, and therefore, they argue against their use in space for any reason. Their preferred method is to simply crash a spacecraft into the asteroid to divert it just enough to miss Earth. It's too late for that."

"Which is why I'm here," interjected Gunner.

"Right, in part. There is another concern that I need to bring up to you. The simulations run through computer models show that an asteroid of this size might reconstitute itself. Yes, the asteroid will crack considerably, with debris flowing outward like a cascade of ping-pong balls. However, despite the fractures caused by the impact, the heart of the asteroid, its core, will not be damaged."

"The gravitational pull will remain," added Gunner.

"Yes. The ejected shards of material will either remain in close proximity to the core, or they'll draw back in to rebuild itself."

Gunner pushed his plate away and took a long drink of sweet tea. After chewing his food, he looked around and saw that some of the astronauts on the mission were eating together in a corner of the room. Their attention was focused on his conversation with Chief Rawlings.

Gunner summarized the tactics. "We've got to get to the core, and the way to do that is pound away at its weakest point. A missile onslaught will give us an opening and then, hopefully, deal it a death blow."

"Like a jackhammer," said Chief Rawlings with a smile. "This is why we needed you. We're turning a planet-killing cannonball into the equivalent of shotgun bird shot. At least with bird shot, we've got a chance."

Suddenly a commotion could be heard near the entrance to the cafeteria. Two NASA security police stomped into the room and began searching with their heads on a swivel. One of the men looked toward Gunner and Chief Rawlings and elbowed the other. They immediately pushed their way through the crowded cafeteria to approach Gunner's table.

"Major Gunner Fox?"

"Yeah."

"You need to come with us. Now!"

"What's this all about?" asked Chief Rawlings.

"Sir, a routine search of Major Fox's room has turned up illegal drugs."

"What the hell? Routine search? This is—" Gunner stood up and confronted the two security police.

Chief Rawlings rushed to his side and grabbed Gunner's right arm before the situation got out of control. "You keep quiet, Major. Let me handle this. Understand?"

Gunner glared at his accusers and then past them to the faces of the other astronauts on the mission. They were giving him looks of disapproval and condescension. Gunner had been exposed to those types of judgmental looks in the past, but this time, they were undeserved.

CHAPTER 23

Wednesday, April 18
Building 9
Johnson Space Center
Houston, Texas

"This is bullshit, Chief!" Gunner was naturally incensed at the allegations made against him. In the so-called routine search, which actually turned out to be an internal, anonymous tip to NASA security, someone had reported they smelled the pungent aroma of marijuana emanating from Gunner's room early that morning just before wake-up call.

Chief Rawlings, advocating on Gunner's behalf, explained to the investigators that Gunner was with him, touring the experimental spacecraft and drinking coffee at the time he was alleged to have been smoking weed.

Nonetheless, NASA's medical team insisted that Gunner be administered two separate drug tests, which took nearly four hours to reveal results. He was cleared of any drug use and released to an awaiting Chief Rawlings.

"Did you say anything while in custody?" he asked Gunner.

"No. Say anything about what? I have no idea what this is about. I don't smoke marijuana. Never have."

"Gunner, I'm talking about small talk with the security personnel. Did any of them quiz you? Try to discuss your private life. Stuff like that."

"No, Chief. They stuck me away in a room, and I sat there with my thumb up my ass while I waited to be cleared. We've lost a whole day of sim training."

"I know, and we're going to get to that. First, let me tell you that I've had my assistant clear your room. You'll be bunkin' with me until Friday morning. Also, so you know, I'm going to ask Jim, um, I mean Acting Administrator Frederick, to let me accompany you to the lunar outpost."

Gunner, still raw from the course of events that both embarrassed and angered him, responded rudely, "Are you my keeper now? Do you think that grass was mine?"

Chief Rawlings stopped and pulled Gunner into an empty office. He slammed the door behind him. "No, Major. That's not the case at all. Like Ghost, I've got your back. Someone wants you or this mission to fail. I'm still working all of this through in my head. In the meantime, we've got to stick together, for your sake and mine."

"Chief, you gotta help me out here. Why would anyone want this mission to fail?"

Chief Rawlings shook his head and paced the room with his hands stuffed in his pockets. "I can only speculate. Some want the Russians to have a chance to save the asteroid for scientific study."

"Save it!" exclaimed Gunner. He was still fuming. "This thing could kill us all."

"Still, there are those who think the best method of diversion is to alter its trajectory or, better yet, force it into either a lunar or an Earth orbit."

"An Earth orbit? Like with the satellites? Playing pinball and wiping out everything in its path. That's freaking brilliant." Gunner reeked of sarcasm, and then he thought for a moment. "Wait, you said *me*. That they might want *me* to fail. What do you mean?"

Chief Rawlings turned to Gunner. "That's the scenario that puzzles me. I can understand some of the anti-nuke scientific community wanting to study this booger. However, Ghost thinks there might be more to it, and the reasons somehow relate to you."

"What the hell have I done? These other guys can't fire missiles, at least not with precision, like me. Are they jealous that I'm even part of the team? Chief, most of them haven't said three words to me except as it relates to my wife."

Chief Rawlings grimaced, trying to understand and make sense of it all. "I don't know, Gunner, but there's no time to waste. We're about to have a late night, and it's time for me to introduce you to someone you'll either love or hate."

"Who?"

"Artie."

CHAPTER 24

Thursday, April 19
Crimean Federal University
Simferopol, Crimea, Russian Federation

Cam and Bear were outfitted for their operation at Fort Belvoir. Their cover was simple because it was one they'd used before when they'd assassinated the chief organizer of the separation movement in Eastern Ukraine.

Roman Lyagin, who had been under the thumb of Putin for years, used Moscow's financial and political support to encourage citizens of Donetsk to push an independence referendum from Ukraine. The ultimate goal of Lyagin, and Moscow, was to bring Donetsk into the Russian Federation.

Since the annexation of the Crimean Peninsula, Putin had sought a land bridge to his newest conquest. Battles raged for years until Moscow sought a more diplomatic strategy by sowing seeds of unrest in Donetsk to undermine the Kiev government.

The underhanded plan was almost successful until the Ukrainian government arrested Lyagin for treason. He was later released to Russian agents in the midst of a bribery scandal, and subsequently resumed his activities of subversion.

That was when the U.S. government got involved to tamp down the effort. Gunner, with the assistance of Cam and Bear, entered Ukraine as part of a foreign contingent of professors, ostensibly to assist in facilitating foreign students into the National University of Life and Environmental Sciences of Ukraine.

Gunner, who had an advanced degree in Earth sciences, could walk the walk and talk the talk. He carried the bulk of the conversations when quizzed by Ukrainian authorities or university personnel. Cam and Bear deferred to Gunner and, fortunately, their cover was not exposed.

Having that trip under their belt, and several stamps on their passports indicating they'd traveled throughout the region, made their ability to travel into Crimea easier. Over the years, as the annexation became accepted as a *fait accompli*, travel restrictions were eased, making way for the duo to gain entry into the Federal Russian Republic that dated back to the Tsarist Empire of the late seventeen hundreds.

There was precious little time to brief Cam and Bear before they left. The Jackal prepared an extensive packet of information that was designed to get them past the Crimean authorities with their travel visas.

The two traveled into the country by boat, arriving at Sevastopol, a major port on the Black Sea for Russia's navy. Given the title *Hero City* for its resistance to the Nazis during World War II, numerous monuments to the city's past military exploits were on full display around the immigration center.

Once they'd cleared customs and immigration, they took a train to the Crimean capital of Simferopol. The two were most impressed with the friendliness of the passengers, who were surprisingly well versed in English. Their fellow train travelers were full of advice on restaurants and points of interest. One man knew the university well and drew them a map of important buildings for them to visit.

"Okay, our guy in Simferopol is Aleksandr Mashchenko," began Cam. "He's a Crimean native and is the vice rector for research. His parents died during the annexation by the Russians, and he's managed to keep that fact hidden from the KGB."

"Is he CIA?" asked Bear, looking over Cam's shoulder as she studied Mashchenko's dossier on her laptop.

"No, he's SBU, Ukrainian Security Service. Fortunately, he wasn't outed before former president Viktor Yanukovych ordered the data on the SBU's officer and informants destroyed."

"Does he speak English?" asked Bear.

"Fluently. German, too."

Bear stretched in his seat to glance out the window. The train was approaching the city and began to slow. "Good. So our target, Karlov, teaches applied physics. What's the play? Does he have a lot of exchange students in his class?"

"Yes, that's the tricky part. Many of them are Chinese. It was part of a large effort by Moscow and Beijing to introduce the two cultures to one another. Over the last two decades, they've become staunch allies and have let their barriers down to the exchange of information. It's worked well for them, frankly, and has served to isolate the U.S."

"Hell, Cam, that geopolitical stuff is way above my pay grade. I'm a soldier. If somebody higher up, like Ghost, can make a national security argument for the op they're sending me on, then I'm in. In this case, if we can help protect Gunner while getting to the bottom of some unanswered questions, then all the better."

The train pulled to a stop at the Simferopol Railway Station. At first, they were confused as to where to go, as none of the signs written in Russian had any directional markers. They tried to follow the crowds toward the exit that was supposed to lead them to a monument of the famed Russian admiral Pavel Nakhimov. That was where their contact from the university would meet them.

Once clear of the station, they asked questions of anyone who could understand Cam's attempt to pronounce the admiral's name correctly. After several attempts, they found someone who led them directly to the monument, just a quarter mile away.

"Let's split up," suggested Cam. "We both know what our contact looks like. Once you spot him, let me approach him first in case the mission has been compromised."

"No, Cam. Face it. I can be taken in, but you have the ability to talk your way out because at least you understand some Russian. I'll just have to rely upon the State Department to fetch me."

Cam smiled and patted Bear on the back. "I can't disagree, but I've got this. When you see me run my hand through my hair, you'll know we're clear. If I quickly walk away, then make your way to the rendezvous point in Pravda. Cool?"

"No problem," said Bear with a smile.

CHAPTER 25

Thursday, April 19
Crimean Federal University
Simferopol, Crimea, Russian Federation

"Professor Mashchenko?" Cam asked as she calmly approached the statue where the Ukrainian agent stood.

He nodded his head and continued to pretend to read the newspaper. "*Da.* I am not sure of your name."

"It's not necessary. Do you have Karlov's schedule for me?"

"*Da.* It's in my vehicle. I must escort you onto the university campus. You are my guests as part of the international exchange program. Once inside, I'll take you near Karlov's building."

Cam ran her hand through her hair, and within a minute, Bear had nonchalantly joined them.

Mashchenko immediately appeared concerned. "He is a large man. Very intimidating."

"So?" asked Cam.

"He will be noticeable. Memorable. I cannot be associated with the two people who interrogate Karlov and might later be described or identified."

Cam leaned into her contact's ear and whispered, "You get us inside; we'll take care of the rest."

Twenty minutes later, Mashchenko wheeled his Chinese-made Bogdan sedan into a parking space and sat quietly for a moment. Finally, he pointed to a building across a large open lawn containing park benches filled with students enjoying the warm spring sunshine.

"Do you see the two-level building across the way with the double wooden doors? That is the science building where Karlov teaches.

There is a side entrance on the right nearest the professor's office building. He will come and go through that entrance most times."

"Does it cross through that thick stand of trees?"

"*Da.* The mulberry trees are overgrown, but the university is prohibited from cutting them. One must lower his head to make his way down the path."

Bear leaned forward from the back seat. "I like it. We'll have cover, and there's probably a place back there for some privacy, if you know what I mean."

"Please allow me to leave my vehicle and then wait until the classes empty out. Students have twelve minutes to move from building to building. That's why the campus seems quiet at this moment. Most students are in their classrooms."

Cam looked at her watch and then thumbed through the notes provided by their contact. "Karlov has a long break after his current class that lets out in twenty minutes. Nobody will be looking for him until his last class of the day this afternoon. That'll be all the time we need to have a chat and then get off the peninsula."

Mashchenko looked them both in the eye. "Good luck to you both. I hope you find the information you seek."

"We do too," said Cam.

With that, the Ukrainian operative exited his vehicle and walked briskly in between parked cars in an effort to distance himself from the Americans. Cam checked her watch again. Just a few minutes until their cover appeared from the buildings surrounding the university common area.

"Okay, I've got the syringes ready," whispered Bear from the back seat. "I don't like messing with this poison stuff. What if I get some on my skin or something?"

"A-234 can be very deadly, Bear. It's the same Novichok nerve agent used to poison the Skripal spies eleven years ago. The KGB loves the stuff, and if Karlov dies, Moscow will be blamed."

Bear leaned forward and looked at the atomizer that Cam rotated through her fingers as she followed the seconds ticking away on her digital watch. "What's in the perfume sprayer?"

"A cayenne pepper solution, one that emulates the feel of the nerve agent on his skin. Karlov will be aware of what A-234 is capable of. I suspect he'll have lots to say in order to stay alive."

"Cam, they're coming out. It's showtime!"

They quickly exited the vehicle and joined the throngs of students and professors who crossed the open space in different directions. The sidewalks met in a large round center area that contained yet another statue of a Crimean dignitary. Nationalism was alive and well in the former Ukrainian oblast.

Cam and Bear walked with a purpose, focused on the area used by teachers to access their classrooms. Their intelligence revealed that Karlov was well-versed in English, and Cam could hold her own in conversational Russian. Her goal was to isolate Karlov in the wooded thicket long enough for Bear to restrain the man and drag him deeper into the woods.

They arrived at the pathway just as the university's staff began to walk back and forth. It was lightly traveled, as most of the teachers in the science buildings remained in their classrooms for another session. The timing of their mission was fortuitous, as they'd caught Karlov on his lightest-scheduled day of the week.

While Cam waited under a tree limb, ostensibly studying some notes, Bear slipped into the woods to search for a place to interrogate the former project manager for Russia's space agency. Less than a minute later, Bear reemerged at the edge of the mulberry trees and provided Cam a thumbs-up, indicating he was ready.

Cam prepared for the ambush. Thus far, Karlov hadn't appeared. She checked her watch and confirmed that the next set of classes were about to begin. She became concerned that Mashchenko was wrong about their target's schedule. Then the thought of a double-cross began to sink in. She nervously began to wander, continuing to study the notes that she planned to employ as a ruse to grab the man's attention.

Then she saw him. He was a smallish man, about Cam's height, with a rotund belly and wire-rimmed glasses. He appeared both professorial and scientific and certainly not one to put up a fight. As he approached, Cam looked up and smiled, immediately causing the nervous man to let his guard down.

"*Privet*," she greeted him as he got closer. She spoke in Russian, but made no attempt to hide her American accent. She'd found on prior missions abroad that their targets who knew English were always eager to use it when approached by an American. "Can you help me? I need directions."

"*Amerikanskiy?*" he asked, with a slight smile.

Cam never got a chance to respond. Bear was surveilling the path and was prepared to pounce on Karlov when the opportunity presented itself. Karlov had barely uttered the word when Bear clamped his massive right hand over the man's mouth and dragged him brusquely into the thicket.

Karlov attempted to shout, kicked, and struggled against Bear's powerful arms, without success. Bear tore through the underbrush, dragging the professor backwards without regard to the beating the older man's body was taking along the way.

Cam picked up Karlov's briefcase and quickly covered their tracks as she followed the swath of broken branches and shrubs left by Bear's abduction. They got to a slight clearing, and Bear forced Karlov to the ground, keeping his large hand clamped down on the man's mouth.

Cam knelt down next to Karlov and revealed the atomizer. "Do you know what this is?"

The man shook his head violently side to side.

"A-234. Do you know what that is?"

Now Karlov was nodding vigorously up and down, his eyes pleading for mercy. Bear reached into his pocket and revealed a syringe. He showed it to Karlov as Cam continued the threat.

"We have questions for you, and all we want are answers. Understand?"

He nodded his willingness to cooperate.

"My friend will release his hand to allow you to speak. If you scream, he will inject you with a lethal dose of nerve agent that will kill you in minutes. If you cooperate, we will tie you up until someone finds you. Will you answer our questions?"

His eyes grew big and he nodded his head vigorously.

"Good," continued Cam. Then she got to the crux of the matter. "Three years ago, you were a project manager assigned to the International Space Station. Yes?"

"*Da.*"

"Do you remember the incident when the communications were terminated for nine hours?"

"*Da.* I don't understand the importance of—"

Cam began to snarl at her captive. "During the communications blackout, an American astronaut died. Do you remember?"

Karlov grew suddenly nervous. He began to struggle, causing Bear to clamp his hand down on his mouth again, and both American operatives shoved their tools of death into the face of the Russian.

Beads of sweat poured off the man's forehead as he began to tremble. His eyes darted in all directions until Cam grabbed him by the jawline and hissed, "Answer my questions or die. Your choice!"

Karlov exhaled, and his body went limp. He closed his eyes momentarily and slowly nodded his head. Cam and Bear had interrogated many people over the years, and this was the telltale sign of their target giving up the fight.

Now, for the answers.

CHAPTER 26

Thursday, April 19
Building 9
Johnson Space Center
Houston, Texas

Gunner had a sleepless night despite having been mentally drained by the false accusations leveled against him the day before. Someone had attempted to set him up, not just for the purposes of removing him from the mission, but also for a myriad of minor drug charges. Possession of marijuana and associated paraphernalia in a federal government facility was much more complicated than elsewhere.

Between the events of the prior day and the building anticipation of his launch into space, Gunner was beginning to have doubts as to whether he would be ready. He needed to clear his head, so, before dawn, he slipped outside into the humid Texas morning and went for a run around the Johnson Space Center.

So as not to alarm Chief Rawlings, Gunner scribbled a note for his host, who'd been assigned a small two-room bungalow that was provided to visiting dignitaries. The two men debated who'd sleep on the couch that evening, an argument won by Gunner via subterfuge. The two men enjoyed a couple of beers, and when Chief Rawlings went to use the bathroom, Gunner pretended to fall asleep on the couch. He'd slept in worse places.

The run felt good and it served to clear his head. He was determined to thwart whoever was responsible for planting the contraband in his room. He was also glad that he'd found an air-conditioning duct in the men's restroom down the hall in which to hide his satellite radio. Call it a hunch, but Gunner did not feel completely secure in his surroundings in Building 9.

He really needed to focus on his final day of training. Working with Chief Rawlings was an amazing experience, but he wouldn't have his crutch, his mentor, to lean on while on the mission. He'd be working with astronauts who might not necessarily like him very much, and foreign crewmates from Russia and the European Space Agency.

After a fleet-footed thirty-minute run, sweat poured out of him. Invigorated by the exercise, he reentered the bungalow and found Chief Rawlings ready to go.

"I wish you wouldn't do that without asking me first," said the chief as he lifted a box off the floor and set it on the kitchen island. "There are restricted areas here, and the last thing I need is to have you hauled into the pokey again."

Gunner laughed. "I wasn't in the pokey, and truthfully, they treated me pretty well, if you consider the silent treatment a good thing."

Chief Rawlings patted the top of the box and smiled. "I've got something for you."

An official navy blue set of coveralls was folded neatly inside the box. The first thing Gunner noticed was the official patch worn by astronaut candidates.

"*Res gesta per excellentiam,*" mumbled Gunner, reading the Latin inscription aloud.

"That's right," interjected Chief Rawlings. "Achieve through excellence. It's the standard for what we do here at NASA. For me, those words represent my commitment to a belief, a frame of mind, that I have the qualities useful to pursue our mission to develop space and reach for the stars."

It was an emotional moment as Chief Rawlings seemed to tear up as he explained the purpose of his life's work. He subconsciously touched his right shoulder and ran his fingers over his own Mission Operations patch.

For Gunner, it was a rite of passage. Until that moment, he was still an Air Force pilot tasked with flying an experimental aircraft. The reality was setting in that, albeit for a short period of time, he was an astronaut, like Heather.

The emotional moment got to him as well. He'd graduated from the khakis and polo shirt he'd been wearing since his arrival. He removed his sweat-soaked shorts and tee shirt, then pulled on the coveralls, zipping it up to a near perfect fit.

"I feel like one of the team now."

"You certainly look the part," said Chief Rawlings, with a laugh. "Before we head into the office, so to speak, we need to talk about your team. I have to make a decision this morning that will leave a lot of folks butt-hurt."

Gunner exhaled. He knew that there was some animosity among the regular astronauts as it pertained to him. For one thing, they'd lost eleven of their friends barely a week ago in a tragic ending to a mission designed to save humanity. In a way, being on this flight and diverting IM86 was a form of revenge for those lives lost. But, also, Gunner was an outsider who hadn't paid his dues. Becoming an astronaut was a long, arduous process, and Gunner had taken all the shortcuts to go to the head of the class.

"How are you gonna deal with it?" asked Gunner.

"Well, for one thing, I'm going to pick a team that compliments you and your limited capabilities, but who can also work together without emotional baggage."

"Works for me. The Starhopper allows for a crew of eight. I understand that the nuclear payload requires us to bring along Russians and European astronauts. Is it gonna be an equal number of four and four?"

"Yes. Three Russians and a Frenchman who are already at the lunar outpost. They are qualified in every manner except they've never trained on the Starhopper. They'll get their opportunity to view the spacecraft and get oriented on Sunday."

"If they know nothing about the Starhopper, why do we even need them on board?"

"Stupid politics. It was the only way to get the United Nations to sign off on us sending nukes into space. They'll sit there, observe, and—"

Then Gunner became suddenly unemotional and his demeanor stony. "They do realize we might not make it home, right? Face it, Chief. This is practically a suicide mission."

Chief Rawlings rolled his head on his shoulders and closed his eyes. This eventuality had never been discussed between them. Gunner had to prepare himself for the worst-case scenario.

"Gunner, if you recognize it, then that's all that matters to me. That said, choosing a crew makes my job all the more difficult. I have to call upon three astronauts from this list, potentially signing their death warrants."

Gunner walked over to his mentor and patted him on the back. It had been an emotional morning for the retired astronaut, who himself had cheated death on one mission.

"Let me look at the list with you. I can at least give you the benefit of my observations."

"Okay, we'll pick three primary members of the crew, and a single backup who doubles as the commander of the Starship tomorrow."

Gunner studied the names and then looked up at Chief Rawlings. "Wait, we've got six seats on tomorrow's launch. This count leaves the Starship short a man."

"That's me," said Chief Rawlings curtly. "I'm gonna be with you all the way until you lift off from the lunar surface, chirping in your ear and keeping your head on straight."

"Do I have a choice?" asked Gunner with a chuckle.

"Nope."

CHAPTER 27

Friday, April 20
Gunner's Residence
Dog Island
Florida Panhandle

"Rise and shine, Major Mills! You too, Staff Sergeant Barrett!" Pop announced his arrival at dawn with a combination of vocal revelry and the aroma of iced cinnamon breakfast rolls. Cam groaned, Bear growled, and Howard simply stretched and nuzzled into Gunner's empty bed.

Pop was relentless. He stood in the center of the large living space and shouted, "Come on, people! That means you too, Howard. Everybody, up and at 'em!"

Bear and Cam had returned from their mission just several hours before. The combination of jet lag, a stressful exit out of Crimea, and the lack of sleep made it difficult for Pop to accomplish his task.

It was a humid, breezy morning on the Gulf, as a storm front was scheduled to pass through the Panhandle later that morning. Pop had been watching the weather for two days, concerned that it might affect today's launch.

Bear came stumbling down the stairs in his football sweats and no shoes. His size thirteen feet barely fit on the treads of the stairs as he lumbered to the main level of the Dog Island beach house.

"Staff Sergeant hungry Bear, present and accounted for, sir!"

Pop had started coffee, opting for a light roast, which was packed with caffeine. The longer coffee beans were roasted, the more caffeine was burned off. Pop suspected Cam and Bear would need the lift in order to be fully awake as Gunner lifted off.

"What time is launch?" Cam's voice was muffled by the blanket pulled over her head.

"Eight. That's less than two hours."

"Huh? How about wake me when it's less than two minutes," she grumbled as she curled up deeper into the mess of pillows and blankets that surrounded her on the sofa. Out of respect for Gunner, she hadn't slept in his bed last night, but she did *borrow* his pillows and duvet.

Bear decided to assist Pop with the wake-up call. He crouched down on one end of the sofa and began to lift it with his powerful forearms. Slowly, the sofa, with Cam in it, was being tilted upright.

"Bear," she hissed from under the covers, "if you spill me out of this thing, I'm gonna kick your gonads into your throat. Do not doubt me on this!"

Bear let out a growl, his best impersonation of a grizzly. He continued to lift the end, causing Cam to slip toward the other side, with the next stop the white bleached-wood floor.

"That's it!" shouted Cam as she emerged from under the covers and scrambled to gain her footing. Bear quickly dropped the sofa back into place and began to run for the kitchen, using the long table as a buffer between him and the crazed animal chasing him.

Cam picked up a plate and threatened to sling it at his head like a Frisbee. Bear ducked and covered his head, falling to his knees, as he was certain she'd do it.

The ruse worked, and Cam used her catlike reflexes to race around the table, playfully kicking her partner in the butt and thighs. To finish off the onslaught, she slapped him in the back of the head.

"I hate you," she proclaimed as she marched off to the bathroom. Both Bear and Pop were out of breath from the melee, but managed to laugh at her feistiness.

"She's always been like that," said Pop, attempting to help the much larger Bear off the floor. "Boys would tease her when she was growing up, especially as a teen when she started to develop, if you know what I mean. I saw her bloody more than one nose when one of them got too touchy-feely."

"I believe it," said Bear as he took his first bite of Pop's baked yummies. "She's a brute. There's no man who'll ever tame that wildcat."

Pop laughed. "Oh, I don't know. When the right one comes along, she'll allow him to tame her, or at least, she'll pretend in the name of love."

Cam returned and muscled Bear away from the cinnamon rolls. Pop encouraged them to go outside and enjoy the sunrise while he prepared a breakfast casserole recipe he'd been working on.

They each filled their coffee mugs, and Bear grabbed the entire tray of cinnamon rolls after Pop grabbed one. They made their way to their usual seats in the Adirondack chairs overlooking the Gulf of Mexico.

Cam glanced to the right and became pensive.

Bear immediately noticed her change. "Are you okay?"

She pointed to the two empty chairs to her right. "It will never be the same without both of them sitting there. Do you realize we've always sat in the same chairs, and Heather's has been left empty?"

"Yeah, come to think about it, you're right. Listen, I feel bad that we can't tell Pop what we've learned. It's not classified or anything like that."

"Yeah, but the news will hurt him deeply, and today's not the day. Plus, Ghost is right. Gunner, unfortunately, needs to be kept in the dark, too. He's gonna need to have his wits about him every second of this mission. A slight mistake and, well, you know ..." Cam's voice trailed off as she set her chin on her fist. She stared at nothing in particular.

"Okay, but what do you think happens next? I mean, Ghost said leave everything to him, but I feel like we need to do something ourselves."

"I can't disagree, but we need to make sure we get Gunner through this first. Plus, I've been thinking, you know, what if?"

"What if what?" asked Bear, confused.

"Well, I did some research on the laptop on the flight home. Bear, we have to be prepared in case this thing doesn't work."

"Gunner will make it happen, no worries."

"I know he will, but even if he succeeds, the planet will still get pummeled with debris, some of which could be as large as a football stadium. Those space rocks will hit us at thirty thousand miles per hour even after they're slowed by the atmosphere."

Bear passed the plate of cinnamon rolls to Cam, but she declined, opting instead to sip her coffee. "It's unpredictable, and therefore, we can't hide from it. I hate to say it, but it'll be pure luck to avoid being crushed by parts of the asteroid."

"I don't even think an underground bunker will shield anyone from the impact. The craters left are enormous. What about the water, though?"

"Tsunamis?" said Bear inquisitively.

"Seventy percent of the Earth is water. The Gulf of Mexico is shallow in comparison to the oceans. If a large piece hits offshore, a wall of water could wipe out Dog Island and everything on it."

Bear glanced over his shoulder to confirm that Pop was still in the kitchen. He was standing over the stove, scrambling eggs for the casserole. "Do you think we need to move Pop?"

"All of us—Howard, Pop, and any of Gunner's personal effects. We've got less than a week to get prepared."

Bear stood and began to pace along the deck's railing. He looked down to the sand. "If a tsunami hits, these pilings might hold, but it's not worth the risk. Do you have a place in mind?"

"My folks left my sister and me a cabin near Delta, Alabama. It's not that far from Cheaha Mountain just east of Birmingham. It's desolate and, more importantly, it's high enough to avoid tsunamis."

"How far from Birmingham?" asked Bear.

"Eighty miles. We'll be able to avoid people spilling out of the city when the madness takes over. Everybody is gonna panic. Don't you think?"

Bear's face turned serious. "They already are."

Pop interrupted their conversation after he turned on the television. The sun was starting to make its way skyward, and the launch of the Starship was about to lift Gunner into the heavens.

"Hey, guys, launch time is getting closer."

The Fox News reporter was providing their viewers an update as the Starship stood proudly on the alternative launchpad employed by SpaceX for this mission.

"*Yesterday, a rocket carrying the critical payload for this mission, the Starhopper, left for the Moon. Aboard a Delta 4 super heavy-lift launch vehicle, part of NASA's Space Launch System, was the Starhopper spacecraft that will be piloted by an eight-person crew consisting of a French male astronaut; two males and one female comprising the Russian cosmonaut crew; and three American astronauts, again two males and one female.*"

"Hey, they're showing Gunner's picture!" shouted Pop, which prompted Cam and Bear to scramble out of their chairs. Gunner had only been introduced to the media yesterday after he'd been cleared of any wrongdoing. The matter had been kept private within the Johnson Space Center, and Gunner had been shielded from interviews during the entirety of his training.

The reporter continued. "*The wildcard in this mission is Major Gunner Fox, a decorated Air Force combat pilot and respected test pilot of the nation's newest experimental aircraft. Major Fox made news in recent weeks when he piloted the new F/A XX aircraft as it disintegrated miles above the Earth's surface. Major Fox was forced to eject, and landed safely in the Gulf of Mexico, but not before he took a harrowing trip from near the stratosphere with nothing but a parachute to stop his fall.*"

Pop suggested they all grab a plate and load up his breakfast casserole, which he'd just pulled out of the oven. Even Howard lumbered out of bed, hoping to have a bonus treat in his bowl in the form of a scrambled egg.

As the group added Cholula hot sauce and sour cream to spice up Pop's recipe, the countdown process continued from the SpaceX launch facility at Boca Chica Village near Brownsville, Texas.

They watched with great interest as the details of the mission were described to the viewers. Cam and Bear had missed most of the coverage due to their mission in Crimea. The feel of this launch was somewhat different, in that the Starship was capable of liftoff without the aid of the massive booster engines that fall off as the spaceship departs the planet.

The spacecraft's design as a point-to-point shuttle made it unique among modern-day spacecraft. Once it lands on the lunar surface and offloads its passengers, it will bring back a payload of minerals mined from the Moon, together with a handful of passengers. The Starship, Gunner's space-based combat jet, was already in place after yesterday's launch, which went off without a hitch.

The reporter's voice became concerned. *"We're on a hold now at T minus twenty minutes, as the winds have picked up here in South Texas. A front was moving through early this morning, and weather forecasters had predicted it to work its way up the Gulf Coast, but remnants of this storm are lingering over Boca Chica."*

"That's gotta be frustrating," said Cam as the three kept their eyes glued to the television. "You know how Gunner is. He gets his game face on and psyches himself up. Sitting there waiting for clearance must be driving him crazy."

An hour passed and the mission continued to be on an indeterminate hold as the weather system stubbornly remained just off the shores of Padre Island. Cam and Bear stood quietly on the deck, watching the surf pick up as storm clouds developed to their west.

"A storm's comin'," said Bear in a hushed tone of voice.

"Bear, how are we gonna convince Pop to leave? He can be stubborn, you know."

"I'll pick him up and take him out the door kickin' and screamin' if I have to."

They sat outside and listened to a panel of experts discuss the psychological impact this delay had on the crew as well as what the delay meant for their plans to intercept the asteroid. They all agreed that NASA had built in a day, or two, as part of a contingency for unexpected delays like this one.

"Bear"—Cam broke the silence—"where are your weapons?"

"In my locker at Eglin. Yours?"

"Tyndall, at the gun range. Ammo, too."

"Should we get them?" asked Bear as he turned to see if Pop was in earshot.

"Yeah, everything we've got. I'll empty Gunner's locker at Tyndall also. Buy all the ammo you can find between here and Fort Walton Beach. I'll do the same."

"Cam, what are you thinking? Do you think the Russians are gonna make a move on us?"

Cam furrowed her brow and shook her head. "Nah, sadly, if the asteroid wreaks havoc, the Russians will have their own hands full. I'm worried about our fellow Americans. Bear, desperate people will do desperate things. We have to protect ourselves and gather any supplies that we can accumulate over the next few days."

Pop suddenly emerged from inside the house. "Well, they've scrubbed the mission for the day. They're gonna try again at the same time tomorrow."

CHAPTER 28

Saturday, April 21
SpaceX Launch Facility
Boca Chica Village
Near Brownsville, Texas

The eight-minute rodeo ride. That was how former Canadian astronaut and Royal Canadian Air Force pilot Chris Hadfield described the eight-minute-forty-second launch process until an astronaut was weightless.

In most circumstances, astronauts remain in quarantine for a week, allowing them to gather their thoughts and remain in a relatively sterile environment. During this time, NASA builds a space suit around the crew members. They check the suit under pressurized conditions, confirm that all communications systems are functioning, and assist the astronauts in taking on board any personal effects, from clothing to talismans.

It might seem incredible to believe that in the world of manned spaceflight and human beings living on the Moon, there were well-documented superstitions and traditions followed by each and every crewmember as if they were performing a sacred rite.

Some invoked spirits of dear, lost loved ones. Others brought holy water. Talismans, objects believed to bring someone good luck and prosperity, were common.

Gunner didn't have a talisman per se. When he flew combat missions, he tried to leave his real life behind and become one with the jet. The same was true when he flew experimental aircraft.

For this mission, Gunner carried a blue canvas duffle bag that simply read GUNNER FOX in bright white letters. The bag contained clothing that he could wear while at the lunar outpost, an electric razor given to him by Chief Rawlings in case he wanted to shave off his disheveled beard, and the satellite phone he'd stashed away for the better part of a week. It was a bag given to him by Heather, and every time he touched it, he thought of her.

He didn't know why Cam had felt compelled to send it to him upon his arrival at Building 9, but regardless of the reason, it had become his talisman as he readied himself to take flight.

The SpaceX launch facility was chosen because of its proximity to the Johnson Space Center and the fact that typically the weather was more favorable. Yesterday's stormy conditions were an anomaly, and Gunner hoped it didn't portend more trouble for the future of the mission.

Located at Boca Chica, Texas, the fifty-acre facility was situated directly on the Gulf of Mexico near the border with Mexico. Nearby, like the rest of Texas, a border wall ran through the SpaceX complex as part of the country's border security plan.

Elon Musk, in an effort to stave off the construction of an ordinary wall, designed one that was less intrusive to the SpaceX operation and that featured a mural of the company's contributions to the space program.

It was just before dawn, and the launchpad was illuminated with large xenon lights, lighting up the Starship like a silver-bullet-designed obelisk. The spacecraft stood proudly, awaiting this opportunity to ferry the important passengers to the Moon on a mission to save Earth from destruction.

Now that the time for liftoff had arrived, the world was sitting on edge once again. The tragedy of a week prior and the dramatic cancellation of yesterday were forgotten. The commander of the starship gave his team a pep talk despite the late addition of Chief Rawlings, who had seniority by virtue of age. The chief of the Flight Directors Office insisted upon the commander being *in charge of this bird*, as he put it. Rawlings was simply a passenger accompanying his fellow crew members to the Moon.

While the commander went through the countdown with the

launch team at Cape Canaveral in cooperation with the SpaceX operations center, Chief Rawlings spoke with Gunner.

"There's no turning back now, Major."

"Good," said Gunner with a chuckle. "No, seriously. I'm ready. Of course, I've played every aspect of my training through my head over and over. Chief, I don't think I slept twenty minutes last night."

"Nervous jitters?"

"No, really, it was more excitement. I was ready yesterday, and the aborted launch really was a downer. That said, it gave me time to review everything again. I'm ready to do this."

Chief Rawlings gave him a thumbs-up, and the two turned their attention to the final countdown. They lowered their visors and settled in to their seats. Gunner clenched his fists in anticipation of the tremendous force the rocket engines would place upon his body. He recalled the words that Commander Hadfield had uttered once, as relayed to him during training by Chief Rawlings.

The eight-minute rodeo ride.

And the ride had begun. The main engines ignited, and the entire spaceship rattled and shuddered like a San Francisco skyscraper during a 9.0 earthquake. A deep rumble shook the cabin as the main engines came up to full thrust.

At T minus zero, the rocket boosters ignited, giving Gunner a massive kick in the back as the Starship blasted off the launchpad at Boca Chica. The pounding of the rocket being propelled toward space shook Gunner continually as they accelerated ever higher at two-point-five g's, ripping through the atmosphere under seven million pounds of thrust.

He closed his eyes, and visions of Heather came into his consciousness. Incredibly, he began to hum a song to himself— Kenny Chesney's "How Forever Feels." As he thought of the lyrics, he inserted Heather Fox in place of Jimmy Buffett and Richard Petty.

Now I know how Heather Fox feels.

Gunner opened his eyes as the Starship reached maximum dynamic pressure, or max q. The engines throttled back up to full thrust with the spine-tingling scream of the slipstream, the wake of air and fluid displaced by the Starship, causing the hair on his neck to stand up. It was the sound of immense power unleashed in barely controlled fury.

The commander of the Starship began to call out the Mach numbers during the final minute: 22 ... 23 ... 24, and, finally, Mach 25.

Done!

The main engine cut off, and thrust dropped to zero in less than a second. The pressure on Gunner's body vanished, and he suddenly began to float within the restraints that held him in his seat.

Every day is a good day when you're floating.

Heather's dream was to be an astronaut. She'd lived her dream, and now Gunner was living it, too. Tears of mixed emotions poured out of him, dripping down his cheeks and into his suit. He closed his eyes in an unsuccessful attempt to hold the tears inside him. He mouthed the words that only he could hear.

Today, I'm leaving Earth, maybe forever.

Just like my wife.

PART THREE

ASTROMETRY

Identification Number: 2029 IM86

Right Ascension: 13 hours 12 minutes 41 seconds

Declination: -18 degrees 31 minutes 09 seconds

Greatest Elongation: 62.23 degrees

Nominal Distance from Earth: 0.19 astronomical units

Relative Velocity: 31,845 meters per second

CHAPTER 29

Saturday, April 21
The Oval Office
The White House
Washington, DC

President Watson was wearing a hole in the rug, figuratively speaking. While his chief of staff, Maggie Fielding, conducted the briefing with representatives of State and Defense, the president's mind was on the mission.

The Starship launch at the SpaceX facility was flawless and without the drama accompanying the liftoff of Falcon Heavy a week ago. Shortly, the American team would join their Russian and French counterparts to begin final preparations for the assault on IM86.

Like most other government officials directly involved in the mission, the president was having difficulty sleeping. As the leader of the free world, it was not unusual to carry a heavy burden as he went through his daily activities.

Most days consisted of a combination of strategic planning sessions and briefings, with the vast majority of decisions having been made before they were presented to the president. His job was to simply reassess alternatives to a particular issue and then give his stamp of approval to move forward.

Upon discovery of IM86, the American government had slowed to virtually a standstill. Congress stopped holding hearings, and no new bills were presented or voted upon. All eyes were on the news, and the news was singularly focused on the Watson administration as it dealt with the crisis.

As was always the case, expert pundits on all sides of an issue were readily available to state their case for handling the oncoming asteroid in one way or another. For every decision made by NASA or the Defense Department, with the seal of approval of the president, there were countless scientists prepared to denounce it.

The Secretaries of State and Defense were ever-present figures in the West Wing, using Fielding's office like a revolving door. The Roosevelt Room had been converted into a war room of sorts. Television monitors, computers, and a whiteboard had been brought in. On a moment's notice, the decision makers in the process could convene, ready to address any aspect of the mission that went awry.

"Mr. President, I can't tell you how important it was for us to form this international coalition," the Secretary of State said, drawing the president into the conversation. "It helped us overcome the debacle of Friday the thirteenth with minimal damage in the eyes of other nations."

The Defense Secretary added, "However, we're still in the dark as to the status of Russia's own mission to the asteroid. They refuse to share video footage, if any, or any kind of update as to whether they've landed."

"Some coalition," grumbled President Watson. "They shoot down our orbiter. They continue to try their own approach. And they're oh so kind enough to allow us to take a shot of our own. I don't trust them. I don't like them. I just can't understand why they think this threat is something to trivialize. Am I missing something here?"

"No, sir," replied the Secretary of Defense. "They seem to have confidence in their approach. Our intelligence sources tell me that Moscow expects to have the asteroid diverted before we arrive there on Monday."

"What can they accomplish in forty-eight hours that they haven't so far?" asked Fielding.

The Secretary of State gave her opinion. "Well, sir, if they've already landed on the asteroid, they may be waiting until they've achieved a modicum of success in changing the trajectory before making an announcement. President Putin is known for his grandstanding."

"That's an understatement," said the president softly. "Let's address the issue of timing. As we know, our Starhopper will be in position on Monday. It's my understanding that we have a specific window of opportunity to blast this thing to either move its trajectory drastically, or at least cause it to break up into many, much smaller chunks of rock."

NASA's acting administrator was unable to attend, so he'd sent Nola Taylor, the head of the Space Technology Mission Directorate. "Mr. President, the mission schedule allows the Starhopper to establish an orbit around IM86 while the spacecraft's onboard computer maps the surface. During that time, data regarding velocity, mass, speed, and rotation will be sent back to Houston for analysis. We'll be able to generate several computer models indicating the points that should be targeted and, at your request, sir, the window of opportunity that minimizes the impact to North America."

President Watson considered the qualifier in Taylor's statement. The president, while cognizant of his responsibilities to help protect Earth from this threat, owed a solemn duty to the people of the United States. His instructions were clear—minimize the impact to America. He looked for confirmation of this issue based upon updated information.

"With a proposed intercept of Monday, does it still hold true that we're better off striking early rather than at the last minute?"

Taylor was prepared to respond. "Yes, sir. The timing of initiating Project Jackhammer will determine where the largest debris field strikes the planet, mostly in the Northern Hemisphere. An early strike will cause the most damage over Russia, the largest country on Earth. A later strike is more likely to spread the debris across North America, from Central America toward the Arctic."

"Thank you, Miss Taylor," said the president with a determined look on his face. "Let's turn to the domestic front. We are preparing for a worst-case scenario, one that will impact us on Friday by all calculations. My question is whether our nation will survive until then? I'm getting reports of hoarding, price-gouging, looting, and violent assaults all across the socioeconomic spectrum. It seems the nation might lose its collective mind before we're in the throes of IM86's remnants pummeling the planet."

"Mr. President, I think we need to make a formal declaration of martial law," said the Secretary of Defense, causing the attendees to grow silent.

"Is Homeland Security ready for that?" asked Fielding.

A representative of DHS responded, "We're ready to deal with unrest, Mrs. Fielding, but FEMA is not prepared for recovery. They are working frantically to get their assets staged uniformly across the country, but as we know, FEMA is a second responder, of sorts. They can move into a region or specific location to assist those in need, but they are not designed to help the entire country at one time. Their personnel and recovery assets are spread too thin."

"Well, can they at least be ready once the remnants of the asteroid hit us? Have Air National Guard at the ready to move them around as needed."

"Sir, um, may I address that?" asked Taylor. "This is purely from NASA's perspective, but we all have to keep in mind that even if the mission succeeds, Earth cannot avoid the catastrophe. While it is true that we can avoid extinction by way of a mile-wide rock hitting us at fifty-some thousand miles per hour, we will still be subjected to thousands of meteorites, the remnants of the asteroid that don't burn up in the atmosphere."

The president furrowed his brow and continued his pacing. "In other words, it's impossible to plan for a specific area of impact, even at the eleventh hour."

"That's correct, sir. And there's another issue that we've been discussing with the Defense Department. Our wired, interconnected world is highly reliant upon satellite technology for everything from communications to national defense. The sheer size of the meteor storm will be devastating to the satellites in low-Earth orbit. We need to be prepared for a loss of communications and, quite possibly, widespread power outages if one or more of our electrical substations around the Continental U.S. is hit. There will be a cascading effect all across our power grid."

President Mack Watson stopped and leaned against the Resolute desk, a nineteenth-century partners' desk used by presidents since the mid-seventies. He stared upward toward the ceiling and slowly closed his eyes. His job just got much more complicated.

CHAPTER 30

Three Years Prior
The International Space Station
Two Hundred Fifty-Four miles above Earth

"Houston, did you see that?" Mere seconds after Heather Fox uttered those words, warning alarms erupted inside the ISS. Confused at first, Heather looked around to seek out one of her fellow astronauts for guidance. The largely Russian crew seemed to stick to themselves as the spirit of cooperation that once was evident aboard the ISS was replaced with the diplomatic chill of the second cold war.

Heather had been frustrated by this and, at first, somewhat despondent. She'd dreamed of traveling into space as a girl, spending her nights gazing through her telescope and her days reading about the history of space exploration.

There was never any doubt about the career path she would choose, and she pursued it with vigor. She understood that her role would be limited on this first trip. It was part of NASA's protocols. Her first trip into space would be intentionally short, full of research projects and mundane tasks associated with the operation of the ISS. While she dreamt of a space walk and envied the other astronauts who had done one just the day before, Heather was willing to pay her dues and wait her turn.

Then things changed in an instant. She'd been studying the solar system through the newly modified Celestron telescope designed to overcome the challenges of observing space from the constantly moving ISS. Up until a few years ago, the Celestron was only used to observe Earth because of the orbital velocity of the ISS. Moving at eighteen thousand miles per hour, the view was designed to focus on the Earth, as the ISS slowly rotates to keep the same side facing the planet.

The design made it very difficult to view the solar system. Given the limited view from one of the windows of the ISS, an astronaut could only observe a region of the sky for about ten minutes. That changed when the Alpha Magnetic Spectrometer was mounted outside the ISS, and with the subsequent Celestron upgrades. Heather was able to focus on a part of the stars and gently adjust her field of view to spend longer than ten minutes on a region. It was fascinating technology, and she spent every available moment using it.

In an instant, her life suffered a massive upheaval. She saw something out of place. It was fast, had a tail like a comet, yet it wasn't on any charts known to NASA. She'd discovered what would later be identified as IM86.

She followed its path across the solar system as it streaked toward the Sun. At first, she didn't say anything into the comms. When she was certain, she asked, "Houston, did you see that?"

Then the alarms rang. Communications had been lost with Earth.

The Russian commander was calm and collected as he assigned tasks to each of his cosmonauts. It took Heather several minutes to find the commander and the top members of his crew. They'd huddled in a closed-off area that contained access to an array of monitors that showed all aspects of ISS operations. When Heather approached, all the monitors were turned off and their screens were dark.

The group nervously broke up and went about the task of fixing the communications system. The commander, who spoke English, explained to Heather what needed to be done. He told her that a complete computer system check needed to be performed, and they also needed to investigate the possibility that space debris had dislodged one of the ISS antennas.

Heather expressed frustration that she was unfamiliar with the computer system and that her ability to assist was limited. That was when she heard the words she'd dreamt about—*we need you to join two members of the crew on a space walk to look for damage caused by debris.*

Heather's heart fluttered as the words soaked in. She felt like a backup quarterback in the Super Bowl with his team down by a touchdown. With tens of thousands of screaming fans looking on, and countless millions around the world watching, that backup quarterback had to lead the team down the field to avoid defeat. He'd practiced, studied, and run simulation plays on the computer against his opponent's defense. He understood what was being asked of him. The fate of the team's season was all up to him.

That was how Heather felt sitting in the air lock of the ISS for the first time. She wasn't supposed to walk in space on that mission, although she'd trained for it. Now the Russian commander had declared an emergency, and Heather became that backup quarterback. He'd entrusted her to search for a problem and fix it, enabling the ISS to continue to function.

There was a reason that the Russian commander was concerned about the external antennae. Years prior, India blew apart one of its satellites orbiting Earth as a test of its ballistic missile defense interceptors. The explosion created hundreds of pieces of orbital debris in an apogee near that of the ISS. It was so close, in fact, that extensive studies were made to determine if the ISS needed to be moved to avoid a collision.

India was condemned and ridiculed for its actions, but it opened the floodgates for other countries to test their ballistic missile defense systems on satellites. At the time, India was only the fourth country to acquire the technology to conduct a test such as this one. After its success, Russia, China, North Korea, and Iran followed suit with similar tests.

The increased debris resulted in Washington issuing a directive aimed at cleaning up space junk. The *Space Fence,* as it was called, enhanced the military's tracking capabilities from twenty-three thousand objects to nearly two hundred thousand.

The concern was real. Moving at thousands of miles per hour in orbit, objects of an inch or larger were capable of causing catastrophic damage to anything that got in their way.

That fact did not deter Heather from getting ready for her first space walk and settling into the air lock. The two cosmonauts had already exited the ISS and were outside, inspecting the massive spacecraft.

Heather was naturally nervous. It was exciting and frightening at the same time. She watched the digital clock tick down, anxiously awaiting it to register zero. Finally, it did. Heather unhooked her suit and she was floating.

She floated over to the air lock's inner hatch and pushed it closed. She pulled the handle down and spun it shut, resulting in a loud clanking sound.

She switched her suit over to its own self-contained battery power and oxygen system. She carefully depressed the air lock, and after a final purge of air from the air lock, she found herself surrounded by a vacuum.

There was no sound. The thud she'd heard when she closed the air lock's inner hatch couldn't be heard now. She could pound on the walls with a sledgehammer, and she wouldn't hear that either. In the vacuum of space, there was no way for sound to travel.

At that point, Heather was ready to take the leap. Nothing held her back except her apprehension, and she fought the fear with anticipation and excitement. She knew that once she opened the outer hatch, there would be nothing between her and an instantaneous death but the space suit she was wearing.

She opened the door to the payload bay and pushed the thermal cover aside. First, she poked her head through to make sure nothing unexpected awaited her. *No little green men. No ugly lizards bearing fangs. No leftovers of the Indian satellite.*

Heather put her hands on the hatch frame and secured her safety tether. Then she pulled herself through, floating on her back, looking up into the heavens.

Everywhere she looked, there was nothing around her but the infinity of the universe. She began to giggle uncontrollably as she realized she'd achieved her dream. She spoke to herself, although the vacuum of space distorted her voice within her helmet. Sound waves travel different at lower atmospheric pressure, causing her voice to sound like a more sexy, throaty Mae West than Heather Fox.

Every day is a good day when you're floating.

She'd dreamed of saying those words, repeating them often to Gunner when she convinced him that she'd be perfectly safe in space. Heather savored the moment, staring upward toward the stars.

Now she wanted to see the Earth. Home. Gunner.

At roughly two hundred fifty miles above the planet's surface, the vantage point didn't enable a spacewalker to fit the whole planet into their field of vision. You can't quite see the curvature of the Earth or its relationship to the universe. However, seeing the Earth through the space station's small windows versus seeing it from outside was like looking at a fish through aquarium glass instead of scuba diving alongside one.

Heather pushed off the ISS slightly to rotate her body toward Earth. As it came into view, her eyes grew wide as she took in the most magnificent view of her life.

There she is, Mother Earth, light and bright in all her glory.

Mesmerized, she tried to force her eyes wider in an attempt to look around the entire image laid out before her, soaking it in to remember for the rest of her life.

And then, it ended.

CHAPTER 31

Saturday, April 21
Aboard the Starship in Lunar Orbit
Earth's Moon

The Starship commander spoke to the crew as they waited to land on the Moon. "We will remain in lunar orbit for another thirty minutes in preparation for our final descent onto Artemis. While we wait, for the benefit of Chief Rawlings and Major Fox, let me provide you a description of what you're seeing."

Chief Rawlings leaned forward and caught Gunner's eye. Gunner responded with a nod of the helmet and a thumbs-up. For a brief period of time, as the Starship sped away from Earth towards its rendezvous with the Moon, Gunner put the task he'd been charged with out of his mind and focused on the magnificent splendor of space.

It was completely pure. There were no buildings or honking cars or millions of people moving about. It was deserted, desolate, and wild. In a way, Gunner thought to himself, it was a shame that man was invading space. *We have a way of screwing things up.*

The commander explained why the two faces of the Moon appeared different. "You've probably noticed that there's a stark difference between the Moon's heavily cratered far side and the relatively smooth, open basins of the Earth-facing nearside. Over billions of years, the Moon has been transformed by space debris. We've learned that the farside has a thicker crust and an extra layer of material. Scientists have suggested that the Moon collided with a dwarf planet at some point in the early history of our solar system, creating this geologic wonder."

Gunner pointed toward a window and asked, "What are the flashes of light emanating from the surface? Is that part of the mining operation?"

"No," the commander replied. "That's been labeled transient luminous lunar phenomena."

"That's a mouthful, right?" quipped Chief Rawlings. "Don't we have an acronym for that? We do for everything else."

"I wish we did, and I also wish we had a full explanation for the light show, but we don't," replied the commander. "We've studied it and found that the phenomena occur several times a week, illuminating part of the Moon's landscape for a brief period before disappearing. We've even observed a reverse effect, which causes the lunar surface to darken. Using artificial intelligence on Earth, we've deployed our lunar vehicles to play an inconsequential game of whack-a-mole. When the light show begins, we dispatch our teams into the open basins in an attempt to identify the source."

"Is there a consensus as to what causes it?" asked Gunner.

"Some believe that small meteors hit the Moon, causing the flashes of light as energy is released on impact. They're too small to register on our seismometers, however. Another theory is that solar activity sends highly charged particles through the solar system that interact with the lunar surface. That might explain why a definite source of the activity can't be pinpointed. You know, the whole *lightning never strikes twice in the same place* concept."

Gunner chuckled to himself. But it does, in actuality.

"Okay, lady and gentlemen, LOP-G is passing beneath us, and as soon as it clears our path, we'll bring 'er down."

LOP-G, the acronym for the Lunar Orbital Platform Gateway, commonly referred to as the *Gateway*, remained in orbit above the Moon although it was scheduled to be decommissioned in two years. The LOP-G performed a similar function to the International Space Station. When it was first launched into orbit around the Moon, it was used as a staging ground for personnel, space machinery, and materials to be delivered to the lunar surface as part of building a base there.

The LOP-G was used for several years to host resupply runs and the delivery of cargo until the lunar outpost was created and operational. At this point, the orbital platform simply assisted in monitoring activity on the lunar surface and acted as a sentinel for incoming space debris like meteor storms, solar activity, and asteroids.

Chief Rawlings leaned over toward Gunner. "So, Gunner, now that you've seen the Moon, here's a last chance to catch a glimpse of Earth before we land. How's it look to you?"

"Light and bright."

*****

Moments later, the Starship was expertly set upon a landing pad in the center of Artemis, the name assigned to the lunar outpost. As the ground control team made arrangements to escort the astronauts from the Starship into the friendly confines of lunar mission control, the newly arriving crew of the mission made small talk.

"Why did they call this Artemis?" asked Gunner.

Chief Rawlings responded, "NASA has always pulled its names of projects from sources like Greek mythology. Artemis was the twin sister of Apollo, as well as the goddess of the Moon. It was a logical name for the lunar outpost, as she embodies our mission to inhabit the Moon.

"In 2024, when the project was begun by navigating a lunar lander to the south pole of the Moon, it was important that a woman be designated the first to step out of the lander. Since then, not only have we established a sustainable habitat on the Moon using resources we found here to build, but we've created a gateway for future exploration."

"Mars," muttered Gunner.

"That's right. Certainly, the mining operation here has become the number one priority as scientists collect rock and regolith samples to return to Earth. However, we've also learned to become self-reliant here. The permanently shadowed craters hold ice that is mined to

157

produce water and rocket fuel. As I mentioned, almost all of the buildings have been built utilizing surface rocks and soils. We've proven that we can convert the natural resources of a celestial body to further human settlements, something that will be absolutely necessary if we're going to duplicate the process on Mars."

The Starship shook as a vacuum-sealed jet bridge connector was attached. Moments later, the hatch was opened and a rush of cool air entered the Starship.

"Welcome to the Moon and Artemis," a uniformed NASA employee proudly announced.

CHAPTER 32

Saturday, April 21
Artemis
Earth's Moon

Gunner's head was on a swivel as he took in the flurry of activity taking place within the mission control center of Artemis. He glanced down at his feet, which stood upon perfectly shaped brick, albeit much larger than standard brick on Earth. Another NASA engineer approached Gunner and Chief Rawlings. His hand was extended and his smile was broad, considering the circumstances.

"Gentlemen, welcome. I'm glad you're here, albeit a day late. Jan Werner, director of mission control here at Artemis. Chief, it's a real honor. When I heard you'd be on board, I told everyone to clean up their cubicles and sweep the floor."

Gunner looked down again and noticed the dusty appearance. "Um, do you have to sweep often?"

Werner laughed. "Not as much as we should, considering. You're standing on, and actually surrounded by, bricks made of moon dust. That's right. One of the first structures built on the lunar surface was a solar concentrator. As the sun rises, electric shutters roll back to reveal a twenty-foot-tall solar array of hexagonal polished mirrors, which, as the name suggests, concentrates the sunlight into a tight light beam."

She nonchalantly tapped her foot on the brick floor, causing just enough moon dust to float around her ankles until gravity pulled it back down to the floor. She continued. "The sunlight is focused into a solar furnace, where temperatures reach five thousand degrees. This is capable of melting most metals, including iron, steel, and titanium.

On approach, you might have noticed the bluish color of *Mare Tranquillitatis*, um, sorry, the Sea of Tranquility. It's abundant with the titanium-bearing mineral called ilmenite. The lunar rocks harbor ten times as much titanium ore than those on Earth. It was a tremendous find and made all of this possible."

She spun around and raised her hands toward the ceiling. The structure resembled a giant igloo, except with all of the modern conveniences of electricity.

"One of the biggest challenges in establishing Artemis was the up-front costs associated with shipping building materials up here," added Chief Rawlings. "The discovery of the titanium, coupled with the technology creating the solar concentrator, allowed NASA to greatly advance the development schedule of Artemis. The building we're standing in was due to be constructed ten years from now, yet here we stand."

"That's right, Chief," said Werner. "Our mining operations are likewise a decade ahead of production. Heck, we're waiting on the private contractors to build rockets so we can start sending our resources back to Earth faster, which, in turn, will start paying for all of this."

"Very impressive," said Gunner. "Where's the Starhopper?"

"We have it inside the hangar, being retrofitted to haul the, you know, payload," replied Werner in a hushed tone. Gunner appeared puzzled, so Werner explained her reasons for lowering her voice. "Major, not everyone here on the Moon agrees with the prospect of blasting the asteroid. They've experienced firsthand what our science and engineering capabilities are because many of them have been with Project Artemis from the beginning. Frankly, they believe the destruction of IM86 is a waste of a valuable research tool."

Gunner smiled. "That's easy for them to say. They're not in the crosshairs of that sucker."

Chief Rawlings shot him a glance and immediately changed the subject. "Director Werner, would you have someone show us to our quarters? I'd like to get our crew settled with a little rest, and then I want to gather up the international additions to the mission so everyone can get a chance to meet one another."

"Ah, yes. Détente," said Werner. "The relationship between Russia and the West has soured on Earth, and some of that has carried forward to Artemis. Don't get me wrong. Everyone gets along and we have a good working relationship with our foreign counterparts. However, once work is done, everyone gravitates back toward their own. Social events are planned and carried out, but generally, the Russians stick together and away from the Americans."

"That's human nature, regardless of what planet or moon you're standing on," said Chief Rawlings. "Point us in the direction of our bunks. We'll need a tour guide until we get our bearings."

Werner held up her hand and stepped away. When she returned, she had a young woman with her who was carrying a computer tablet and a portable communications device.

"Jennifer will assist you in gathering your belongings off the Starship, and take you in one of our lunar transports to the housing complex. The astronauts have their own section, separate from the commissary, dining hall, and recreation facilities, so that you can have more peace and quiet. You'll come back here to conduct briefings, and we have an annex that contains the flight simulator delivered along with the Starhopper. Practice makes perfect, right?"

Gunner rolled his eyes and shook his head. He'd had enough of the all-too-chipper Director Werner. He wondered to himself if she secretly might enjoy the Earth getting blasted to smithereens, leaving her as Queen Bee of humanity, snug as a bug on the Moon.

"Actually," began Jennifer, "I'm having your things brought to your quarters. It'll take a while for the crew to unload them off the Starship amidst all of the gear that you brought with you. This way, please."

Gunner and Chief Rawlings followed the young woman, with the remainder of the American contingent following close behind. She led them through a series of windowless hallways toward a transportation center that resembled a taxi stand, except all of the vehicles were designed like Humvees with five-foot-tall tires.

Gunner was anxious to see the lunar surface, so he asked, "There aren't any windows. Don't you guys get claustrophobic?"

Jennifer laughed. "No, sir. We get used to it. The windows would have to be brought up from Earth, and to be safe from incoming space rocks, they'd have to be extraordinarily thick. As a result, you'd not be able to see anything or, at least, it would all be distorted."

She stood to the side and pointed toward one of the behemoth lunar transports. A twelve-foot-tall platform ladder was pushed up against the machine, where the driver waved Gunner and the rest of the American astronauts forward.

"Jennifer, where are the Russians? I thought the lunar outpost was manned at fifty-fifty American to international personnel."

She nodded and waved the last person up the ladder. "They work mainly in the mining operations. From the beginning, their interest in Artemis was less about the prospects of reaching Mars and beyond, but rather what resources are available here on the Moon."

Gunner thought to himself, *Here and now, one thing at a time. Let someone else spend trillions of dollars and lose their astronauts' lives exploring the Great Beyond.*

CHAPTER 33

Saturday, April 21
Artemis
Earth's Moon

Jennifer the Jolly Tour Guide chattered away as the lunar transport hauled the American astronauts to the housing facility. She didn't have a care in the world, Gunner surmised, because her world wasn't in danger. Or maybe they weren't fully aware of the threat? Did the inhabitants of Artemis wake up in the morning and turn on the local news, sports, and *weather on the 8s?* Was Artemis the true utopia that people dreamed about? One without financial worries, social pressures, or family conflict?

From time to time, Gunner's mind would wander back into the present as Jennifer pointed out something of interest. Jennifer, who was knowledgeable and cute, was explaining the background for the development of Artemis.

"One of the keys to making Artemis a reality was our ability to have a space-based supply of propellant. Yes, mining is an important factor in the lunar outpost's development, but we, I mean, NASA has always set its sights on access to the inner solar system.

"The vision established in 2018 and 2019 to place man on the Moon again turned out to be one of the great advancements for mankind. The discovery of lunar polar volatiles resulting from that first walk on the Moon since 1969 made all the difference."

A volatile, as it relates to planetary science, is a chemical compound with a sufficiently low boiling point that it can be converted into a form of energy. These chemical elements are usually associated with a planet's or moon's crust, and are most abundant near the poles. When NASA successfully landed at the south pole of the Moon in 2024, scientists were astounded at the opportunity to create a supply line of propellants. Refueling at the Moon transformed the potential for deep-space travel.

"There's more," continued Jennifer. "Thanks to the Moon's shallow gravity well, water-derived products such as hydrogen and oxygen can be exported to be used for life support, as well as being combusted for rocket propulsion. I cannot overstate the importance of the 2024 mission and the advancement in space exploration that resulted from it."

The transport made a wide sweep around a massive rock pile, and suddenly the mining operation came into full view. To their left, several small vehicles with solar arrays attached were scurrying about the surface.

"What are those things doing?" asked Gunner.

"Oh, of course," began Jennifer. "Those are some of our *Skylights*. You see, the lunar surface has been assaulted for millions of years by space objects, some bigger than others. Craters are formed and, over time, so are fissures and crevasses. Each Skylight, solar powered of course, is equipped with a high-resolution 3-D camera capable of mapping a lunar feature.

"The resulting computer-generated model shows us whether it's safe for a human or a larger unmanned rover to descend below the lunar surface to explore its attributes.

"One of the first discoveries after the Skylights were deployed was ice. As you know, for humans, water is life, and the ice discovered in the shadows of these long, narrow openings in the lunar surface has provided us an invaluable resource. If you look ahead, you'll see one of our Skylight Maximus vehicles at work."

The driver of the transport slowed as Jennifer pointed out a much larger version of the Skylight rover. The Maximus model contained a large solar array as well as a device akin to the railguns deployed on U.S. naval destroyers.

"The Maximus was based upon a concept called the Mini Bee. It was a method of optical mining designed to harvest resources from asteroids. The technology was applied to the Moon, except on a much larger scale, hence the name Maximus."

"What does it do?" asked one of the astronauts.

"It's quite simple, actually. Using the power of the sun, a laser beam is generated that wears away at the surface, separating the dust from the valuable resources identified through the Skylight rover's analysis. The generated minerals are collected in an inflatable bag and returned to the central mining facility. The moon dust residue is gathered in one of our sweepers and used to make more bricks, the building blocks of future development on the Moon."

While Gunner was truly enjoying the tour of the Moon, his cynical side began to wonder how long it would take before county commissions, and metropolitan planning commissions, and building inspectors, and homeowner's associations, and environmental groups arrived on the Moon to ruin Jennifer the Jolly Tour Guide's utopia.

"Here we are," she said cheerily as a sprawling complex of buildings appeared before them. "This is our housing unit. Each space is the same, by design. There is no hierarchy here. Age, rank, wealth make no difference at Artemis. We've found that eliminating bragging rights like the biggest house, car, or nicest sofa makes the stresses of living in relatively close quarters more, well, habitable and hospitable."

The lunar transport pulled into a large single-stall garage and waited while a roll-down door closed behind them. The solar-powered engine idled, allowing oxygen to circulate through the compartment. A minute later, the driver announced that pressure and oxygen levels within the garage had equalized, and they were clear to exit the transport.

"Okay, let me spend a few minutes showing you around the common areas, and then I'll lead you to your quarters."

Gunner held back to wait for Chief Rawlings as he exited the transport. "Whadya think about all of this?"

"Truthfully? I find it both remarkable and chilling. Don't get me wrong, I'm proud of what NASA has accomplished here. I'd like to think that I've been a part of bringing it to fruition. But did you get the sense that our escort has been drinking the Kool-Aid?"

Gunner nodded and leaned in to his mentor. "She's so tickled to be here, Earth is just a foreign country she never plans to visit. Is it that great up here that nobody gives a rat's ass about friends and family they left behind?"

"It sure sounds like it," replied Chief Rawlings. "Listen, call me a pessimist, but any place that's full of people, especially in close quarters, whether it's a submarine, a spacecraft, or Artemis, there's always an undercurrent of jealousy, discontent, and hostility."

Jennifer chastised the men. "Gentlemen! Try to keep up, please."

Gunner continued to whisper. "It's very *Stepford Wives*. Too perfect. I'd prefer to deal with the devil I know instead of the devil I don't."

"Amen, brother," said Chief Rawlings as he encouraged Gunner to walk ahead of him.

As they walked through the common area, which was filled with people eating dinner and engaging in conversation, Chief Rawlings and Gunner both noticed a group of cosmonauts sitting alone at a corner table. Rather than wearing the customary blue NASA coveralls, they were dressed in red uniforms, the adopted color of communism and the Bolsheviks, symbolizing the blood of the working class.

Chief Rawlings nudged Gunner. Before he could speak, Gunner said, "I see them. Recognize them, too."

"Yeah, Sokolov, Chernevsky, and Semenova," added Chief Rawlings, who continued to stare ahead nonchalantly. "I'll never forget. Do you think they noticed you?"

Gunner looked down at his feet, emulating Chief Rawlings's attempt to pretend they didn't notice the group. He whispered his response. "Oh, yeah. Every head at the table snapped up. I'm sure they remember my choice words in the media and the congressional hearings."

"You had choice words for everybody, if I recall."

"Yessir. That I did."

CHAPTER 34

Sunday, April 22
Defense Threat Reduction Agency
Fort Belvoir, Virginia

"Good morning, Agent Cuccinelli," greeted Ghost as he entered the office that had been temporarily assigned to the FBI agent on loan to the DTRA. The Jackal was supposed to have been returned to the bureau a week ago. However, after the discovery of IM86, and the ongoing efforts of Ghost to follow a hunch, he arranged for the cyber specialist to remain at Fort Belvoir for the foreseeable future, such as it was.

Unlike other government agencies, who furloughed their employees for the upcoming week due to the anticipated impact event of Friday the twenty-seventh, Ghost, and those within his charge, didn't stop performing their duties. He had confidence in Gunner's ability to perform as requested. What he wasn't sure of was whether NASA's plan of diversion would work. Computer simulation was one thing. Reality was another.

"Good morning, sir," she responded. "Sir, I've just received information via my contacts in Moscow. The Russians will be announcing their three-person crew this afternoon for Project Jackhammer."

"I'm surprised they haven't done that already," said Ghost as he set a carton of Krispy Kreme doughnuts on the Jackal's desk.

She quickly snatched up a cruller and munched on it. She chewed it down and then addressed his comment. "Sir, they've been very tight-lipped about their intentions, both with respect to their attempts to land on IM86 and the crew announcement. I get the sense they're hedging their bets."

"Why do you say that?" asked Ghost.

"Well, they've made no public statements about landing on the asteroid. Now, it's presumed that they have not, because Putin has been silent on the issue. His ego prevents him from admitting failure, but it also would prompt him to make an announcement the moment it happened."

"I agree."

"That leads me to my next observation," she continued. "As you know, I've been frustrated at my lack of ability to tap into the Russian Space Agency's servers. Once the Russians began their transition from the World Wide Web to their country's own internet, *Runet*, our ability to hack into their systems has been hindered."

"Yet you're still able to do so," countered Ghost.

"True, sir, to an extent. Naturally, the CIA has operatives throughout Russia, some of whom are highly placed within the government. That said, the Kremlin's censor, *Roscomnadzor*, has been very effective in segmenting portions of the government's operations so that one cannot reach the other. Very smart, frankly, but something the public would never allow in America. Our nation is all about open government, hence the reason we're not like Russia."

Ghost paced the room in frustration. "So you have no inkling as to the status of the Russian mission or their intentions?"

"No, sir, I didn't say that. I have a suspicion, based upon newly discovered information I gleaned from their communications."

"Please, what is it?" he asked.

"I don't believe they've landed yet, although they must be close to pulling it off. My guess is that they need more time."

"Do they not realize that the world is running out of time? Friday, for Pete's sake, is coming like a freight train. And the asteroid won't hit the brakes."

"Sir, NASA tells us that the Russians may have until Tuesday to achieve their dual goals of landing and diverting. If the diversion method they utilize doesn't have an effect by Wednesday, then our strategic bombing is the only option."

"We're scheduled to do that on Tuesday, with Wednesday the drop-dead deadline, pardon the godawful pun."

"Correct, sir. We're at cross-purposes with the Russians, and the crew that they intend to announce this afternoon indicate they want to play hardball right up until the last minute."

Ghost stopped wandering the room and leaned on the desk with both hands. "Who are they?"

"Chernevsky, Semenova, and Commander Sokolov."

"Their henchmen," growled Ghost.

"Yessir."

"I've gotta talk to Colonel Robinson with the DOD. He's familiar with these three because he was at Houston Mission Control when that all went down."

The Jackal leaned back in her chair and finished her doughnut. She stared at her monitor and grimaced.

"What is it, Cuccinelli?"

She looked up at him and then reached for the remote to a television monitor mounted behind Ghost. "Let me show you."

The monitor powered up and the Jackal began typing furiously on her keyboard. Seconds later, a chart that resembled a whiteboard in an FBI field office during an organized crime investigation appeared.

"Sir, sometimes, I fall back on my investigative roots with the bureau to solve a problem. I realize this might appear somewhat confusing with the names and circles and lines connecting them together."

"To say the least," he muttered. "I do see one name located in the center of the graphic."

"Robinson," said the Jackal. "You see, I've been trying to piece together this whole thing for a couple of weeks now."

"Wait, what? A couple of weeks. You've only been involved—"

"That's right, sir. Since Gunner and his team went to Far East Russia. I hope I haven't overstepped my bounds, but please allow me to explain."

"Sure," said Ghost, who sat in a chair across from the young FBI agent to give her his full attention.

"I could sense how troubled Major Fox was and also noticed the inordinate amount of confidence you placed in him. I took a peek at his psychological profile, and honestly, you know, I'm supposed to remain unemotional during any investigation, but, um, I felt sorry for him. What he and his wife had was special, and the events of three years ago have changed him."

Ghost nodded. "I knew them both. Gunner and Heather were more than a married couple, they were a team who supported one another with love, encouragement and advice."

The Jackal continued. "Anyway, I decided to delve further into the events. When you approached me about investigating Professor Karlov in Crimea, I'm ashamed to admit that he was already on my radar."

"You knew about Karlov before I instructed you to do the background for Cam and Bear's mission?"

"Um, yessir. I apologize."

"Who else is on your radar, as you put it?" Ghost was not annoyed but, rather, intrigued by the mind of an FBI agent.

"I gathered all the information I could on the personnel on duty that day, both in the ISS and in Houston. Then I accessed the classified files from the House Subcommittee that conducted its own hearings and found the names of the Russians, both named and unnamed, involved in Russia's space agency. I discovered a common thread."

"Robinson?" Ghost leaned forward and gritted his teeth. There was something sketchy about that guy, he was sure of it.

"Because of the overall hostilities between the two nations and the circumstances regarding lost communications in the past on the ISS, Colonel Robinson became the liaison between Moscow and Houston. Everything passed across his desk or through his ears."

Ghost leaned back in his chair and took a deep breath. He exhaled and then asked, "Agent Cuccinelli, are you saying that Colonel Robinson knows something about what happened that day?"

"Sir, I think he might know everything."

CHAPTER 35

Sunday, April 22
Artemis
Earth's Moon

"Well, it's official," began Chief Rawlings as he joined Gunner for coffee. "Commander Sokolov will lead his team of Chernevsky and Semenova on board the Starhopper. Two males and a female, to counter our contingent. The Frenchman, Jean-Louis Favier, will be the sole European on board. By previous agreement, our people will have complete control over the mission, from liftoff, to detonation of the nukes on the surface, to your return to Earth. The Russians and Favier are nothing more than political figureheads to create a false sense of cooperation."

"Very false," snarled Gunner. "I don't want anything to do with those three ass-clowns. In fact, I'll stay in my quarters until it's time for me to pull the trigger, if it's all the same to you."

Chief Rawlings laughed and finished off his coffee. He glanced around and slyly reached into his pocket to pull out his pack of Levi Garrett chewing tobacco. The three-ounce bag generally lasted him a day or so. After he'd packed some in his cheek, he slipped it back into his pocket.

"I'm not the only one capable of carrying contraband," he said with a smile as the nicotine entered his body.

"That wasn't my marijuana," Gunner protested.

"I know, Major, relax. I have my suspicions, but it doesn't matter at this point. In forty-eight hours or so, this thing will be over, and I'll be joining you at Vandenberg for a beer shortly thereafter."

Vandenberg Air Force Base, located in Santa Barbara County,

California, was home to the 30th Space Wing of the Air Force Space Command. It's fifteen-thousand-foot runway was ideal for landing the Starhopper under these circumstances.

The modifications being made to the spacecraft to carry the nuclear weapons also required specialized landing gear to be installed. The engineers at SpaceX were up to the task, as they'd already designed the modified version upon a request by the Air Force years ago.

Mounting the nuclear armaments had to be done on the Moon, as the risk of detonating the devices was too great upon liftoff from Earth. Escaping the gravitational pull of the Moon took far less power and thrust.

"Chief, I'm ready. I've forgotten about all that crap on the ground. In fact, our tour guide kinda helped me transition from the troubles on Earth to the mission ahead of me."

"Well, I think you and I are both ready to see the new design of the Starhopper and get to know the rest of your crew," said Chief Rawlings. "Let's take the high road and greet our Russian comrades, maybe putting a thaw on the cold war. Whadya think?"

"Chief, you don't wanna know what I think, but, in the interest of goin' along to get along, I'll be on my best professional behavior."

The two men gathered up the remainder of the American astronauts and made their way to the Russians' table. Commander Sokolov was unusually cordial, but the other two astronauts, not so much. They finished their breakfast and barely made contact with the Americans. During the small talk with Sokolov, the French *astronaute*, Favier, joined them. After several minutes, the group of eight, led by Chief Rawlings, left for the transport garage and crammed in one together.

"Thankfully, the Starhopper has more room than this," said Chief Rawlings jokingly. "This reminds me of the old Apollo spacecraft. They were before my time, but I have taken the opportunity to sit in them."

He was doing his best to defuse the tense atmosphere in the transport. Chief Rawlings didn't care if these people liked each other.

He just needed them to work together to put Gunner in a position to do his job. After a twenty-minute ride through more of the mining operations, the transport approached a launch facility that could be seen by lunar mission control from a distance.

Once inside, they took a brief tour of the Starhopper's modifications, led by a SpaceX engineer. Other members of the retrofit team were on hand, including a space engineer familiar with the nuclear missiles. After a brief explanation of the modifications and how they might affect the spacecraft's maneuverability, he addressed the issue foremost on everyone's minds—the nuclear missiles.

"Without going into the debate of whether the use of nuclear weapons to attack IM86 is the proper method of diversion, I will say that we may not have much of a choice at this late juncture."

The three Russian astronauts talked among themselves, revealing an angry reaction to the engineer's lack of confidence in their still ongoing mission.

Undeterred by their attitude, the engineer continued. "Nonetheless, we've been tasked with pulverizing this asteroid, or at the very least, sufficiently dismembering it to either divert it from its present trajectory, or minimize the magnitude of the impact event. We've studied this in computer simulations for years. The opportunity to test it has never come about until now.

"Let me say this, it will take the force of ten atomic bombs to completely destroy IM86, and that's based upon certain assumptions. We know that asteroids are mainly comprised of iron and rock, but we have very limited data on their surface and interior composition. The study of Bennu a decade ago shed some light on this, but Bennu's size paled in comparison to IM86.

"The space rock that you're going to tangle with is likely very old, stripped of most loose material after numerous trips around the sun. This explains why IM86 has a very low reflective nature."

"We'll have onboard AI to determine the asteroid's points of vulnerability," added another scientist. "In a laboratory setting, we set up experiments using high-speed cameras to predict how rocks on

Earth fissure and crack when struck with a projectile. We then extrapolated that data, accounting for the low-gravity environment that exists in the limited atmosphere around the asteroid."

The space engineer continued. "Geologists have studied the results of the testing. What they found was a spider vein effect. By that, I mean that the first crack leads to a collective behavior of cracks, all trying to move really fast, interacting with each other. Now, the resiliency of the asteroid will determine how numerous and quickly these cracks spread across the outer surface.

"That leads to the second aspect of this mission. Once the asteroid has been mapped, using AI, and your points of vulnerability have been established, you'll begin unloading your nuclear arsenal."

He turned around and pointed toward the Starhopper. "As you can see, there are four nuclear weapons mounted to the sides of the spacecraft. Earlier I said that it would take ten to pulverize IM86. That hypothesis still holds, but you'll only have four at your disposal."

The astronauts began to talk among themselves, questioning whether they were going into this mission without sufficient firepower to be successful.

"Will the computer update the targets after the initial strike?" asked Gunner.

"Very astute question, Major. You're spot on with it. Once the first missile strikes the asteroid, its composition will change. The cracks and fissures that I mentioned will begin to race around the surface. Your vulnerability points will still be identified, but most likely reprioritized. In other words, it'll be up to you to pick and choose your targets for maximum effect."

"How much firepower do we have?" asked Gunner.

"We've supplied you with eighty gigatons of TNT, containing roughly the equivalent of four million Hiroshima-size bombs, or for our Russian friends, that's nearly two thousand Tsar Bomba devices, the most powerful nuclear weapon ever detonated. It's four times more energy than previous estimates of what it would take to destroy an asteroid of this size."

"Because?" asked Chief Rawlings.

"Chief, this new estimate by our geologists takes into account the complex interactions between the surface fissures created on impact and the depth of the blast. It's possible that a second strike in the same location will cause the asteroid to split. Then a third and fourth strike of the two halves will divide it even further, revealing the core."

"Then that's what we'll do," commented Gunner.

The Russians laughed among themselves. One of them muttered, "*Samouverennost'.*" This was translated to mean overconfident.

The space engineer, who was fluent in Russian, disregarded the remark but took it upon himself to remind Gunner of the difficult task he faced. "Major, one thing that you'll have to remember is that IM86 is going to fight back. In the vacuum of space, Newton's third law will apply, and the action of blasting the asteroid will send debris in all directions around it. You will have to fly through the debris, avoiding being struck by the material, so that you can return to take that second shot.

"After your second missile launch, assuming that you've been successful, the amount of space debris increases significantly. The last two missile strikes may be impossible under these circumstances. You'll have to be careful."

"I intend for all of us to live through this, and do our duty," said Gunner proudly.

"Well, Major, then there's one more thing you should know. After you are successful, the remaining parts of the asteroid will hurtle towards Earth at even faster speeds. The nuclear detonations will act to shove it towards the greatest source of gravity in its vicinity, Earth. While you're circling your target, aiming to take the shot, part of IM86 will likely be streaking ahead."

The space engineer paused and looked at each member of the Starhopper crew. "To put it simply, you'll be in a race with a massive meteor storm to get home."

CHAPTER 36

Sunday, April 22
Artemis
Earth's Moon

The act of killing another human being had its own gravitational pull. Once you get the taste of taking another human being's life, you're drawn to killing a little closer. Soon, after several kills, you've stayed on the dark side of humanity too long, and you can't break free.

For Russian space commander Anton Sokolov, murder became an easy, acceptable means to solve a problem. He'd never forgotten his first kill. He had been vying with another cosmonaut to ride into space as part of the early group of Russians to man the International Space Station when it was launched in 1998.

Sokolov saw his opportunity slipping away as his rival continually outperformed him in both written and practical testing. So he reverted to a method he'd learned from his father in the KGB—poison.

Exotic poisons have been a mainstay of Moscow-ordered assassinations dating back to the days of the Czars. Castor bean, a KGB favorite, was an exotic addition to any garden. With beautiful, oversized tropical leaves, many Russian gardens contained this plant. One of the features of the castor bean plant, its bizarre seed pods, produced a bean that contained ricin.

Ricin, one of the most deadly and toxic substances on Earth, caused acute gastroenteritis. The bean itself closely resembled a coffee bean and was easily smuggled by Russian agents until it was ground up and ingested by an unsuspecting victim. It was the poison of choice for Commander Sokolov and had served him well over the years.

He'd perfected the dosage, knowing exactly how much to use to cause death, or simply a bad case of gastroenteritis, an inflammation of the lining of the intestines often associated with a virus or bacteria. Commonly referred to as the stomach flu, gastroenteritis can be treated with medication and bed rest.

Commander Sokolov was a highly respected Russian cosmonaut who'd been associated with international space programs for thirty years. He was a loyal soldier, willing to carry out whatever Mother Russia called upon him to do. Unlike Gunner and Chief Rawlings, who had to use subterfuge to bring their contraband into Artemis, Commander Sokolov simply put in a request for his favorite coffee, several bags of which were always on hand in his quarters.

Until now, he'd not found a reason to dig into his preferred problem-solving tool. Certainly, the Americans at Artemis annoyed him from time to time, but overall, he and his top lieutenants, Chernevsky and Semenova, stuck to themselves with the other Russian scientists on the Moon.

That evening, he had little time to execute his plan. He enlisted the aid of Russian kitchen personnel in the housing unit, who were sworn to secrecy and bribed through perks given their families back home.

Their window of opportunity was brief. One of the waiters in the dining hall was instructed to offer coffee to the American astronauts after they finished dinner. The Russian baker who worked in the kitchen was instructed to create a coffee whip dessert made up of heavy whipping cream, miniature marshmallows, and coffee from grounds.

The coffee of choice for both after-dinner treats—Sokolov's Special Blend, laced with ricin.

He didn't want to kill the Americans. That wasn't necessary to accomplish his purpose. Severe gastric problems would ground them for days, more than enough time for his comrades to land on the asteroid and proudly plant the tricolor flag on the surface. The

Americans might have beaten them to the Moon, but Mother Russia would claim the asteroid as their own and reap the benefits.

Like the night before, the Russians sat at their usual table tucked in a corner of the dining hall. They intently observed the Americans as they ate, laughed, and engaged in conversation in the center of the room.

Khorosho, he thought to himself. *Good. Let the Americans feel comfortable and loose. Let your guard down and enjoy the moment. Your arrogance will soon cost you days of agony in the infirmary.*

First, coffee was offered and served to only two of the American astronauts. Sokolov scowled at the waiter as he sent a subliminal message for him to insist upon pouring a cup for everyone. Still, three declined, including Chief Rawlings and Gunner.

Sokolov lifted his own cup of coffee and took a sip, hoping to make eye contact with Chief Rawlings. He was successful and provided the American elder statesman of space exploration a pleasant smile. Chief Rawlings smiled back, but still didn't take the hint.

"Piz-dets!" he mumbled to the others at the table. *Dammit!*

Only Chernevsky and the beautiful cosmonaut Semenova were left sitting with him now, both of whom were aware of the operation to poison the Americans. If their efforts to ground their military man Major Fox failed, Semenova would take more drastic measures, using her sexuality to get close to the handsome combat pilot.

The waiter approached the table with a tray of the coffee whip desserts topped with ricin. Rather than offer them to his guests, one was placed in front of each of the astronauts, together with friendly words of encouragement to try the delicacy.

Once again, the two astronauts who partook of the coffee dug into the dessert. Sokolov chuckled to himself and stifled a smile. They'd get the worst of what ricin had to offer. The infirmary was ill-equipped to diagnose the poison and most likely would assume their illnesses were isolated due to poor hygiene.

He became more frustrated when he saw Major Fox push the dessert to the side and begin to leave the table. As he was saying his goodbyes, Sokolov patted Semenova on the thigh and whispered to her, "You make love to him, and when he sleeps, three drops of this into his mouth or allow him to breathe it in. He will never awake."

Sokolov slipped a small vial of polonium-210 into her hand. Po-210 was a radioactive isotope used by the Russian space program for decades in its lunar landers to keep the spacecraft's instruments warm at night. It was also a deadly poison more toxic than hydrogen cyanide. The radiation travels through the body and immediately begins to decay vital organs.

"*Da.* I will." Semenova turned on the sex appeal. She sashayed across the dining hall, swaying her hips and drawing the attention of every male in the room. She picked up the pace in an effort to catch Gunner as he made his way down the hallway to his quarters.

Semenova glanced over her shoulder to confirm she was alone with her target, and then called out to Gunner, "Major, may I speak with you for a moment."

Gunner turned around to face the Russian muse.

Semenova was fluent in English, having taken acting classes in which she learned to drop her Russian accent when speaking the Americans' language. In this moment, however, that wouldn't serve her purpose. She wanted to be exotic, exciting, and mysterious. She spoke in softer, hushed tones. Her Russian dialect was intended to be enticing, irresistible to the handsome man who lived alone.

Her touch was soft, loving, graceful as she reached out to Gunner's arm in an attempt to make physical contact. She almost succeeded in sucking him into her web of deceit. A black widow with a deadly poison in her pocket.

But Gunner was uninterested. To be sure, this was a challenging moment for the man who'd not shown any interest in another woman since Heather. He was in a foreign world, far away from anyone whom he was close to. It was the night before his mission to save Earth would likely lead to his death.

And it was for that reason that he recoiled from her touch. He would not disrespect his wife by giving in to the sexual advances of a stranger. He didn't need the touch of a woman's body to make it through the night.

Gunner Fox said goodnight, entered his quarters, and brusquely shut the door behind him, locking it as he did.

CHAPTER 37

Monday, April 23
Artemis
Earth's Moon

It was launch day and Chief Rawlings was full of nervous anticipation. He'd tossed and turned all night, thinking of every minute detail of the mission and certain aspects that he'd reinforce with his crew during their prelaunch briefing. The wild card in all of this was Gunner's ability to perform. He'd been tasked with the near impossible—the precision bombing of an asteroid tumbling through space at sixty thousand miles per hour.

Chief Rawlings refreshed himself with a wet washcloth and looked into the mirror. Tired eyes returned his stare. He laughed and said aloud, "And did I mention that we're using the largest nukes ever detonated on Earth, all at once?"

He began to wipe his hands on the towel and gave his uniform one final adjustment when a hard knock on the door startled him. Whoever was outside incessantly pounded on his door, demanding his attention.

"I'm coming!" shouted Chief Rawlings angrily as he stomped out of the bathroom. *What is the hellfire emergency?*

He flung open the door and was greeted by one of the mission control directors. Standing several feet behind him was a doctor from the infirmary dressed in all-white scrubs.

"What's happened?" Chief Rawlings asked.

"Sir, two members of your crew have fallen ill," replied the mission control director. "I'll have the doctor explain." He stepped aside and the female doctor stepped closer. She was holding two aluminum-covered medical charts and opened the first one.

"Sir, during the night, we were called to the quarters of Martin and Andrews. The two men had complained of abdominal cramps, watery diarrhea, and a low-grade fever. We took both men to the infirmary, where their condition has worsened. They are now on intravenous fluids to prevent further dehydration, together with essential salts and minerals to stem further damage to their immune systems."

"What caused this?" asked Chief Rawlings.

"That's still to be determined, sir," the doctor replied. They are symptomatic of many types of gastrointestinal disorders. Pinpointing the exact cause will take some time. Unfortunately, there's no specific medical treatment for their symptoms. Antibiotics aren't effective against viruses. Bacteria can't be identified without further testing. Norovirus is a possibility, as it is the most common cause of foodborne illness worldwide, but we have no other patients exhibiting these symptoms."

Chief Rawlings ran his fingers through his thinning hair and looked at the floor. He didn't want to appear unsympathetic, but he had to consider the big picture. "Doctor, you're aware, of course, that we have a launch this afternoon. Can these two astronauts be available, and if not, when?"

"Sir, without further testing, I can't give a definitive answer. However, I can state that they're not capable of going to the bathroom on their own at this point, much less into space again. It'll likely be days."

"Shit!" exclaimed Chief Rawlings, startling the two Artemis personnel. He leaned back against the doorjamb and closed his eyes. They were down two astronauts. NASA only had the commander of the Starship as backup and nobody within the ranks of Artemis personnel on the Moon. He sighed and turned to the mission control director. "I need a secure line to Washington. Where can I call Acting Administrator Frederick?"

"Come with me, sir."

Chief Rawlings entered the offices and waited for the call to go through. He'd lost track of time on Earth, leaving his watch behind as an unnecessary burden to carry. Now he had a bigger one to overcome.

"Sir, I have Mr. Frederick on the phone for you."

"Thanks," he said, closing the door as the mission director left. He turned his attention to his boss. "Jim, we've got a problem."

"I just heard about it, Chief. It's too late for us to get two alternates up to you. One obvious solution is to plug in the commander of the Starship. He's a seasoned astronaut and more than capable."

"Agreed. That still leaves us an empty seat, and this mission is too important to go into it a man down."

"There's a French backup on Artemis. He could fill—"

"No, thanks, Jim. If a critical decision has to be made that requires a crew consensus, the French will fold and side with the Russians every time."

"Well, I might as well tell you this now so that you're not blindsided with it," began Frederick. "We've already been contacted by Roscosmos. They consider the addition of two new untrained astronauts to the mission to be an unacceptable risk. They're willing to wait for us to ferry replacements up to Artemis, but it will be tomorrow before they can arrive. They want us to scrub or, rather, delay the mission for another day."

Chief Rawlings, who'd been standing during the duration of the phone call, rolled his eyes and flopped into a side chair next to the desk. "Jim, they're stalling. They'd rather try to lay claim to this booger, and if they fail, they don't seem to care if Earth gets hit head-on."

Frederick paused on the end of the line, causing Chief Rawlings to pull the handset away from his ear to determine if it had lost power. "Jim?"

"Yes, Chief, um, well, there's good reason for that. Now that we're a hundred hours away from the impact event, Houston has provided me a more precise window of time for IM86's entry into our atmosphere, and the most likely location for destruction."

"Let me guess. North America."

"That's correct, Chief. We cannot wait for the Russians to land on the asteroid's surface and begin their own diversion tactics. We have to move forward with the nukes."

Chief Rawlings took a deep breath and winced. "Jim, I'm gonna take that last seat. Nobody is better qualified than I am. Heck, I trained them, remember?"

"Chief, I appreciate you for offering, but you know our protocols regarding retired astronauts. I mean, age matters when you're in space."

"That's a bunch of bull, Jim, and you know it. Besides, we're not talking months aboard the ISS. I can make the argument that my presence aboard the Starhopper will increase our chances of success rather than lessen them. I don't like the way it came about, but I almost wish this had been the plan all along."

"Why's that, Chief? Have you lost confidence in Fox?"

"No, not at all. It's just that the two of us have a bond I can't describe. We see eye to eye and understand each other. I also think that I can have a calming effect on him during the mission. Frankly, with due respect to my sick boys in the infirmary, this may have worked out for the best."

Frederick paused, and then he rendered his decision, without enthusiasm. "Okay, Chief. Welcome aboard."

CHAPTER 38

Monday, April 23
Artemis
Earth's Moon

Chief Rawlings gathered the eight astronauts and cosmonauts who'd be manning the Starhopper into the conference room at the lunar mission control center. It didn't take long for the Russians and the lone Frenchman to notice the change in American personnel.

"I'll get right to the point," began the formerly retired astronaut. "Two of our crew have been stricken with some kind of stomach flu and are therefore grounded. Because time is short, we've changed our team. You all know the commander of our Starship. If I recall, he's undertaken missions on the ISS with each of you at some point in time."

Gunner was unaware that two members of the crew were ill. He was as surprised as the others that a personnel change was being made, although it didn't matter for purposes of his role. Then he did a quick head count and noticed that either the Starship would embark on the mission down a man or—

Chief Rawlings continued. "And you know me. I've volunteered to take the last seat on the Starhopper to see this thing through."

—*and then there's that*, Gunner thought to himself.

For the next half minute, the Americans congratulated Chief Rawlings for joining the mission. He was revered by everyone at NASA, and his presence on board the Starhopper would boost the confidence of the astronauts.

The Russians, however, were not as celebratory. Commander Sokolov seemed to be prepared with his rebuttal.

"I, for one, see no reason to celebrate your fallen comrades. By design, the three cosmonauts from the Russian Federation have been excluded from the planning of this spaceflight. We have not been given, nor were we offered, an active role in the operational duties of the mission. You are now asking me to applaud the loss of two trained crew members in exchange for a retiree?"

One of the Americans charged toward Commander Sokolov, and for a moment, Gunner thought the men were going to come to blows. For his part, Gunner admired the restraint he showed. He was close enough to knock the mouthy Russian out himself, but he hid his clenched right fist behind his back.

After cooler heads prevailed, Chief Rawlings addressed Commander Sokolov. During his remarks, Gunner began to admire his mentor even more. He was no-nonsense and didn't mince words.

"Let me explain something to you, Commander. If you don't like the American crew that's been designated for this mission, then you are welcome to ground yourself and your fellow cosmonauts. We can certainly accomplish our mission without you and your interference."

Commander Sokolov grew red in the face. He was used to being the bully, and now someone was pushing back. "The agreement between our two countries was to include—"

Chief Rawlings cut him off and walked forward so that he was standing in front of the much taller, muscular Russian. "That part of the arrangement was a handshake deal, *comrade*," he began sarcastically. "The United Nations agreement was for an international contingent made up of four Americans and four from other nations. If you don't want to fly, I'm sure there are French, Japanese, Canadian, or Indian alternatives to choose from around here."

"They don't have the experience—"

Again, Chief Rawlings interrupted. "All they have to do is sit there and stay out of our way, Commander. Just like you three."

Chief Rawlings walked away from his Russian counterpart and led the Starship commander by the arm toward the door.

"Where are you going?" Commander Sokolov demanded. "This isn't over."

"Yes, it is. The decision is made and the two of us have to get outfitted in our space suits. When I get back, we will review the mission one last time and then board the Starhopper for a newly scheduled liftoff in eight hours."

Commander Sokolov. "A delay of only two hours? I insist that you and this new crew member take more time to prepare yourself for this critical mission!"

Chief Rawlings laughed. "We were born ready, right, Commander?" He slapped the second senior-most member of the American crew and walked out the door without looking back.

Gunner had thoroughly enjoyed the exchange. Chief Rawlings was not only coming on the mission, a comforting thought for Gunner, who had to remind himself of the difficult nature of their task, but he'd backed down the commander of the ISS during Heather's first flight into space.

A man he considered partly to blame for losing his wife.

*****

It had been fifteen minutes since Chief Rawlings had left, and the tension in the room was unbearable. The other American astronaut and Favier huddled in one corner while the trio of Russians talked among themselves in the other.

From time to time, Gunner, who mainly wandered the room looking at printed materials related to the operation of the Starhopper, glanced in the direction of Semenova. Unlike last night when she was in her sex-kitten mode, today she appeared to be all business, not even giving him a second look. Gunner found it odd that she could turn off her desires like a light switch, but eventually shrugged it off as he got bored and wandered out of the room.

Gunner decided to explore the mission control complex of Artemis. Other than the fact his surroundings resembled a large igloo, the activity was no different from what he'd observed on television at Houston's mission control during a manned spaceflight.

Occasionally, one of the Artemis staff would smile and say hello to him as he casually walked around the building. He entered the long hallway where he and the other Americans had exited the Starship the day they arrived. A group of uniformed personnel were assisting some new arrivals. A decidedly unexpected group, in Gunner's mind.

Men, women, and children were being hastily escorted out of the spaceport and away from him toward the lunar transports. They were dressed in civilian clothes and came from all nationalities and races.

"Children?" Gunner mumbled to himself as kids ranging from six to sixteen were instructed to stay close to their parents. Curious, he approached the group, and one of the Artemis personnel halted his progress.

"I'm sorry, sir, this area is off-limits for now," he began, taking a moment to study Gunner's attire. "Say, are you one of the astronauts for the asteroid mission?"

He'd asked the question loud enough for some of the new arrivals to hear him. A couple snapped their heads toward Gunner as they continued to be hustled away from the spaceport.

Gunner made up the best lie he could. "Yeah, sure. Listen, I was told a new spacecraft had arrived, and I just wanted to take a look."

"Oh, you haven't seen the Spacebus yet?" asked the young man. "It's quite spectacular. Basically, it's a larger version of Spacecab. Designed by Bristol Spaceplanes, it's become the world's most used general-purpose passenger launch vehicle."

"Is this something new? I haven't heard about it before."

"Well, sir, everything is experimental until it's not. In a way, that's why you're here, right?"

"I suppose that's true," replied Gunner.

"Let me clear this group of new arrivals, and then you can enter the spaceport to see it. Be sure to check out the four turbojet engines that power that sucker. It can accelerate to Mach 4 in a blink of an eye, and then, after separation of the rocket boosters, hit Mach 6. It's a real head-snapper, if you know what I mean."

Gunner chuckled. Indeed, I do. A *real head-snapper*. As the civilians cleared the hallway, Gunner stuck his head around the corner toward the spaceport. He turned to ask the young man why these people were being brought to Artemis, when he heard his name called out.

"Major Fox! Chief Rawlings is looking for you back in the conference room."

CHAPTER 39

Monday, April 23
Artemis
Earth's Moon

It was two hours before launch time, and all members of the Starhopper crew were on board. The mission would take them two days from liftoff, to intercept the asteroid, and then return back to Earth, where they would land in California.

The design of the Starhopper was not quite as spacious as its larger cousin, the Starship. There was seating for eight crewmembers, and accompanying sleeping quarters. A combined bathroom and shower was designed very similar to those found on midsized motorboats in which the entire encapsulated area included a fiberglass molded toilet, sink, and shower with a centrally located drain.

There was ample storage for the crew's gear and personal belongings. Food and supply storage was abundant, as Starhopper was designed for trips to Mars and back to the Moon.

With the three powerful Raptor engines pushing the Starhopper through space at a comfortable speed of seventy-two thousand miles per hour, the traveling time from the Moon to Mars when they were at their closest approach was twenty-two days. The benefit of using the Moon as a starting off point for Mars missions was the fact that far less fuel was burned to break free of the lunar gravitational pull compared to Earth.

Finally, on board the Starhopper was a recreation area for the crew to relax, prepare meals, and access computers. Throughout the spacecraft were workstations for the astronauts to access. All in all, the Starhopper was a faster, more space efficient version of the space shuttle, and was capable of interplanetary travel. Its use for Project Jackhammer not only provided Earth the opportunity to survive the threat posed by IM86, but it was also a test run for the next great mission—a trip to Mars.

"Chief, we're on a hold at T minus two hours," announced Mark Foster, Mission Control director in Houston. Ordinarily, for shuttle flights between Earth and the lunar surface, the mission control team at Artemis handled the liftoffs. Not to diminish their capabilities in any way, NASA elected to take control of Project Jackhammer from start to finish, especially in light of the fact that there would be a period of time in which the Starhopper would lose contact with Artemis as the Moon's orbit around Earth took it in a different direction.

"Do we have a problem, Houston?" asked Chief Rawlings, who'd assumed command of the mission although the commander of the much larger Starship would be handling the navigation of the spacecraft from the pilot's seat. He'd been instrumental in providing SpaceX feedback on the navigational controls and overall design of the spacecraft's flight deck, and therefore was the most experienced of the entire crew in the Starhopper's handling.

The entire crew waited in nervous anticipation as Director Foster paused for a considerable amount of time in his response. Finally, he provided his reasoning for the launch delay.

"Chief, the Sun has decided to complicate matters. A strong solar flare was emitted late yesterday evening. At this point, the SWPC is issuing a G3 warning, although their unofficial comments indicate this storm could increase to a G4."

The SWPC, an acronym for the Space Weather Prediction Center, was a division of NOAA, the National Oceanic and Atmospheric Administration. They provided meteorologists around the world with up-to-the-second information on weather on Earth. In addition, they provided NASA and world governments with details on space weather conditions resulting from solar activity.

Space weather impacted numerous facets of everyday life, from air travel to land-based communications. Geomagnetic storms resulted from solar wind shock waves following a coronal mass ejection, a large release of plasma from the Sun that is carried through space with the solar wind.

Solar storms and associated corona mass ejections have been known to alter the dynamic of celestial bodies, including asteroids, comets, and the Moon. Solar storms have sandblasted the lunar surface, removing a surprisingly large amount of dirt and debris as the CMEs pass over the Moon.

The SWPC had just issued a warning that a strong G3 or severe G4 storm was headed toward the Moon. During a G3 geomagnetic storm, surface charging occurred on satellite components, causing increased drag. A G4 storm was more likely to damage a spacecraft as highly charged, hot electrons associated with the storm pelted the outer shell, causing a negative charge to build on its surface.

Like walking on a carpet and then touching a doorknob, an electrostatic discharge could occur, knocking out the spacecraft's communications systems and its ability to map the surface of the asteroid. Without an accurate identification of the weakest geologic points on IM86, Gunner would be firing nuclear missiles on a wish and a prayer.

"What's our time frame on this, Houston?" asked Chief Rawlings.

Gunner could hear the frustration in his mentor's voice. He also caught a glimpse of something that Chief Rawlings was too preoccupied to see. When the hold was announced by Mission Control, Chernevsky provided a noticeable thumbs-up to Commander Sokolov, who immediately raised his hand as if to block the gesture from view. Gunner, however, saw it and began to process why the Russians would be interested in delaying the launch.

"Stand by, Chief," came the response.

Several minutes passed and then the dreaded words came through the comms. "I'm sorry, ladies and gentlemen. We're gonna call it a day, holding at T minus two hours. We will modify our launch window as soon as possible, but most likely will try again in the morning."

Frustrated, the astronauts shuffled in their seats. They slammed their heads against the seatbacks or pounded their fists on the arms holding them snugly in place.

The cosmonauts' reaction was quite different. They looked toward one another, and Gunner detected a barely discernible nod of approval from Commander Sokolov.

Within ten minutes, the entire crew had disembarked and headed toward the housing unit in separate vehicles. Gunner held Chief Rawlings back, as well as the other two American astronauts.

"Chief, may I make a suggestion?" asked Gunner, who motioned for the group of four to stand in the far corner of the staging area, where they were out of sight of the French astronaut.

"Sure, Gunner, what is it?"

"Chief, guys," he began his reply, looking each one of them in the eyes, "I have a hunch. It may sound conspiratorial, but it may be spot on."

"What is it?" Chief Rawlings asked.

Gunner paused, gathered his thoughts and glanced around one more time before he spoke. "I want the four of us to be careful until we're in the air. I watched the body language of the Russians when the delay was announced. Instead of being irritated with the delay, they seemed almost, um, pleased."

"What are you thinking?" asked Chief Rawlings.

"While we were waiting on Houston to make a decision, I got to thinking about the timing of the mission and especially our planned missile strikes of the asteroid. The earlier we hit it, the more likely it is that the meteorite debris will hit Asia in the Northern Hemisphere, right?"

"That's correct," responded Chief Rawlings. "That would certainly explain their reaction."

"There's the other issue," continued Gunner. "They're hell-bent on planting their flag on the surface of IM86 first. I can't imagine why they haven't so far, but we've presumed the Russians were arguing for a delay after our guys fell sick to give their mission time to succeed."

"So another delay would be to their advantage," surmised one of the astronauts.

"Exactly," said Gunner.

Chief Rawlings was puzzled. "Gunner, you're not suggesting that they conjured up the solar storm, are you?"

"No, Chief, of course not. I am saying that the delay forces us to spend another night here at Artemis. One more night like the last one, and we could easily be down two more astronauts, if not more."

"Come on, Major," began the Starship commander. "Are you implying that Sokolov or someone under his control poisoned our boys?"

"Commander, Russians love to use chemicals and poisons. They're experts at it. If they wanted a delay, or even a cancellation, then what better way is there than to take out the only people capable of implementing Project Jackhammer?"

The two astronauts started peppering Gunner with questions and counterarguments, and Chief Rawlings held up his hands to calm everyone down.

"Gunner has a point, one that we should at least consider. Until the mission prelaunch briefing early in the morning, let's stay confined to quarters. I will speak with the Artemis security team and the outpost's administrator. I want our meals prepared by Americans and under the supervision of security."

Gunner set his jaw. He had a number of options swirling around in his head. "Or let me deal with them. We don't need them on board anyway, right?"

Chief Rawlings smiled and patted Gunner on the shoulder. He'd read every aspect of Gunner's dossier and knew exactly what this young Air Force Major was capable of. He fully understood why Ghost considered him to be one of the most valuable assets in the American military.

"Gunner, without proof, let's not create a diplomatic incident that will bring the heat down on Artemis. Watch each other's backs, and tomorrow, we'll go after the real enemy."

CHAPTER 40

Monday, April 23
Gunner's Residence
Dog Island
Florida Panhandle

"I can't believe this has happened again." Pop lamented the postponing of the Starhopper's liftoff. "First, a weather delay for strong winds kept them in Texas an extra day. Now a weather delay for solar winds? This is ridiculous."

Pop had a tendency to get excited about important events, and when they were delayed, it threw him off-kilter, putting him in an ornery mood.

"This really adds a lot of pressure on Gunner," said Cam. "Based upon what we've seen on the news over the weekend, it's gonna be difficult to hit his targets with a whole day to map the surface and establish a game plan. Now he has to attack IM86 with no practice runs and limited analysis."

Bear tried to reassure his partner. "Get in, get out, Cam. We've done it before."

"I understand that. I don't doubt Gunner's ability to get the job done. It's just that there are so many variables and unknowns here. Seriously, the so-called experts aren't one hundred percent certain how the first nuke will alter the asteroid. Gunner may not get another shot. Or worse, the debris from the nuclear detonation may throw up all over the place, damaging the spacecraft."

"What? What do you mean by that?" Pop was unaware of this risk and began peppering Cam with questions.

Bear shot Cam a disapproving glance and then responded,

"Nothing, Pop. It's not gonna happen that way. Let's sit down for a moment because we have something to talk with you about."

"Okay. What's on your minds?"

Cam, who inwardly chastised herself for allowing her emotions and concern to show, helped Bear change the subject. "Here's the thing, Pop. Even if Gunner is successful—"

Pop interrupted her. "When my son is successful."

"Yes, of course. When Gunner is successful in breaking up this thing, all the analysts say that we'll be in the line of fire of the remains of IM86. As we've seen discussed this weekend, the timing of the destruction is important, especially as it relates to what part of the Northern Hemisphere takes the brunt of the asteroid residue. This delay makes it more likely that the debris field could hit our neck of the woods."

Pop shrugged. "It is what it is. We can't exactly hide under the bed, right?"

"True," began Bear in response. "But we can minimize the threat. The Gulf of Mexico is a great big target for the remains of IM86. A tsunami is a very real possibility. We have an idea for moving to higher ground, you know, until it's over."

Pop wasn't so sure. "Gunner built this house on steel-reinforced concrete pilings that are sixteen feet above sea level. It's withstood two major hurricanes. I think we'll be fine."

Cam scooted up on the sofa and looked Pop in the eye. "If a large chunk hits the Gulf, sixteen feet won't be high enough. Dog Island will be underwater, and the surge will likely knock all of these houses down."

"But where will we go?" he asked.

"Do you remember my folks' place in Alabama? We called it Fort Mills. Gunner came and stayed with us that one summer when you and Mom went to Europe."

"Sure, I remember. I thought, um, sorry, after both of your folks passed that it was sold or something."

"After my dad died in the helicopter crash in Afghanistan, my mother, you know, well, she didn't deal with it very well." Cam began to well up in tears, causing Pop to reach out and squeeze her hand. "Anyway, as you know, my mom couldn't deal with the grief, and then there was the car wreck and she ended it."

"We don't know that for sure, dear." Pop knew her parents, and Cam had always been a member of the Fox family, just as Gunner had been close to her parents growing up.

"Anyway, my sister and I inherited it, but I only go up there once in a while. She moved out to Colorado, so it stays vacant most of the time."

Pop leaned back on the sofa. "You two think we should go there?"

"We do, Pop," replied Bear. "It's only three hundred miles from here straight up past Tallahassee. The elevation is around two thousand feet, so tsunamis won't be an issue, and it's sparsely populated."

"There are a lot of pluses," said Cam. "It's on the lake created by damming up the Ketchepedrakee Creek. Our property fronts the creek and the lake. It's perfect for hunting and fishing. It's remote and completely off the grid. We've got solar power, a well, and a root cellar to store food."

Pop thought for a moment. "We could come back when the coast is clear, right?"

Bear reassured him. "We sure can, Pop. I'll drive down and make sure everything is cool; then we'll come back."

Pop was warming up to the idea. "How big is the lake? Maybe I can bring my plane?"

Cam shrugged and looked to Bear before responding, "You know, that might be a pretty good idea. We've got a boat dock and fuel stored underground. I'm sure we could tie off the seaplane as well."

"I say yes," added Bear. "We can cram the H1 and one of our cars with supplies. Pop can also bring some things. It's a win-win."

Pop stood and walked toward the open doors overlooking the beach. It was deserted. He turned around and addressed the power issue. "I like the fact that it has solar power. The news people seem to think that the electricity transformers will be damaged, meaning it could take weeks to fix."

Pop had barely finished his sentence when the skies became eerily dark despite the fact it was a cloudless day.

"What the hell?" bellowed Bear as he shot off the couch and ran onto the deck.

"Don't look up!" warned Cam. "If it's a solar eclipse, you could damage your eyes."

"I can't believe we haven't heard about this coming today," said Pop. "I mean, we've been watching the news nonstop for days."

Cam was recording the shadow with her iPhone as it passed over the sun and then darkened parts of the Gulf of Mexico. As the sunshine returned, she slowly walked toward the deck railing.

"Guys, that wasn't an eclipse. Something blacked out the sun. Something really big."

Pop had retreated to the living room and turned up the volume on the television. He shouted for them. "Cam! Bear! Quick!"

Howard responded with a bark-howl and excitedly ran into the room. Cam was the first to arrive and read the chyron aloud. "Shadow of occultation blots out Sun."

"What does that mean?" asked Bear.

Pop turned up the volume again as a scientist on the panel of CNN explained.

"To our viewers, what we've just experienced across the eastern half of the United States is known as asteroid occultation. Basically, when an asteroid occults a star, cuts it off from view, it has the same effect as an eclipse. Many of you may have witnessed a shadow that passed nearby, even after the Sun reappeared. That is known as a shadow path."

The CNN host frantically fired off several panic-stricken questions. "What does that mean? Was this IM86 passing us by? Were the calculations incorrect, which means we're in the clear?"

The expert responded, "No, Alisyn, none of the above. Certainly, the length of time that the Sun was obscured combined with the size of the shadow we just viewed through the windows here in the studio is indicative of the close proximity of the asteroid. Our viewers have to remember, IM86, a very large asteroid, is on a pace and trajectory to hit Earth on Friday. The shadow of occultation we just experienced is a grim reminder of that."

"Well, that's gonna send the crazies to the top of the mountain and off the edge of the cliff," said Bear with a chuckle. He turned toward Cam and noticed Pop was hustling toward the elevator.

"Hey, Pop, where are you going?"

"Home, to pack. We need to get to Fort Mills."

PART FOUR

ASTROMETRY

Identification Number: 2029 IM86

Right Ascension: 14 hours 29 minutes 52 seconds

Declination: -15 degrees 24 minutes 58 seconds

Greatest Elongation: 58.02 degrees

Nominal Distance from Earth: 0.11 astronomical units

Relative Velocity: 33,338 meters per second

CHAPTER 41

Tuesday, April 24
Gunner's Residence
Dog Island
Florida Panhandle

Bear was out of breath as he reached the top of the stairs. He'd been tasked with loading the final boxes of provisions into Pop's seaplane. After the seventh trip on the unusually warm spring day, he was beginning to complain. "I don't know why we couldn't have locked off the elevator after I was finished loading the plane."

"I'm sorry, Bear," replied Pop. "I have this checklist, you know, for when hurricanes are due to hit. We always have to park the elevator cab on the highest possible floor so that the walls can break away during a storm surge."

One of the requirements of coastal construction was to avoid building solid wall construction at sea level. When a major storm came onshore, it often brought high waves crashing over the protective dunes that lined the beach. This storm surge could easily knock over a house that was built at sea level, or even one on pilings if the ground-level walls were solid and attached permanently.

Breakaway construction allowed the surge to tear through the lower structure without knocking out the support pilings. An elevator cab would be bashed against the pilings, causing the supports to lose their structural integrity.

"What about the hurricane shutters, Pop?" asked Cam.

"We don't usually bother with those, dear. The windows and doors are impact-resistant to meet a sustained wind with debris of one hundred seventy miles per hour."

Cam thought for a moment and then said, "Let's lower them all anyway. It's not the water that concerns me. It's looters. I know Dog Island is not accessible by car, but that won't stop people coming onto the island by boat and breaking into homes. The steel roll-down windows will at least act as a deterrent."

"Not a problem," said Pop. "They operate at the push of a button, or a hand crank when the power goes out."

Bear guzzled down a Red Bull and crushed the can. He'd recovered from his frequent loading trips and was now ready to relax before the newly scheduled launch of the Starhopper.

"Let me tell you," he began. "Gunner's Hummer is loaded down, as is the U-Haul trailer I rented yesterday. My SUV is stacked so full of canned goods that I can't see out the windows."

"Oh, that reminds me," said Pop. He hustled into the kitchen and grabbed two portable, handheld can openers. He tossed them into a beach tote full of kitchen utensils. "You know, just in case the power goes out. They're old school, but we'll be glad we've got 'em."

Pop had warmed up to the idea of bugging out to Fort Mills. Gunner had raved about Cam's family vacation spot, and the thought of riding out the aftermath of the asteroid threat there was comforting.

"I don't believe that we've forgotten anything," said Bear. "I packed every tool I could find and all of Howard's stuff."

"Wait! I almost forgot something." Pop rushed into the kitchen and ducked into the pantry. He emerged with a yellow metal box that looked like it had been dropped off the back of a semi and kicked down the interstate during rush hour.

Bear laughed. "What the hell is that?"

"This is my baking toolbox," Pop replied. "It's got all the essentials for cooking and baking. I put this together for when I went into Apalach for bake-offs."

Bear took the handle to the metal case and muttered, "It's heavy." He lifted up the battered case to study it and paused to read the inscription marked on the top. "Wait, are you kidding me?"

Pop laughed and shoved his hands in his pockets. "You read

correctly, Sergeant. This once held a guided missile launcher test set. It was used to check the firing sequence of the LAU-7 guided missile launcher. They're used for the Sidewinder and Sidearm missiles."

"Where did you get this?" asked Bear, setting the heavy box containing kitchen utensils on the wood floor.

"I found it at a yard sale in Fort Walton Beach. Crazy, right?"

Cam flopped on the sofa next to the snoring basset hound. "What about Howard? Who's he riding with?"

"He hates to fly," Pop quickly replied.

"I'll take him in the Hummer," answered Bear. "He's familiar with it, so I made him a cubbyhole in the middle of the back seat to curl up in."

"He misses Gunner," observed Pop. "He seems to sense that his best pal is off doing something more dangerous than the usual missions. Dogs have a sixth sense about people, you know. Howard isn't around other people much, so he doesn't necessarily identify someone as having negative energy. He can sense a negative vibe, however. In this case, a situation that is making us all uncomfortable."

"Does he act nervous?" asked Bear.

"No, he just sleeps."

"Pop, he's always sleeping," said Cam with a chuckle.

"I know, but this is different. He becomes totally uninvolved in his surroundings. It's as if he wants to tune out the world until Gunner returns."

Cam increased the volume on the television, and everyone turned their attention to the screen.

The reporter described the scene. "We are in the final countdown of the delayed launch of the Starhopper. There are launch parties around the world, waiting in great anticipation of this moment when the international crew from the United States, Russia, and France begin their twenty-five-hour journey to intercept asteroid 2029 IM86 as it speeds toward Earth."

T minus thirty seconds.

"The countdown has been somewhat different from the rocket

launches we've all been used to seeing for decades. The Starhopper is designed very much like the space shuttle, except with its own Raptor rocket engines capable of taking it to Mars and back some day. For now, it will embark on a mission that will likely determine the fate of our planet."

T minus ten seconds. Nine. Eight. Seven. Six. Five. Four. Three. Two. One. Zero.

Raptor engines have ignited and we have liftoff of the Starhopper!

"There he goes!" Pop said excitedly with tears in his eyes. "My son can do this, guys. I know him. He can do it."

Cam and Bear moved in to hug the man who'd been a father to them both over the years. They watched as the Starhopper lifted off from the Moon, the orange glow of the Raptor engines powering the spacecraft toward the stars and a rendezvous with the planet killer.

Chapter 42

Tuesday, April 24
On Board the Starhopper

Unlike the space shuttles that had been retired, the Starhopper was designed for carrying passengers for extended lengths of time. The space shuttle was a workhorse, operating under a crew of seven astronauts and capable of hauling lots of cargo. The sixty-foot-long cargo bay, the rocket engines, and the fuel tanks made up eighty percent of the space shuttle's length. The one-hundred-twenty-foot-long Starhopper was laid out more efficiently, befitting its design for deep-space exploration. It was considered more luxury motor coach and less eighteen-wheeler.

It was also designed with advanced technology to partially eliminate the challenges of living in a completely weightless environment. In television programs, and on the big screen, viewers always saw the ship's crewmembers stably on the floor of the spacecraft, seemingly denying the lack of gravity in space.

In space, unless you were orbiting the Earth to use as a point of reference, you had no way of knowing which way was *up* as there was no gravitational force pulling you *down*. With the Starhopper, SpaceX pioneered the technology known as intra-vehicular artificial gravity.

It was built with an inner shell, part of its overall composition, that constantly rotated. This continuous rotation created centrifugal force that generated artificial gravity. Centripetal acceleration created by the constantly rotating inner shell gave its human occupants the feeling that the outer hull of the Starhopper was pushing them towards the center.

The technological breakthrough also paved the way for travel to distant planets in the near future. Remaining weightless took an incredible toll on the human body, subjecting it to a horrific biological wear-and-tear process like bone loss and space blindness.

By building a gravity-producing shell, the astronauts were protected from the forces of ultra-rapid acceleration necessary for lengthy space travel, and the attack upon IM86.

The interior of the Starhopper was also unparalleled. The flight deck contained four seats, with a front row occupied by the commander and his pilot. Both of these astronauts had access to the same control panel, a mirror image for both left seat and right seat. In an emergency, the controls could be manually piloted from either astronaut's position.

Immediately below them at mid-deck was a lounge area and kitchen galley. Toward the rear of both levels were the crew sleeping modules, storage, and the bathroom. Moving about the spacious Starhopper was easy once liftoff occurred and it had escaped the gravitational pull of the Moon.

Initially, the four seats on the flight deck were occupied by the Americans. Chief Rawlings occupied the commander's seat, with Gunner sitting directly behind him, while the commander of the Starship, who'd been enlisted onto this flight at the last minute, piloted the Starhopper with the female American astronaut sitting behind him.

Mid-deck, the Russians and the French astronaut were able to monitor the progress of the launch on eight monitors that provided them simultaneous data and telemetry feeds.

"We have separation, Chief," said the commander, a highly respected family man who'd flown dozens of space shuttle missions and was well versed in the operations of the Starhopper. "I've got us locked in on IM86, and now we are weightless."

"Thank you, Commander." Chief Rawlings gave him a thumbs-up and then turned to address the second group. "Listen up, folks, before we get settled in for this long flight. I want two of us at the helm at all times. I can't keep our guests out of these two rear seats, but I can insist they stay away from the controls. If a seat is empty, the temptation to occupy it will be too great to resist."

"Roger that, Chief," said Gunner. "They'd freak out if we restricted them to mid-deck, wouldn't they?"

"Without a doubt. Keep in mind, this mission is our baby, and we're not turning back now. But, out of respect for the president, who pulled this all together, we don't need to leave him a diplomatic mess to deal with that could be just as devastating as IM86. This second cold war ain't no joke. We have more powerful enemies than we did in the sixties and seventies."

"Got it," said Gunner.

The commander added a comment. "Our passengers aside, I think we need to provide Major Fox as much time in the right seat as possible. Granted, the Starhopper flies itself most of the way, kinda like the old space shuttles. We didn't have to do any work until the last four or five minutes. But sitting here, as opposed to the simulator, will give him the opportunity to get comfortable with the flight controls. Not to mention this panel that was added in the center console."

He tapped a display that was combined with a series of buttons and a small keyboard. This was the launch control panel for the nuclear missiles. It was almost identical to the controls contained in the military's modern combat jets for air-to-surface missiles, except the ordnance was far more powerful.

"I agree, Commander," said Chief Rawlings. "Gunner, eat and get some rest. As we get closer, you're gonna want to stay up here the whole time. One of us will come get you when it's time for a switch in personnel."

"Chief, shouldn't somebody hang out with the Russians to see what they're up to? I don't like them roaming around without some sort of supervision."

"The three of us will keep an eye on our guests. You rest and get your mind ready."

CHAPTER 43

Tuesday, April 24
On Board the Starhopper

Gunner slept well. The night before their second launch attempt, he'd racked his brain considering all of the possibilities associated with the sudden gastrointestinal illness suffered by the other two astronauts. He considered getting Ghost and the Jackal involved to conduct research on the various poisons, but there was little time before he was required to board the Starhopper again.

Chief Rawlings woke Gunner up by gently tapping on his sleeping module door. He had taken some time to rest as well so that the two of them could command the Starhopper for the final stretch to the asteroid.

After a stop by the galley and an abrupt conversation with Commander Sokolov, Gunner and Chief Rawlings relieved the other two American astronauts and settled into the flight deck.

"Okay, Gunner, we're gonna guide this thing to our point of intercept using a combination of manual controls and the onboard computer system. But before we do, I think it's time for you to spend some time with Artie."

"A stowaway?" said Gunner with a chuckle.

Chief Rawlings smiled and then changed his tone. "Engage artificial intelligence support."

A second later, a computer-generated voice with a Scottish accent replied, "At yer service, Commander."

"Hello, Artie," said Chief Rawlings.

"Hullo."

"Artie, please welcome Major Fox."

"Wylcome, Major Fox. Hoo's it gaun?"

Gunner busted out laughing and then played along. He tried to imitate a Scotsman's dialect, using a poor imitation of Scottie from the old *Star Trek* shows. "A'm daein fine, whit abooty yersel?"

Artie replied, "No' bad, Major Fox. Do I detect a wee bit of a Scotsman in ye?"

Gunner laughed uproariously, perhaps the most genuine belly laugh he'd had in years. "Chief, I like this guy. Did you pick the Scottish accent?"

"Yessir. I've always been a Trekkie. Who didn't love Scotty?"

Gunner nodded and looked around the upper control panels as if expecting to see Scotty, or Artie, looking down upon him. "Where are his controls? I mean, how do I turn him off?"

Chief Rawlings furrowed his brow and turned his seat to face Gunner. "Off? Um, why would you want, um, well, you can't."

"All right, let me ask this a different way," began Gunner. "Does this thing, Artie, have the ability to override my control of the spacecraft?"

Chief Rawlings shrugged. "Well, of course there are certain safeguards built into the system to prevent a catastrophe."

"Such as?" asked Gunner.

"Well, erratic navigation, for one. If AI senses that you have become incapacitated or unable to perform, in a way that poses a risk to the spacecraft and crew, Artie can assume command of the Starhopper to avoid danger."

Gunner sighed. He didn't want to pick a fight with Chief Rawlings. The two had established a close-knit relationship. It was just that Gunner had a certain way of doing things, and he didn't completely trust computers to make decisions that only a human's individual experience could make.

"Chief, we created artificial intelligence to help us, not lead or control us. No machine can replace what's in my head."

"I understand, Gunner. You have to understand. We can't turn Artie off."

"Major Fox, dar ye want ony lei dither than Scots? American English?"

"You've been eavesdropping on our conversation?"

"Ay, a wee bit, while on the flight deck only."

Gunner shook his head and shot an *I-told-you-so* glance at Chief Rawlings. "Yes, Artie. I like speaking to a Scotsman when we're playing, but I prefer American English when we are working."

"As you wish, Major Fox," Artie responded with his perfect narrator's Midwestern *no-accent* voice inflection.

"Artie, is there a command I can give you that means no?"

"No means no, Major. If I ask you a question, and you say no. It means no."

"Artie, can I tell you not to do something? A command to stand down."

"Stand down in military parlance means go off duty in some cases. I cannot go off duty."

"Artie, can you do nothing if I command you?"

Artie paused. Gunner could feel the machine thinking, processing the question, its intended meaning, and the myriad number of potential answers. Finally, Artie responded, "Major Fox, with the permission of the commander of the Starhopper, I can create a command that will only be recognized if it comes from your voice."

Chief Rawlings looked to Gunner and whispered, "What do you want me to say?"

"Chief Rawlings, my sensors can discern a whisper at the same auditory levels as a scream," interrupted Artie. "May I make a suggestion?"

"Yes, Artie, go ahead."

"If Chief Rawlings approves, I can create a command based upon Major Fox's voice for the words *Artie, stand down*. If I hear such a command from Major Fox, I will not perform the function that I'm programmed to do."

Chief Rawlings shrugged and looked at Gunner.

"Works for me," said Gunner.

Chief Rawlings gave the order. "Artie, create a command for Major Fox to override your functions by using the words *Artie, stand down.*"

"Yes, Commander. Major Fox, please say the words slowly and distinctly."

"Artie, stand down."

Artie paused for a moment and then spoke. "Your words have been recorded, and your voice can change its tone, inflections, and level of emotion without altering my ability to recognize it."

"Thank you, Artie," said Gunner. He was beginning to warm up to his new friend.

Suddenly, Commander Sokolov appeared at the rear of the flight deck. "Chief Rawlings, another member of your crew has fallen ill. It is Favier. He is complaining of stomach cramps and pain."

Chief Rawlings stood and walked toward Sokolov. "Where is he?"

"In his sleeping module. He has spent the last thirty minutes in the toilet."

Chief Rawlings turned to glance at Gunner and then pointed toward the rear of the spacecraft. "Take me to him."

"Someone must remain with the major. He is not an astronaut. He cannot be trusted to command the ship in your absence. I will stay with him."

"That won't be necessary, Commander Sokolov." A voice came from behind him toward the cargo hold. It was the American Starship pilot who'd been resting. "I will occupy the flight deck with the major while you gentlemen attend to our friend from Paris."

Commander Sokolov appeared frustrated. He began to badger Chief Rawlings. "This is not acceptable to Russia. We are at risk on this spacecraft because you and your crew have brought an infectious disease on board. It was during your command of the International Space Station in 2019 that many astronauts fell ill due to bacterial infections. I will not risk my crew suffering the same fate as your astronauts!"

Gunner had had enough of the mouthy Russian and was ready to do something about it. Chief Rawlings sensed that and quickly raised his hand to stop Gunner from continuing to rise out of the pilot's seat.

"Let me assess the situation, and we'll follow proper medical procedures to help him."

Sokolov didn't back down. "You and your crew should be quarantined before the mission is compromised. I am capable of piloting this craft and, with the help of onboard intelligence, completing the mission."

Chief Rawlings sighed, but was firm with Commander Sokolov. "I am in command of the Starhopper on a United States-sanctioned mission. I will make these decisions, and for now, I am instructing you to clear the flight deck area."

The chief pushed his way past the much larger man, and the void he left was quickly occupied by the other American commander on board, who immediately crossed his arms in front of his chest.

"You heard our chief. Clear the flight deck."

Commander Sokolov glared at Gunner, grunted, and stormed out.

CHAPTER 44

Tuesday, April 24
Fort Mills
Near Delta, Alabama

Delta, Alabama, population two hundred, was a small unincorporated community in Central Alabama in Clay County. Nestled on the edge of the Talladega National Forest on the southern edge of the Appalachian Mountains, Delta was known as a gateway to Alabama's highest natural point, Cheaha Mountain in the Cheaha State Park.

The area was beloved for its scenic vistas and beautiful waterfalls. Nature trails were abundant, and in the areas bordering the state parks, bowhunters were granted limited access to hunt deer and wild turkeys.

Pop was given the coordinates to the lake at Ketchepedrakee Creek that ran across the western border of Cam's family cabin. Bear and Cam drove the vehicles along the back roads, avoiding large towns and certainly steering clear of Tallahassee, where unrest had been reported at banks and retail stores.

He took his time preparing his Cessna for flight. Dog Island was practically deserted, as most of the full-time residents had headed inland in search of food and supplies. The story was the same around the county. Americans hoped for the best. They wanted to believe that Project Jackhammer would succeed. Most were prepared to take their chances that the resulting meteor storm would either burn up in the Earth's protective atmosphere, or any meteorites that found their way through would impact the planet elsewhere.

Nonetheless, as reports of looting, food shortages, and gas stations running empty hit the news, it became every man for himself. Pop watched with disbelief as people fought over shopping carts full of bottled water in grocery store parking lots. A woman had her baby knocked out of her hands as she attempted to buy formula at a Walmart. Looting was rampant, with everything from televisions to tennis shoes being stolen in preparation for IM86's arrival.

Pop was confident in the plan laid out with Cam and Bear. His focus of concern was for his son. He prayed relentlessly for God to keep Gunner safe. To be sure, Gunner was receiving heartfelt prayers to succeed in his mission, but nobody wanted him home safely more than Pop. It was a topic that the father and son had discussed many times throughout their lives together.

He'd said to Gunner, "You can risk your life for your country, but oftentimes, they'll judge you by your successes, not by the level of risk you place yourself in."

As a result, Gunner began to realize that upon his return from flying experimental aircraft, the questions always surrounded the plane itself and not Gunner's surviving the test. Heather's career was similar. Certainly, when NASA suffered tragedy, they came together as a family to offer solace. But when a mission was completed and the crew arrived safely, only family said, "I'm glad you're home alive."

It saddened Pop to see how Gunner had changed in the last three years without Heather. A large piece of his soul had been lost that fateful day, and he wondered if his son would ever recover. But, for now, he wanted to make sure Gunner came home, to Earth, alive. And when he did, Pop would hug him like he'd never hugged him before.

After one final look around Dog Island, wondering what it would look like when he returned, he made the lonely walk down the dock to the Cessna and climbed into his seat. As was his custom, he prayed for a safe flight and added a few words for their home. Then he took off into the sky, focusing his eyes on the heavens and wondering if his son was holding up okay.

*****

"I hear the plane!" shouted Cam as Bear emerged from the cabin. He'd volunteered to carry in all of the supplies if Cam promised to find a place to store everything. The smallish, twelve-hundred-square-foot log cabin home contained three bedrooms, two bathrooms, and a large open living area that included the kitchen, a stone fireplace, and a cast-iron wood-burning stove with a cooktop.

Cam's father had been in the military and over time became somewhat of a conspiracy theorist. He frequented websites like Infowars and Zero Hedge, soaking in all of the latest theories concerning activities in Washington and relating to the threats America faced.

Stationed in the Middle East until his unfortunate accident resulting in his death, he learned from several members in his unit about the concept of preparedness and the likelihood of societal collapse in the event of a catastrophic event.

Their cabin in the woods soon took on a different look from when Cam was a young girl. In between deployments, Cam's father had modified the cabin so that it was completely off the grid. A solar array was installed first, followed by alternative heating and cooking methods. He had a well dug and installed a pump that was tied to the solar array. As backup, he purchased a tri-fuel generator that could operate using diesel fuel, solar power, or propane gas.

As a teen, Cam and her family would practice bugging out from their home to Fort Mills, the name that was adopted after her father began to prepare in earnest. Cam wouldn't say that her father was obsessed, but he was certainly committed to protecting his family in case the nation suffered a catastrophic event.

Now, he and Cam's mom had died, and she was facing a planet-killing asteroid that would arrive in just three days unless her best friend in the world could successfully divert it.

"Sure enough," said Bear as he ambled down the grassy hill toward the dock. Earlier, Cam had moved their fishing boat around to make room for the Cessna to taxi up to the dock. It was a tight fit, but without the issues of tides causing the water levels to fluctuate, the plane should be secure. "I'm so impressed with the way he handles that little plane. Did you know he refuses to let me fly it?"

Cam laughed. "Gunner has probably told him about what you've done to some of the aircraft you've flown."

"Hey," he protested, giving his partner a playful shove. "I can't help it if we get shot down sometimes. Or run out of gas."

"Or clip the tops of those kapok trees in Brazil. Do you remember how far we had to walk through the jungle to meet the extraction transport?"

"Yeah, well, at least we made it. The Russians were pissed that we took out their munitions depot in Venezuela."

Cam started walking toward the dock, still reminding Bear of his piloting exploits. "I told you we were flying too low."

"Blah, blah, blah, Cam. I got us out of there and that's all that matters." Bear pouted as he caught up to Cam, who was waving Pop over to the dock.

Cam wrapped her arm around the muscular teddy bear of a man. "I'm just bustin' your chops. Listen, before Pop arrives, I wanted to tell you that I spoke to Ghost briefly a moment ago. He's given me several secure frequencies to contact him and the Jackal if necessary. He tells me Washington is very concerned about the state of affairs around the country. If we get slammed by the leftovers of IM86, whatever that might look like, he thinks it might be difficult to get Gunner here."

Pop was waving his arm out the window as he idled toward the dock. Bear got into position with the dock lines to tie the plane off. He turned to Cam. "Maybe I should go out to Vandenberg and meet his, um, whatever the hell that spaceship is called."

"Starhopper," offered Cam.

"Yeah, that. Starhopper. I could help Gunner get here, you know, the two of us working together."

"I already brought that up. Ghost said that, depending on the circumstances, they'd be able to give him a lift. But, Bear, there is something else."

"What?"

Cam hesitated and spoke quickly as Pop cut the engines to the seaplane. "If Gunner can't outrace the asteroid, then Vandenberg may not be an option for him to land."

"Where else would he go?"

Cam took a deep breath and responded, "Anywhere he can find a place to set it down."

CHAPTER 45

Wednesday, April 25
On Board the Starhopper

Mark Twain once wrote that the two most important days in your life were the day you were born and the day you found out why. Gunner Fox felt that he was born for this moment, a single day in his thirty-four years on Earth, plus now five days in space. He set his jaw, determined to focus on the next eight hours until he could get up close and personal with the asteroid heading toward its bull's-eye—Earth.

"All right, Gunner, we can get a pretty good look at this booger now," announced Chief Rawlings, who'd been working with Artie to align the telescope to focus on IM86. The passing solar storm had left a wake of solar particles that distorted the horizon in space, causing IM86 to mysteriously appear and disappear for several hours.

At first, Chief Rawlings was beginning to believe that the Russians had succeeded in their mission, and Houston was simply unaware of what they'd accomplished. Artie dashed his hopes by making the necessary adjustments so that IM86 was now on clear, full display for Gunner and Chief Rawlings to observe.

"It's different than what I expected," said Gunner as he leaned toward the monitor to get a closer look. "I expected it to be smoother."

"Artie, please transmit these images to Houston."

"Yes, Commander Chief Rawlings."

"Gunner, this is the first close-up look we've had of the asteroid. We're really pissed at the Russians for not sharing their findings, which is part of the reason that I don't give a rat's ass that Sokolov is butt-hurt over how I'm handling this mission."

"Chief, look at it. The surface is much stonier than I expected, and the debris field has created a defined tail, a lot like a comet, although much smaller."

"We'll get a better look as each hour passes," said Chief Rawlings. "However, the makeup will have an effect on how we attack this thing."

Gunner remained focused on IM86. "It looks like it's exploding, doesn't it, especially at the rear. As it tumbles, it appears to be spewing out dusty, gravel-sized debris."

Chief Rawlings chuckled. "That gravel-sized debris, as you call it, is gigantic boulders the size of a football field. Any one of those could destroy a midsized American city when it strikes the planet at this velocity."

"It's the result of its tumble," commented Gunner. "Think about when you picked up a clod of dirt and threw it as a kid. Sure, the bulk of it hit the side of a tree, or whatever, but as it flew along, loose pieces fell off in all directions. The difference with the asteroid is that the pieces are being pulled along by its gravity."

"Exactly," said Chief Rawlings. He addressed the artificial intelligence to make adjustments in the telescope. "Artie, please zoom in to the point that the lens loses focus."

Artie complied, bringing the view much closer to reveal the rocks and boulders of various sizes and chunky and irregular shapes, instead of being sleek and smooth.

Gunner studied the image, which continuously blurred and then refocused. It was difficult to get a sustained look because of their distance from the asteroid.

"Artie, are you too far away to map the surface?" he asked.

"Yes, Major Fox. To provide you an accurate analysis, we will have to establish an orbit."

Gunner glanced over his shoulder to confirm they were alone.

Then he whispered, remembering that Artie could not differentiate between the decibels a voice projected, "Artie, can you determine if the asteroid is inhabited?"

"I must allow for several rotations in order to scan the surface for life on unexpected objects."

Chief Rawlings smiled and looked at Gunner. "Great question."

Suddenly, the image began to blur again, and the telescope struggled to find its focus. The point of view kept widening, pulling back on its zoomed-in view of IM86 until the ability to see the detail provided by the first image was lost.

"Major Fox, I cannot make a determination at this time."

"Artie," Gunner whispered again, "please continue to analyze the surface and look for evidence of human beings or spacecraft on the surface. Also, please scan the asteroid's surroundings in search of an orbiting spacecraft."

"Yes, Major Fox."

Chief Rawlings, who'd dug out his pouch of Levi Garrett earlier, spit into a Ziploc bag and quickly sealed it up before the liquid floated through the flight deck. He leaned over to Gunner and whispered, "Are you thinking what I'm thinking?"

"Chief, the debris could be because the Russians are already breaking up the asteroid by attempting to divert it. That means they're already on the surface and have managed to keep tight-lipped about it."

"A first," mumbled Chief Rawlings sarcastically. "But a brilliant strategy. Which begs the question, why would they acquiesce to this mission?"

Gunner leaned back against his seat and continued to stare at the monitor as Artie tried to make adjustments. "They couldn't say no. They had to know the president would move forward anyway, and their excuse of AI error on shooting down Falcon Heavy wouldn't fly a second time. If they shot our second launch out of the sky, nukes would be flying and the planet would be destroyed before IM86 got the chance."

"So they allowed us to move forward. Secured three seats on

board, led by a sketchy commander in Sokolov."

Gunner finished his thought. "And then do everything in their power to delay, hinder, or otherwise sabotage our mission. They can claim we failed and their mission saved the day. A win-win because they have control of the asteroid and significant bragging rights as well."

Chief Rawlings shook his head in dismay. "They don't want us to succeed, which means they'll pull out all the stops to bring about failure. We've got to stick together and make sure they stay out of this flight deck."

CHAPTER 46

Wednesday, April 25
On Board the Starhopper

Semenova had used the same sexual enticements against the weaker French astronaut, Favier, that she'd unsuccessfully attempted upon the American major. It took less than five minutes of pretend lovemaking to watch him lose his inhibitions, and then lose his life. The lethal dose of ricin could easily be discovered in an autopsy, but his body would have to be recovered from Russia, where the cosmonauts intended to land the Starhopper after the Americans' mission was foiled.

Chernevsky had stationed himself just behind the entrance to the flight deck, eavesdropping on the conversation between Major Fox and Chief Rawlings. They were only three hours away from intercept, and the onboard telescope was beginning to provide detailed images of the asteroid's surface. When Chief Rawlings and Gunner began to discuss the fact that the Russian orbiter was nowhere to be found, Chernevsky slipped away to locate his commander.

Sokolov gathered his team and issued his orders. One by one, the others must be eliminated, by incapacitation or death. Semenova was to lie in wait for the next person to check on the Frenchman. Chernevsky would ambush the Starship commander while he slept.

For his part, Sokolov would pull his favorite diversion tactic—technical failure of communications. There could be no witnesses to the sabotage of Project Jackhammer. It was a method of subterfuge he'd used before with success.

*****

Chernevsky prepped his injection. He would not use the inhalation method preferred by Semenova. The risk of an accident resulting in his own death was too great. He quietly went toward the crew quarters while Sokolov made his way to the lower deck where the advanced avionics were housed.

He'd arrived in the sleeping quarters before Semenova and found the Starship commander's sleep module empty. He immediately made his way to the galley and recreation room. The element of surprise was still available to him, as he doubted the American astronaut expected to be attacked face-to-face.

Chernevsky casually entered the kitchen galley, where he found the commander of the Starship making an ISSpresso, a soluble coffee available for use in space. The aroma was enticing to Chernevsky, and for a moment, he considered sneaking the ricin into the zero-gravity espresso carafe for all to enjoy, except his comrades, of course.

However, there was no time to waste waiting for the commander's body to respond to the diluted poison. Within minutes, Semenova would have made her second kill and the communications between the Starhopper and Earth would be lost.

"Greetings, new friendship," said Chernevsky, feigning a lack of fluency in the English language. He, in fact, had a greater command of vocabulary and grammar than his Russian comrades.

The commander laughed at the misuse of words. "Yes, a new friendship, indeed," he replied, forgetting the distrust he had for the cosmonauts. It would prove to be a fatal mistake. "Comrade, would you like some coffee?"

"*Da!*"

"Cream or sugar?" asked the American.

"*Nyet.* But you will enjoy yours this way!"

Chernevsky rammed the needle into the base of the commander's skull and scowled as he quickly depressed the plunger. The larger man swung around in a last-ditch effort to defend himself. As his eyes rolled into the back of his head, he dropped the carafe of hot coffee onto the floor, causing his feet to slip out from under him.

"*Chert!*" grumbled Chernevsky. It would be impossible to clean up the mess and hide the man's body. He took a deep breath, retrieved the commander's coffee off the counter, and took a sip. He stared down at the dead body, giving the American's head a slight kick, checking for a response. "American scum!"

Another sip of coffee later, and Chernevsky was dragging the dead man across the mid-deck.

*****

Semenova positioned herself in a sleeping module across from Favier's. She took long, deep breaths, forcing her body to relax as the adrenaline coursed through her veins. Killing was not difficult for her anymore, at least, not after the first one. She'd never done it on Earth, but in space, she became a different person. *Assassin. Black widow. Hunter.*

The female American astronaut nonchalantly made her way into the sleeping quarters of the Starhopper. She was completely unaware of Semenova's presence in the shadows of the module. The woman stuck her head into Favier's module first and called out his name. "Jean-Louis? Are you feeling better?"

Semenova managed a sly smile and thought to herself, *No, you twit. He's dead.*

Semenova readied the syringe, placing it in her right hand like an assassin's blade, to be plunged into her victim's back. Her motion would be swift and decisive, landing into the base of the woman's neck, immediately forcing the deadly poison into her spine, causing paralysis.

Now! She moved across the hall and raised her arm high as the female astronaut began to panic over the discovery of Favier's dead body. She couldn't manage a scream, but instead, recoiled out of the sleeping module and crashed into the approaching Semenova.

There was, however, no struggle. Semenova acted quickly and stuck the needle into the American's throat before depressing the syringe. The lethal dose of ricin burned into her body, causing her mouth to open wide as it gasped for air. Death would come fast for this one, unlike the other two on the Moon. By now, their bodies were rotting away from the inside out.

With her task completed, Semenova dragged the dead body to another sleep module and unceremoniously dumped it on the floor. She kicked the astronaut's lifeless limbs in order to clear the door, which she gently pulled shut.

She looked in on Favier and whispered, "Sleep tight, sweet prince. You were a good kisser." Semenova glanced in the mirror, adjusted her space suit, and fixed her hair. She allowed herself a smile. It was time for another kill.

*****

When Commander Sokolov arrived in the isolated part of the spaceship, he immediately became confused. The Starhopper's systems were unlike anything he'd seen on the space shuttles or within Russia's own space fleet. Hundreds of individual buttons, knobs, and dials were mounted on three walls toward the nose of the spacecraft. Despite advanced technology being available to create the Starhopper, there was still a remarkable amount of old-school hardware on board.

Sokolov took his time to study the panels that controlled navigation, management of the flight deck consoles, and hundreds of other functions that powered the spacecraft. He was tempted to sabotage them all, but that might be akin to sentencing himself to death.

Then he found it. He tapped on a panel box labeled DSN—Deep Space Network. The DSN consisted of antenna complexes at three locations around Earth that made up the ground segment of the communications system for deep-space missions. The challenges posed to any communications system between a spacecraft and the antennas on Earth were created by the distance.

The transmitters on board a spacecraft were limited in their power due to lack of space on board. The Jet Propulsion Laboratory at CalTech had addressed this issue with the development of optical communications capable of powering large amounts of data via laser technology.

Sokolov carefully opened the panel to view the microcircuitry inside. It would not be as easy as flipping a switch, something he'd done before. The new DSN systems were more complicated.

Frustrated, his forehead began to break out in sweat. He'd been on the lower deck too long. So he just began destroying the communications hardware by pulling out the resistors and scraping away solder jumpers. Anything loose was torn away or twisted. Nobody on board had the tools, much less the know-how, to make the repair.

With a laugh, Commander Sokolov pushed the DSN panel closed and hustled back up to the mid-deck. He gathered himself, took a deep breath, and reached into his pocket for his own vial of ricin. Like Chernevsky, he preferred the needle as his weapon of choice. It wasn't just the safety factor, but also the ability to look into his victim's eyes, when they grew wide and the realization set in that they were about to die.

It was an unforgettable experience.

CHAPTER 47

Three Years Prior
The International Space Station
Two Hundred Fifty-Four miles above Earth

There was a time in the early development of the space programs when space walks were considered risky and even feared. As NASA ramped up the space station project in the early nineties, many experts voiced concern that astronauts couldn't safely pull off three or four assembly space walks on every shuttle mission, several times over the course of a year, for nearly a decade. Scientists called the schedule of extravehicular activity, or EVA, the *Wall*, as it was roundly considered an insurmountable obstacle.

Yet NASA tore down the *Wall* in spectacular fashion. Space walks became routine, and perhaps the most incredible statistic about NASA's EVA record of over eleven hundred hours during the ISS missions was there had never been a serious accident other than bruised knuckles, droplets of water mixing with the protective coating of an astronaut's visor that found its way into his eyes, and a preventable incident in which a water leak within the space suit nearly drowned an Italian astronaut.

Even Hollywood's favorite space disaster scene, during which Sandra Bullock floated off alone, wasn't considered much of a risk due to NASA's EVA protocols, similar to the buddy system employed by scuba divers.

These protocols—in which everything was checked, double-checked, and then inspected again by your *buddy* on the space walk—were designed to prevent mishaps and provide a quick response to unforeseen accidents.

Spacewalking was akin to mountain climbing in many respects when it came to tethering to the framework of the ISS. There was one long safety tether that was part of a spring-loaded reel, plus smaller, supplemental ones as backups.

Even if these tethers failed, the astronaut's suits were equipped with a mini-jetpack called SAFER, an acronym for *simplified aid for EVA rescue.* The propulsive backpack system enabled astronauts to conduct space walks untethered or, in the event of a tether-system malfunction, allow the astronaut to navigate back to the hatch for reentry into the spacecraft.

No one had ever died while conducting an EVA thanks to these well-honed procedures and the use of the buddy system. The only way the SAFER system could fail was if all of the backups and redundancies malfunctioned.

Or if it was murder.

Heather was mesmerized by her view of the Earth. She hadn't taken the time to locate her fellow spacewalkers, her *buddies*, Chernevsky and Semenova. But they certainly kept their eyes on her.

It happened in a flash, catching Heather completely off guard. The two Russians slipped in behind her, hidden from her view by the lack of peripheral vision afforded a spacewalker due to the large helmet, and in this case, Heather's first look at Mother Earth while floating.

Every day is a good day when you're floating.

With precalculated efficiency, Semenova expertly disconnected her American victim's tethers from the space station's frame. Chernevsky slipped in behind Heather and grabbed the handheld controller attached to the front of her space suit. He jerked it toward him, extending the connecting wire, and within seconds, using the pistol-grip tool that was a mainstay of the spacewalker's toolbox, he powered the Dremel attachment at thirty-five pounds of torque.

Before Heather knew what was happening, she was drifting away from the space station, looking back at Chernevsky holding her controller, with Semenova by his side.

"Help me! Help me! I'm off structure!"

She waved her arms in a futile attempt to get her attackers' attention. Confused, she asked, "Please, why did you do this?"

Heather's heart raced and her anxiety levels hit the red zone. If she'd been connected to the ISS, or if communications had been working with Houston's Mission Control, alarm bells would be screaming that an astronaut was in distress. But she was on her own.

Floating.

Her screams for help were unheard except for the echoing through the inside of her helmet. She desperately tried to wave her arms in a swimming motion, a panicked reflex that was ineffectual in the vacuum of space. Her demands for assistance went unanswered.

She kicked at her tethers, thinking they would provide her sufficient counterforce to send her floating back toward the ISS. That failed, only serving to get her feet tangled, which caused her to spin slightly.

Tears were streaming down Heather's cheeks and floated throughout her helmet. She rubbed at her visor in a futile, subconscious attempt to clear her vision. She tried to focus on the illuminated gauges and digital displays that provided data regarding her space suit.

TEMP 59F RADIATION MINIMAL WARN OXYGEN 69% LIFE SUPP BATT 61%

Heather felt around the front of her space suit. She hoped to find some kind of backup system to operate the nitrogen-powered backpack or a way to contact Houston directly.

There was nothing, but deep down, she knew that.

What was happening to her had never been contemplated by NASA or any other space agency—murder. She was being murdered. A slow, emotionally agonizing death that would end when her oxygen levels reached zero, or the life-support battery drained, resulting in her freezing to death. Or both.

TEMP 59F RADIATION MINIMAL WARN OXYGEN 56% LIFE SUPP BATT 54%

Oxygen fifty-six percent? Or was it sixty-six percent? She begged for the tears to stop. They floated through her helmet, obscuring her view of the digital displays. Could I have used that much oxygen in that short a period of time?

Heather forced herself to relax. She was breathing too fast, burning up valuable oxygen at a rate faster than the life-support batteries were being drained.

Why? Heather asked herself. Her mind raced as she tried to understand why the two Russian cosmonauts would want her dead. She'd barely spoken to them since her arrival. They had been cordial, although their commander, Sokolov, was standoffish. But she certainly hadn't done anything to deserve to die.

She held out hope. Hope that someone on board the ISS would notice her missing. They could undock the space shuttle and retrieve her. She was sure of it.

But the ISS grew smaller and smaller as it continued its orbit around Earth without her. The tears had stopped flowing from her eyes, but those floating within her helmet had found their way back to her throat and chin, joining her anxiety-created sweat.

TEMP 61F RADIATION MINIMAL WARN OXYGEN 38% LIFE SUPP BATT 43%

Heather's body slowed its gyrations, giving her a perfect view of Earth—home. The atmosphere was clear above North America, and she could easily make out the United States and the Florida peninsula.

Remarkably, an odd sense of calm came over her. She smiled as she reached out and traced the coastline with her index finger. From Tampa to Cedar Key, around Florida's Big Bend until she saw the barrier islands of Florida's Panhandle.

Dog Island.

Gunner.

The tears flowed again as the realization set in. She would never see Gunner again. She'd never enjoy his laughter, his touch, his kiss.

Her helmet filled with fluid and she began to breathe heavily once again. She tried to force herself to calm down. She needed oxygen. She needed to buy time. They would come back for her. She'd accept their apology.

No harm, no foul. It's all good.

But deep down, she knew. Her days weren't numbered. Her minutes were. She didn't know whether anyone could hear her. Maybe there was a recording device built in to the space suit that could be given to Gunner when they …

Heather's thoughts trailed off as she realized that nobody would ever find her, nor would they look. She'd either float in orbit like the tens of thousands of other pieces of space debris, or eventually, she'd be cremated as her body was sucked through the atmosphere toward the planet's surface.

TEMP 63F RADIATION MINIMAL WARN OXYGEN 20% LIFE SUPP BATT 31%

She closed her eyes and summoned everything within her to send Gunner a message. She imagined typing a text, or an email, or even writing a letter. She found humor in the moment as she imagined creating a message in a bottle that someday would float up on the beach of Dog Island, behind the home they'd built together with love.

"Dear Gunner," she said aloud, causing her to begin laughing as her tears of sadness turned to joy. "Well, I'm floating, but this wasn't exactly what I had in mind. Um, the bad news is that I'm about to die. In fact, the race between oxygen depletion and battery failure is no longer a close one. You can put down cause of death as asphyxiation.

"That's if I don't die of sadness first. Gunner, I love you with all my heart and I am going to miss you.

"Thank you for loving me. You have given me an awesome life, especially by supporting me as I pursued my crazy dreams. We have lived our lives to the fullest, and neither of us should have regrets over the choices we've made.

"I want you to remember our fantastic life together and don't focus on the loss. Remember the day we got married, the first time we made love, and the last. Remember our walks on the beach, the rides in the boat, and our vacations. Laugh at the memories we made and the fun we had."

TEMP 61F RADIATION MINIMAL WARN OXYGEN 11% LIFE SUPP BATT 23%

Heather briefly considered dictating her love letter to Gunner in her head to save oxygen, but she visibly shook her head side to side as she continued. It wouldn't be the same unless it was aloud.

"Take care of Pop. He will miss me, as I will miss him. Howard, too. All three of my guys need to stick together.

"Gunner, I've been unbelievably lucky to spend almost half of my life with you, and I'd promise God everything if He could find a miracle that placed me back in your arms one last time. You are truly the best husband in the universe. You are a hero to your country. There aren't enough words to express how loved and respected you are.

"Hold me in your heart, my love. I will surround you with my love through the rest of your life. Just know, if you stop and look hard enough, you'll see that I'll be there with you. You are my soul mate and the best wingman a gal could have. And know this, if ghosts are real, I'll be there happily haunting you for the rest of your days. I'll try not to make it creepy, lol."

TEMP 58F RADIATION MINIMAL WARN OXYGEN 04% LIFE SUPP BATT 14%

"Oh, God, Gunner. It's almost the end for me. Please don't forget that every day matters. Never take your moments on Earth for granted. That is my single biggest regret—that we didn't spend every minute of every day by each other's side.

"I'm certain that someday, we will find each other again. Either in the afterlife, or back on Earth in different bodies. Just look for my smile and adoring eyes. Until then, my love, I will be waiting, loving you from afar, and protecting you in any way possible. Meanwhile, I'll be floating, counting the days 'til we're together again.

"Because every day is a good day when you're floating, even if it's my last one."

OXYGEN 01% LIFE SUPP BATT 11%

Heather took her last breath and held it. With a gentle smile on her face, she closed her eyes and held onto her memory of Gunner for her final moments above Earth.

Then, she floated.

CHAPTER 48

Present Day
Wednesday, April 25
On Board the Starhopper

Chief Rawlings intently studied the data streaming from the onboard telescope through the computer monitors that were positioned at eye level on the center console. Artie was analyzing the images at unimaginable speeds, creating a digital map of the asteroid's surface. With every tumble of IM86 as it sped closer to Earth, Artie's analysis changed. Now, coordinates were being marked as the weak points on the asteroid's surface, generating a series of targets for Gunner to focus on.

"Obviously, your first target will be pretty straightforward," he commented, glancing over at his protégé to gauge his level of intensity.

Gunner rarely blinked as he studied the screen. "Chief, most people would be surprised at the amount of time combat pilots take to prepare for a mission. Usually, from takeoff to landing, a sortie's duration is around one plus fifteen—an hour and fifteen minutes. This is no different, except the variables are poles apart. I can predict how a bogie will react to a near miss or a partial hit. I can tell you how surface-to-air missiles can be avoided. But this asteroid is gonna require flexibility and quick reaction."

"What do you mean by flexibility?"

"Well, let's take what Artie is doing for us now," replied Gunner. "The mapping process is a huge help, but everything will change with the first strike."

"Artie will help you there," said Chief Rawlings.

"I'm sure of that, as long as he doesn't argue with me."

The two men grew silent for a moment as the timer marking the interception point ticked down. Chief Rawlings grew antsy in his seat, turned around, and craned his neck to see if anyone was hovering outside the flight deck.

"You know, I'd feel better if we were all together for the last two hours. This spacecraft has all the bells and whistles but no internal communications system. Then again, I don't think they envisioned calling out *all hands on deck* during a trip to Mars."

"Chief, you can go get them. Nobody is gonna sit in your seat, trust me."

Chief Rawlings nodded, stood, and patted Gunner on the shoulder. Then he paused and said, "Gunner, there's no doubt in my mind that you'll knock the shit out of this booger. Stay calm and trust your training and your instincts."

"Thanks, Chief. I feel good."

Chief Rawlings left Gunner alone in the crew module and made his way toward the back of the Starhopper. He poked his head into the hallway of the sleep modules and saw no activity, so he made his way through the ship until he reached the recreation area.

"Arrrgh!" growled Semenova as she emerged out of nowhere to attack Chief Rawlings. In his late fifties, the retired astronaut's reflexes were slower than when he was a younger man, but he still managed to fend off the attack.

He grabbed her with both arms and pushed her into a series of cabinets that opened using push latches. Her body weight caused the doors to depress inward, and as she bounced to the floor, the doors swung open abruptly, causing food supplies to tumble on top of her.

Enraged, Semenova crawled toward Chief Rawlings and grabbed his pant leg, yanking his right leg out from under him until he crashed downward. He struck his forehead on the corner of a cabinet door, causing blood to run down the left side of his face.

He frantically tried to wipe the blood out of his eyes and cleared his vision just enough to see Semenova lunge at him with a syringe held high over her head. She thrust her arm down toward his face, but he raised his arm in time to deflect the blow.

She rolled to the side and he crawled on top of her. She continued to jab at him with the needle, and Chief Rawlings reached for her wrist to stop the assault. As he focused on her arm, she raised her knee hard into his groin, causing him to gasp for air and double over in pain.

Semenova had the upper hand again, using catlike reflexes to take another stab at Chief Rawlings with the syringe. She aimed for the right side of his face, but he turned it just in time to avoid being punctured. She tried again, but he whipped his head the other way, again avoiding her attempt.

Her arm slid along his cheek and Chief Rawlings didn't hesitate to bite her wrist, causing her to shriek in pain as he punctured her skin, drawing blood. Semenova was infuriated and lost control.

Still holding the needle, she flailed away at Chief Rawlings, landing body blows with her free hand, but being thwarted by the older man's ability to block the arm holding the needle.

Then Chief Rawlings squirmed, using his body weight to throw her off balance. He was back on top of her again and grabbed her wrist that was holding the syringe. He gritted his teeth and forced the needle toward her face, using all of his weight to push it downward.

Semenova's eyes grew wide as she saw the sharp tip of the needle grow closer. This just provided Chief Rawlings a bigger target. With one final effort, he grunted and plunged the syringe into her right eye, not bothering to find the plunger. She screamed in pain as he crammed the needle into her eyeball with a circular motion, forcing it deeper into her head until she released her grip. When she did, he pushed down on the plunger, emptying the deadly poison into the optic nerve and directly into the brain, killing her in seconds.

Chief Rawlings relaxed and scrambled off Semenova's dead body. He tried to hold the blood back from the cut on his forehead, to no avail. He wiped it off his face the best he could as it continue to hamper his vision, but it only served to distract him as two sets of powerful fists began to pummel him from behind.

With blow after blow, Chief Rawlings was beaten by Sokolov and

Chernevsky. They were merciless, hurling insults and cursing the revered astronaut who'd served his country, and humanity, in space.

He tried to warn Gunner by calling out his name. "Gun—" But a heavy blow to the mouth silenced him, causing him to choke on his blood.

Soon, he was powerless to defend himself against the brutal beating. In less than a minute, his eyes were swollen shut, his face was bleeding profusely, and he was having difficulty breathing.

Sokolov, out of breath, gave instructions to Chernevsky. "Go, comrade. Put down that dog, their hero. Kill him. Now!"

Chief Rawlings tried to struggle under the weight of the much larger Sokolov. He tried again, in vain, to warn Gunner. His mind was fading, along with his ability to fight, as the heavy blows caused his brain to concuss.

Sokolov returned to the beatdown. He stood over Chief Rawlings, whose limp body was no longer able to protect itself. He growled and stomped the defenseless man. Chief Rawlings was unable to move. After several kicks to his groin, his bladder released, and the excruciating pain came to a merciful end as he drifted toward unconsciousness, a growing darkness, and then his mind faded to black.

CHAPTER 49

Wednesday, April 25
On Board the Starhopper

"It's been too long," muttered Gunner as he twisted in his seat and glanced through the back of the flight deck toward the common area leading to other parts of the ship. He'd become concerned for Chief Rawlings and the rest of the crew, but he didn't dare leave the flight deck of the spaceship unattended.

Gunner turned toward the console to initiate communications with Flight Control One in the Mission Control Center. He hadn't had direct communication with Mark Foster thus far because Chief Rawlings and the other American astronauts took the lead on piloting the spacecraft.

"Houston, this is Starhopper, Major Fox."

No response.

Gunner studied the control panels to ensure that he was operating the communications system properly. Unlike the astronauts charged with the operations of the Starhopper, Gunner did not have comms built into his space suit.

He tried again. "Houston Mission Control, this is Major Gunner Fox aboard the Starhopper. Does anybody read me?"

Gunner scowled and began to run his fingers along the vast array of complex switches and dials. Had he missed something during his training in the simulator? Lost communications and the protocols to follow were never discussed. It was always assumed that the other crew members would handle those issues.

"Where the hell is everybody?" Gunner asked aloud, and then he saw a shadow pass across a reflective surface on the Starhopper's navigation console.

The light that normally reflected off the console emanating from the hallway was eclipsed. Gunner turned his head to find the cause of the shadow and quickly snapped his head back the other way just as Chernevsky swung his clenched fist downward. He was holding a syringe like a dagger.

Gunner was not belted into the seat, so he was able to twist his body to get into a defensive position. Chernevsky, on the other hand, lost his balance as a result of the missed blow. His face crashed into the navigation console, giving him a bloody nose and causing alarms to sound in the crew module.

"Artie, do something!"

"Yes, Major Fox."

Gunner reached for the cosmonaut, grabbed the collar of his space suit, and flung him backwards onto the floor between the second row of seats. He launched himself out of the pilot's seat and pounced on his assailant.

Chernevsky managed to hold onto the syringe and made a stabbing motion toward Gunner's face, which he easily blocked with his forearm. Chernevsky reared back for another try, but Gunner punched his wrist, forcing the attacker to lose his grip on the syringe.

Both men saw it bounce across the steel floor and roll under one of the second-row seats. A scramble full of tangled arms and legs ensued as they both tried to reach the deadly poison.

Gunner was faster and grabbed the syringe just before Chernevsky. They struggled and Gunner forced the needle toward the younger man's neck. He could see the veins popping out as Chernevsky used all his strength to hold Gunner's hand away, but, with one final push, Gunner plunged the needle into the Russian's neck.

Then Gunner lost his balance, and the needle broke off in Chernevsky's neck. The Russian was feeling the effects of a small amount of the ricin that entered his system, but it wasn't enough to kill him. He tried to fight Gunner, but he was weakened.

Gunner retrieved the syringe and saw that the needle had come out. He grabbed Chernevsky by the hair, straightened his face so they could see one another, and he tried to shove the syringe into the man's mouth.

The Russian clenched his mouth shut and flailed about to avoid consuming the poison. Gunner was pressing harder, closer to forcing the syringe in Chernevsky's mouth. Then he chose another option.

He rammed the needleless syringe into the killer's nose and forced the plunger down, emptying the deadly ricin deep into the nasal cavity. Chernevsky loosened his grip and began to shake uncontrollably. A white mucous substance flowed out of the Russian's mouth, and then the expected blank stare of death told Gunner he could relax.

For the moment.

*****

Gunner got to his feet and turned to the console that was still processing the images and data from IM86. During the fight with Chernevsky, Gunner had been unaware that the warning signals screaming throughout the flight deck had stopped.

He took a deep breath and stared out the front windows of the Starship, still seeing darkness ahead of him. He had to find Chief Rawlings.

Suddenly, it felt like a battering ram crashed into his spine, knocking him forward against the pilot's seat, crushing his sternum against the headrest.

He gasped for air and tried to gather himself when Commander Sokolov grabbed him by the shoulders and pulled him to the floor of the flight deck. He tried to stomp on Gunner's face, but missed.

Gunner rolled over and crouched onto his knees. Sokolov tried to kick again, but Gunner was ready this time. He grabbed the Russian's leg and twisted it, causing him to lose his balance and fall backwards on top of Chernevsky's dead body.

"I will kill you!" the Russian shouted as he scrambled to his feet.

Gunner, who'd recovered from the initial blow, was ready for his assailant. The two men rushed each other, crashing like two Sumo wrestlers. Toe to toe, they exchanged blows. Gunner took a shot to the kidneys, but he returned the favor with a solid blow to Sokolov's mouth, causing two teeth to fly out.

Bloodied, but undeterred, Sokolov grinned, revealing the lost front teeth. He reached into his pocket and retrieved two syringes, one for each hand.

"It is time for me to kill another American Fox!"

Gunner was stunned. His body relaxed at first as he tried to understand. "What?"

"Oh, yes, Major Fox. You will be my second kill of a Fox! Arrrgh!"

Sokolov leapt toward Gunner, holding both syringes high into the air. Gunner jumped off the floor with both feet and double kicked Sokolov in the chest, knocking him backwards, but the force also propelled Gunner into the Starhopper's console again, setting off more alarms.

"Artie! Fix that."

"Yes, Major Fox."

Sokolov was undeterred. He climbed to his feet, but realized he'd lost one of the syringes. He paused, giving Gunner the opportunity to strike first. He kicked the Russian's right knee, causing his leg to buckle and the killer to scream in pain.

Gunner jumped on top of Sokolov, who attempted to stab Gunner with the syringe, repeatedly missing his face.

"What did you do to my wife?" Gunner screamed his question as he pounded the Russian's face with blow after blow.

Sokolov lost his grip on the syringe and began to cackle. An evil, loud laugh that made him sound demented. Blood spat out of his mouth as he talked. "She floated, you fool! We cut her loose and she floated away!" He continued to laugh, which enraged Gunner. He pounded the man's face and head, landing blows with both hands until his knuckles were bruised and bloodied.

"Floating ..." said Commander Sokolov, Heather's killer, with his last breath as Gunner landed a crushing blow to his temple, ending his life.

CHAPTER 50

Wednesday, April 25
On Board the Starhopper

Gunner lost it. For three years, he'd bottled up his emotions, going to dark places where no human being should go. Attempting to find answers to why the love of his life was taken from him. Blaming God. Blaming NASA. Blaming himself. Even, at times, blaming Heather. That was when he hurt the most. He begged to go back in time. To have an opportunity to keep Heather on Earth and not in space where he couldn't protect her.

And now he'd learned the truth. She hadn't died in a freak accident. It wasn't some unpredictable mishap during which fate got in the way of what should've been a routine space walk to repair the ISS communications system. She'd been murdered.

Gunner spun around and began to kick Sokolov's dead body, forcing blood out of his face until the entire floor of the flight deck was covered in it. His anger took hold as he kicked again, this time slipping and falling onto his back next to Chernevsky's dead eyes staring at the ceiling.

Gunner began to bawl. Tears flowed out of him and he shuddered uncontrollably. These men had killed his beloved wife. A woman he adored with all of his being. His partner. His best friend. An adorable, loving woman who'd planned to grow old with him on Dog Island, picking up shells or swimming with the dolphins.

She was gone, murdered, and he'd exacted his revenge against the people responsible. So why didn't he feel better? Shouldn't he have a sense of relief? Why was the pain worse than ever?

Gunner allowed himself time to cry and grieve again.

Then Artie brought him back into the present. "One hour until intercept."

Gunner wiped his face and lifted himself off the floor. He was covered in blood, and his agony of learning the truth about Heather's death was now replaced with a sense of dread. Throughout the brutal battle with the two Russian cosmonauts, nobody else had emerged from the bowels of the Starhopper.

Were they all dead? Chief Rawlings too?

Gunner gathered himself and entered the hallway leading to the sleeping quarters. He checked each room until he found the dead Frenchman and one of his fellow astronauts. He closed his eyes in disappointment as he witnessed two more good people taken by the hands of the soulless Russians.

He carefully made his way to the mid-deck, being vigilant as he watched for Semenova, the woman who'd intended to kill him that night at Artemis. She could be waiting to attack him.

He eased into the recreation area and found a massacre. Semenova's dead body lay sprawled in a pool of blood, a syringe protruding out of her eye, bloody sputum trailing out of her mouth and nose.

Nearby, he saw the leg of the Starship commander—a man who, like Heather, had responded to the call of duty at the last minute to aid his country—hanging out of a storage room. Gunner didn't need to check his pulse. He too was dead.

Gunner shouted, "Chief! Are you here?" He looked around the room and then made his way into the galley.

Nothing.

He studied the blood on the floor. It appeared a body had been dragged toward the laundry and refuse room. Gunner's chin dropped to his chest. He closed his eyes and sighed.

"Please, God, no," he said as he walked through the blood and slowly opened the door.

Chief Rawlings was doubled over, lying on his side with his face crammed against a cabinet. Gunner approached him and then he saw

Chief Rawlings breathing. His chest rose ever so slightly, but he was alive!

"Chief! Chief!"

Gunner dropped to his knees and slowly rolled his friend over to see his battered face. *My god*, thought Gunner. His eyes were swollen shut. His nose was contorted from the cartilage being broken in several places.

Yet he was still alive.

"Chief? Can you hear me?"

The badly beaten NASA veteran wiggled his fingers. He tried to speak but began to hack up blood.

"That's okay. Don't talk. Let me try to set you upright."

Chief Rawlings's body was limp, so Gunner had to lift him by himself. His fingers stung from beating Sokolov to death, but it was a pain that suddenly felt glorious.

Gunner reached into the cabinet and retrieved some bath towels. He gently wiped the blood off Chief Rawlings's face.

"I'm gonna get you some water and clean you up," whispered Gunner as he lovingly set a clean towel in the older man's lap.

"Careful," he whispered back.

"It's okay, they're all dead."

"Ours?"

Gunner exhaled. "Yes. Everyone but us. I'll be back."

Gunner raced to the kitchen and grabbed several bottles of water. He spent the next few minutes cleaning the blood off the commander of the Starhopper. Revived, Chief Rawlings began to show signs of life, so Gunner left him for a moment to gather first aid supplies.

Ten minutes later, both men's uniforms were still covered in blood, but they were no longer bleeding from their own cuts.

Unexpectedly, Chief Rawlings's swollen eyes opened wide as the realization set in that they still had a mission to perform.

"How much time?" he asked, coughing as he spoke.

"Less than an hour. I have to get to the crew module."

Chief Rawlings pushed off the floor and quickly sat back down.

He held his head and grimaced. "Damn headache. Help me up."

"Why don't you stay here and rest?"

"I can help. Please, just pull me up."

Gunner stood and reached under his armpits, hoisting the badly beaten man onto his feet. His legs gave way at first, and then he found the strength to stand on his own with the assistance of Gunner.

"I'll help you get up there and seated. Don't overexert, Chief. I'm gonna need a good wingman."

Chief Rawlings smiled, revealing the gap from the teeth he lost during the beating. "I think you can manage with Artie's help. I just don't want to miss the show."

He began to cough, spitting up a little blood in the process. As they made their way to the crew module and the flight deck, Chief Rawlings offered Gunner some words of encouragement.

"I believe in you, Gunner, and I know you believe in yourself. There is something inside you that is extraordinary."

Chief Rawlings began coughing again, with more blood coming out of his mouth. He seemed light-headed and complained about his head aching again. Then he somehow caught his breath and continued. "I know about your struggles and the loss you've suffered. It will pass. Heather will help you through it. Talk to her. It's okay. You aren't crazy. It will help. I promise."

He began coughing so hard that Gunner stopped and offered to set him on the floor to rest. Chief Rawlings refused, adamant that he would be all right if he could just get into the commander's seat.

A minute later, Gunner got him situated in the left seat, helped him drink some water, and moistened a towel for him to use to wipe his mouth. He affixed his mentor's harnesses and gave him one last look over to make sure he was comfortable.

He turned and dragged the dead Russians out of the crew module. He growled at the dead bodies as he did. "You don't deserve to be in here."

Gunner took a moment to rush back to his sleep module and retrieve his duffle bag. He quickly peeled off the blood-covered space suit and donned a pair of khakis and the white, long-sleeve NASA shirt sent to him by Ghost with the words *watch your back* scribbled inside.

When he returned, he stood and took in the entire flight deck. The clock was ticking down to under thirty minutes. He took a deep breath and smiled. He was ready.

"Okay, Artie. Let's do this!"

"Do what, Major Fox?"

Gunner rolled his eyes and laughed as he strapped himself into the pilot's seat and ran his fingers across the nuclear missile launch panel. He flexed his fingers and studied the mapping of IM86.

Channeling Chief Rawlings, he replied, "Kill this booger."

CHAPTER 51

Wednesday, April 25
On Board the Starhopper

Gunner Fox put his game face on.

He checked on Chief Rawlings, who'd fallen asleep in the commander's chair to his left. He checked his pulse and temperature. He considered changing his mentor's space suit for a fresh one but chose not to for fear of aggravating his injured, battered body.

"Okay, Artie. It's just you and me, pal."

"Yes, Major. We are alone. Houston is offline."

"Artie, have you completed the mapping process?"

"Yes, Major. Would you like the precise composition of 2029 IM86?"

"No, that won't be necessary. Approximate dimensions will suffice."

Gunner went through a number of systems checks as he conversed with the onboard artificial intelligence.

Artie provided him the data. "Length is seven thousand six hundred thirty-two feet. Width at its greatest point is five thousand eighty-eight feet."

Not that it mattered because he had a job to do, but Gunner was curious about how mean this bastard was. "Do you have an estimated impact energy?"

"Yes. The impact energy is estimated to be two hundred four thousand megatons. It registers a nine on the Torino scale."

Gunner shook his head in amazement. "What would it take to be a ten?" he muttered to himself.

Of course, Artie heard him. "A kinetic energy of ten to the power of five, Major. A much larger object."

"Artie, what is its speed?" asked Gunner as he looked at his console. He was now tracking the asteroid on a parallel path towards the Earth. The good news was that the constant rolling motion of the asteroid alleviated the necessity for him to circumnavigate it for artificial intelligence to get an accurate picture of its surface.

"Major, the velocity has remained steady at fifty-two thousand four hundred miles per hour."

Gunner glanced at the console and confirmed the information. It was moving slower than the scientists on Earth estimated. That worked in his favor, but only by a few hours. He was feeling the pressure of the delayed launches, both at Boca Chica and from Artemis. He was urged to strike quickly so the debris field was largest on the opposite side of the Northern Hemisphere from the U.S., namely in Russia and China.

"Got it. Artie, have you identified the weakest points in the asteroid's structure?"

"Yes, Major. There are nine points of attack identified in order to destroy 2029 IM86."

Gunner glanced over at Chief Rawlings, who was still asleep. He leaned across the center console and felt his mentor's wrist. His pulse was weak, but there.

"Artie, I only have four nukes. We can't hit nine bull's-eyes."

"Major, it requires nine points of attack to destroy 2029 IM86."

Gunner took a deep breath and exhaled. "Artie, have you ranked these nine points of attack by order of priority?"

"Yes, Major."

"And, Artie, after the initial strike, are you able to analyze the damage inflicted upon the asteroid?"

"Yes, Major. The asteroid has three distinct layers. The outer layer of silicate minerals produces the stony appearance. The intermediate zone consists of cellular nickel-iron and silicate minerals. The dense nickel-iron core cannot be destroyed without nine points of impact."

"Artie, after the first strike breaches the outer layer, can you then reprioritize the remaining points of attack?"

"Yes, Major. The list may increase, or decrease, depending on the accuracy of the first strike."

Gunner laughed. "Nice CYA, Artie."

"I'm sorry, Major. I do not understand."

"Your ass, Artie. You just covered your ass."

"I do not have an ass, Major."

Gunner chuckled and checked the time. He was past the window of opportunity to begin the attack that minimized the number of remnants hitting North America. However, with the asteroid travelling slightly slower than predicted, he might still have some success. The bottom line was just to kill it, or in the absence of total obliteration, break it up into many pieces so that the impact event on Earth was survivable.

He reached for the nuclear launch control panel and manually activated all four missiles. Protocol required him to set them to ready on an as-needed basis. He'd scoffed at that statement during his training.

First, did they really expect him to haul ass home with a nuke still strapped to the Starhopper's belly? Second, were they on a budget? Gunner had already decided he was gonna fire off the entire load just to make sure. It appeared, per Artie, four of the most powerful nuclear missiles ever assembled still might not be enough.

Gunner rolled his head around his shoulders in an attempt to ease the tension. One at a time, he removed his hands from the console and wiped his sweaty palms on his khakis. This mission was affecting him like no other. In a combat aircraft, he was completely at ease, one hundred percent confident in his abilities. Flying the Starhopper, with the fate of the world in his hands, caused him quite a bit of apprehension. He hoped it would dissipate once he began the attack.

"Game on, Artie!" he shouted as he took over the controls, manually flying the spaceship from this point forward.

He brought up the mapping coordinates on the large navigational panel in front of him. He also continuously looked through the windows that provided him a limited view of the asteroid, except where the nose of the spacecraft was pointed.

Gunner turned toward the asteroid and immediately picked up speed. The gravitational pull of IM86 had a greater effect on his approach than he expected.

His pulse raced as the planet killer grew larger, filling the one-hundred-eighty-degree view afforded by the Starhopper's windows.

He slowed the spacecraft, focusing on his first mark. Then he glanced at the asteroid and caught a glimpse of something out of the ordinary. It was the Russian space vehicle on the surface of the asteroid.

Gunner grimaced and gritted his teeth in anger. He pulled up and away from the asteroid, causing the g-force on his body to push him back against the seat. The sudden maneuver also jostled Chief Rawlings awake, who let out a groan.

"Sorry, Chief. We had to abort the first run."

"Um, Gunner. I can't see. My eyes are swollen so bad I can't open them."

"You rest, Chief. I've got this."

"I wanna know what's happening in case I can help. Is Artie online?"

"Yes, Commander Chief Rawlings, I am online."

Gunner reached over and felt the battered astronaut's pulse again. It had increased somewhat, not necessarily a bad sign.

"Gunner, can you describe your actions so I can follow along?"

Gunner circled the asteroid and brought the Starhopper back into position for another run at the first target.

"Chief, the Russians did land on the asteroid, and they are within a tenth of a mile of our primary target. When the nuke hits, they'll be turned to dust."

Chief Rawlings managed a chuckle and then winced in pain. "That's not our problem, son. Do what you have to do."

Gunner hesitated. "I thought I'd do a flyby. You know, give them a heads-up as to what's about to come their way."

"There's no time, Gunner. Even if they heeded your warning, their delay in evacuating the asteroid will put us and the planet in danger."

After a moment, Gunner agreed. "We can't help them. I'm going in."

Gunner focused on the target a second time and navigated directly for it, watching his speed more carefully during his approach. The trial run had given him confidence, and he noticed his palms were no longer sweating.

He squinted his eyes and focused his concentration on the asteroid's surface and his control of the Starhopper. Hitting a moving, spinning target required coordination and proper timing. Gunner took a deep breath and held it. He slid his hands onto the launch controls.

His mind wandered, ever so briefly, to his days as a combat pilot. The code word *Fox* was used by NATO pilots to signal the release of air-to-air missiles during combat. Gunner always appreciated the irony that his last name represented the destruction of another aircraft, or in this case, a planet killer flying toward Earth.

He depressed the first button and announced, "Fox 1 is away."

CHAPTER 52

Wednesday, April 25
On Board the Starhopper

Gunner pulled up and away from IM86, using every aspect of the technologically advanced maneuverability to clear the impact of the nuclear missile on the surface. Had circumstances been different, Gunner would have programmed the nuclear missile to detonate just a few hundred yards above the surface. The irradiation of the surface of the asteroid would undergo a superheating effect, altering the composition and causing it to move off its trajectory.

The time had passed for alternative means besides brute force.

"Artie, provide me the results of the first strike."

"Major, the first strike missed the target by approximately nineteen meters. I am analyzing new data."

Gunner shrugged and brought the Starhopper back into a parallel trajectory with IM86. The impact of the nuclear missile had a profound effect on his visibility. A combination of dirt and boulders had erupted from the surface, flying in all directions as the blast wave of the nuclear missile spread.

He anxiously awaited Artie's analysis. He turned to his commander. "Chief, I missed by sixty feet or so."

He smiled and coughed his response. "I heard. Pretty good shooting under these conditions. You gotta keep pounding away, Gunner. Don't give the gravitational pull time to draw the debris back in."

"Major Fox, I have my results and revised coordinates for the second strike. It requires a repositioning of the Starhopper to the far side of 2029 IM86."

Gunner didn't hesitate as he pulled the Spaceship higher and farther away from the asteroid's surface to avoid the continuously spewing debris.

"The Russians?" asked Chief Rawlings.

"We can't see the surface, but they never knew what hit 'em. It was probably better that way."

Gunner established his flight trajectory in preparation for the next strike. The other side of the asteroid was experiencing some large debris orbiting the surface as IM86 continued to tumble.

"Remember, Gunner. Jackhammer. You have to keep pounding away until you chisel the core."

"Roger that, Chief," said Gunner, who then turned his attention back to Artie and the navigational panel. "Show me the new coordinates, Artie."

"Yes, Major."

Gunner studied the information provided by the computer's analysis and then began his rapid descent toward the surface. He used visual navigation more this time in order to avoid any ejected materials resulting from the first detonation. With each missile launch, his task would become more difficult, requiring more reliance on his senses of sight and touch, and a hint of luck.

"Fox 2 is away!" Gunner exclaimed as he continued to get caught up in the excitement of the mission. His first strike hadn't been delivered with pinpoint accuracy, but he learned from it. He began to apply his experience of being in dogfights with other aircraft to the hunting of IM86.

As before, he pulled the Starhopper upward, using all of his effort and the spacecraft's capabilities to avoid being caught up in the nuclear explosion on the surface. He was a lot closer to the asteroid on this missile launch, and the shock wave was felt as he retreated into space. The last two missiles would require him to push the limits of the Starhopper—and his anxiety threshold.

"Talk to me, Artie. Provide me a status of the second strike."

"Major, the second strike missed the target by approximately fifteen meters. I am analyzing new data."

Chief Rawlings slurred his words this time as if he was sleepy or slightly intoxicated. "Well done, Gunner. You're getting better."

"Thanks, Chief. It appeared that Artie directed me to a point immediately opposite the first strike."

Gunner held his breath, hoping that Artie would tell him that the core of the asteroid was exposed, its weak underbelly ready for a decisive blow and the end to this mission.

"Artie?" asked Gunner impatiently.

The AI responded, "Major Fox, I have my results and revised coordinates for the third strike. It requires a repositioning of the Starhopper to the third side of 2029 IM86."

Gunner had noticed that the irregular-shaped asteroid had features that rendered it somewhat triangular in appearance. It was logical that Artie would focus on cracking the asteroid all the way around before giving it a final, hopefully decisive blow.

He glanced over at Chief Rawlings, who was fading in and out of consciousness. He resisted the urge to pause the mission and attend to his mentor and now close friend. Time was crucial during this juncture of the attack, and the repeated warnings from the space geologists about the asteroid reconstituting itself rang through his head.

"Artie, show me the coordinates," instructed Gunner as he turned the spacecraft upside down relative to IM86 and looked upward toward the dark side that was hidden by the rays of the Sun.

As he navigated into position, he got a visual of the debris field that had formed around the asteroid. IM86 had appeared to grow exponentially. It now had a tail that was longer than its original mile and three-quarter length.

A large chunk had split off and was racing ahead of the much bulkier remains. Gunner considered that this piece was of sufficient mass to have a devastating impact on the planet by itself. He could only hope that it sailed off the current trajectory, which, according to the onboard telemetry, indicated a direct hit for an area just above the Tropic of Cancer to near the Equator.

Gunner set his jaw, clenched his fists around the Starhopper's manual navigational yoke, and dove toward the surface, not bothering to slow his speed on this run. His confidence had grown and he was ready to end this fight.

"Fox 3, away!"

This time, rather than pull up, which would have led him into the path of the asteroid, Gunner banked hard right, taking him a greater distance away from the asteroid's path towards Earth. As Artie analyzed the results of this third strike, he wanted to get a visual of the total picture—the asteroid, its debris field, and home.

CHAPTER 53

Wednesday, April 25
On Board the Starhopper

Gunner forgot about what had brought him to this critical moment
in his life. He stared past the enormous asteroid that was now broken
into many thousands of pieces of varying sizes. He saw Earth ahead.
Large, blue, and peaceful. He was awestruck by the realization that
humanity, and everything that he'd ever known, existed on a fragile
blue orb surrounded by vast darkness. It caused him to reflect on
how he felt about life. He wanted to live—for himself, for Pop, and
for Heather. She was proud of him and was standing behind him
now. He could feel it in his soul.

"Major Fox, I have the updated coordinates for the final strike.
The dual cores of 2029 IM86 are not exposed. I have determined that
it does not have a homogeneous structure."

"Wait. Artie, are you saying it's been fused or spliced together?"
asked Gunner.

"It is a possibility, Major Fox. It is possible that 2029 IM86 was
formed by the collision of two bodies that bumped together and
merged into one many millions of years ago."

"Artie, have you found its structural weakness so that I can strike
the core with the final missile."

Artie hesitated. "Major, 2029 IM86 does not have a homogeneous
structure; therefore it does not have a single core. It has two separate
and distinct cores, neither of which are exposed."

Gunner tensed up at this new revelation. He wanted to know why
this couldn't have been determined in advance, but perhaps he had to
chip away at the surface in order to provide artificial intelligence a

better look.

"Well, shit. It is what it is." He lamented the newfound information. He thought for a moment and then addressed Artie. "Artie, can you identify a point that is most vulnerable to attack that will yield a division of the two fused asteroids?"

"Yes, Major. I can."

"Artie, please do that. I can see the asteroid attempting to pull itself back together."

"Yes, Major Fox. I have compared 2029 IM86 to my knowledge database of other binary asteroids. I have identified a point of impact that could result in a splitting of the asteroid into two separate, homogenous bodies."

Gunner looked over toward Chief Rawlings. "Chief, are you awake. Whadya think?"

Chief Rawlings didn't respond. His breathing was slow and shallow. Gunner elected not to wake him. He was prepared to go it alone, as always.

"Give me the coordinates, Artie."

Artie complied and Gunner adjusted his orbit. He got a visual of the rubble pile that had formed around the entire asteroid. It wasn't disintegrating, and Gunner didn't expect that it would. But it was expelling debris in all directions as it seemed to be flying apart. His best result at this point was to split it in two, with one or both parts sailing off in different directions.

"I'm going in," announced Gunner. On this final run toward the surface and the last target, he'd fly completely using his visual acuity. The first three approaches to the surface of the asteroid had taught him about the movement of the rubble. All speeds are relative to one's surroundings, so he put out of his mind that the debris was flying all around him at fifty thousand miles per hour. He'd dodge it as if it were standing still.

He was speeding toward the surface when warning lights and alarms sounded on the console. They were the kind of ground proximity warnings employed in aircraft. Whenever an airplane was functioning properly, but nonetheless flew into a side of a mountain, it was because the plane was off course or the pilot had lost track of its position. The technical term was *controlled flight into terrain*, or CFIT. Artificial intelligence had been employed to avoid CFIT accidents.

The Starhopper's AI was programmed to include a version of the GPWS—ground proximity warning system. In the event of a potential impact with the ground based upon the spacecraft's speed and angle of descent, artificial intelligence would assume the pilot had been incapacitated.

Artie's warning was more than that. It was a signal of AI's intention to take over the controls of the Starhopper. Artie's robotic voice blared through the flight deck speakers.

"Terrain. Pull up. Terrain. Pull up."

"No, Artie. I've got this." Gunner continued his speed and current course toward the target's coordinates, flying the Starhopper closer to the surface like a Japanese kamikaze pilot attacking Pearl Harbor.

"Terrain. Pull up. Prepare for automatic control override. Automatic control override in five seconds. Four. Three."

"No, Artie. Stand down! Stand down!"

"Three seconds and holding."

Gunner continued to head toward the surface. "Artie, stand down."

"I am not programmed or authorized to self-destruct."

Closer.

"Stand down."

Gunner swerved between debris the size of skyscrapers, and he could now see the surface without the aid of the external video cameras. A distinct fissure had formed, and Gunner knew he had the target in sight.

Artie continued his count. "Three. Two."

"Stand down! Fox 4 away!"

Gunner pulled up on the controls, managing to evade the detonation that rocked the Starhopper back and forth, almost causing him to crash into the rubble. Within seconds, the blast wave of the nuclear explosion reached the spacecraft, pushing it forward and causing Gunner to fight for control.

A cloud of dust consumed them, making his visibility difficult, but he focused and persevered. He sped forward, wondering when the rubble would dissipate and he'd be clear of the massive debris field that surrounded him.

Banking left and right, he undertook every evasive maneuver he'd learned in the simulator and during his first three missile launches. The only one he didn't utilize was slowing down. Slowing down was not an option.

CHAPTER 54

Wednesday, April 25
On Board the Starhopper

"Hell yeah!" exclaimed Gunner as he broke free of the gravitational pull of the asteroid and soared upward through the ever-burgeoning debris field. He pumped both fists into the air. "We did it, Chief! We blasted that booger!" Gunner honored his mentor by using the term that he'd heard a hundred times, if he'd heard it once.

Gunner, in a rare show of emotion since Heather died, clapped his hands together repeatedly, applauding the result, allowing himself to savor his victory over the planet killer. He knew he'd hit the mark, but he was interested in hearing Artie's own expert analysis.

He glanced over at Chief Rawlings, whose head was leaned back against the headrest of the commander's seat and turned away from him. Gunner reached over to wake him up. When he felt his hand, he knew.

He wanted to close his eyes and try again, but he had to continue to navigate away from the asteroid in the midst of the rubble. He hoped his touch betrayed him, so he shook his mentor's arm.

"Chief, wake up. It's almost over and I'm taking you home. Chief?"

With one eye on the rubble flying all around him, Gunner stretched and pulled Chief Rawlings's head toward him. A trickle of blood had poured from the left side of his mouth and his left ear.

He fell back into his seat and looked at the ceiling to speak to God. "Dammit. We did it. I was taking him home. You couldn't have waited?"

Of course, Gunner didn't get a response. He rarely did, at least that he noticed.

He shook his head and sighed. He gathered himself and slammed his fist on his armrest. He had to keep it together—there was still work to do.

He took a moment to get a good visual of the spacecraft's surroundings. He felt like a NASCAR driver at Talladega Superspeedway. At two hundred miles per hour, the cars rode alongside each other, counting on the experience of their fellow drivers not to make a mistake. One wrong move. One lapse in judgment. One inadvertent lift off the throttle, and half the field would crash into each other.

The Starhopper was boxed in by meteoroids of all shapes and sizes, the resulting debris field of his attack upon IM86. Some passed him while others collided with each other before shooting off in different directions. They were in a race toward Earth, one that began millions of years ago when IM86 was formed, likely from a collision between space rocks much like what he was witnessing all around him.

It was not possible for Gunner to leave the flight deck. He couldn't risk turning over the controls to an autopilot that wasn't programmed for this scenario. Plus, he had a bone to pick with Artie.

"Artie, what part of stand down do you not understand?"

"Major Fox, I am not programmed to self-destruct. In human terms, that is considered suicide."

"Artie, I told you a time might come when I'd need you to stand down. We made a deal."

"Major Fox, deals are made to be broken."

"What? Artie, who told you that?"

"It is part of my programming. Many axioms are."

Gunner rolled his eyes and shook his head side to side. "Artie, I needed you to trust me. Remember, I've got this."

Artie fell silent. He hadn't been asked a direct question, but he was programmed to enter into conversation when appropriate. Gunner surmised he was at a loss for words.

"Major Fox, you have not lied to me. I trust you. I will stand down when requested."

I don't need you to now, Gunner thought to himself, but he didn't want to argue with artificial intelligence. It was bad enough that he was engaging in a conversation with it. He wondered if Artie would become his *Wilson* from the Tom Hanks's movie *Cast Away*.

"Artie, can you provide me an explanation of why we can't outrun the debris field?"

"Yes, Major Fox. The four nuclear detonations created a high level of kinetic energy on 2029 IM86. The resulting blast wave forced the rubble at speeds close to one hundred thousand miles per hour, not uncommon for meteoroids."

"Artie, can you provide me any estimate at this time on when and where the bulk of this debris will strike Earth?"

Artie hesitated. Gunner could feel the AI processing the data, likely using the Starhopper's external radar, telescopes, and sensors to analyze every piece of debris heading toward the planet.

"Major Fox, I am sorry, but I cannot provide you a precise response. Much of the debris field has moved too far ahead of our current position for me to analyze. The gravitational keyhole will have a significant impact on the field as it approaches. The satellites in low-Earth orbit will partially obstruct the rubble as it approaches. The atmosphere will serve to protect Earth from some of the meteoroids."

"Artie, I understand there are a lot of variables. Can you at least provide me an educated guess?"

"Major Fox, I am not programmed to guess. I am prepared to make a hypothesis based upon my knowledge base as supplemented by the current experience."

Gunner was exhausted and exasperated. "Artie, please provide me your hypothesis."

"The debris field will most likely extend as far south as the Equator and as far north as fifty-eight degrees North latitude. It will circumvent the globe, with some regions experiencing a greater impact event than others."

Gunner recalled seeing the larger chunk of IM86 expelled from the leading edge following the first two nukes. "Artie, I observed a piece of the asteroid broken off from the asteroid. Were you able to map its size, velocity, and trajectory?"

"No, Major Fox. It was obscured from our detection within seconds by the rubble field."

Great, thought Gunner to himself. *I just turned one planet killer into three.*

CHAPTER 55

Thursday, April 26
On Board the Starhopper

It was a new day, as evidenced by the clock on the Starhopper's console. As the digital clock ticked past midnight eastern time, Gunner realized that in space, only your body could tell you if it was night or day, or time to sleep or be awake. His mind, and body that was still pumping with adrenaline, didn't care that it had been over twenty-four hours since he'd slept.

"Gimme a freakin' break!" yelled Gunner in frustration as the Starhopper continued to get battered the closer he got to Earth. NASA tracked in excess of twenty-two thousand pieces of space junk in Earth orbit at any given time.

That was on a normal day. This day was not normal.

The meteoroids raced well ahead of the Starhopper, leaving a swath of destruction in their wake. The rocks crashed through the satellites inhabiting low-Earth orbit like bird shot through a cardboard target. The extremely lightweight materials, such as aluminum and composite alloys like nickel and cadmium, never stood a chance against the pummeling.

The Starhopper was much sturdier than the small communications satellites in orbit, but it was only able to take so much abuse or it might suffer the same fate as Gunner's last test flight in the F/A XX. This time, like a tight-roping Wallenda walking between two skyscrapers without a net, Gunner didn't have a parachute to find his way to planet Earth.

"Artie, give me a damage report. I'm having difficulty controlling—" He cut off his sentence as a large piece of IM86 sailed past the spaceship, causing Gunner to reflexively duck.

"Major Fox, three exhaust gas ports have been damaged. Two of the missile supports have been partially removed from the Starhopper, which is causing drag as we approach Earth's atmosphere."

"Artie, all of this is causing us to veer off course."

"Major Fox, your speed is too great."

"No shit, Artie! It's either run or get run over."

"Major Fox, may I suggest a different landing destination. My analysis of the western United States renders it unsafe for landing. Your speed is too fast for the planned California location."

Gunner knew about the speed issue, but only Artie was capable of analyzing the projected impact of the rubble sent hurtling through space from IM86.

"Major Fox, T minus four minutes until orbiter rotation."

As the Starhopper returned to Earth, it was designed to rotate tail-first in the direction of travel to prepare for the orbital maneuvering system engines to fire. Referred to as the deorbit burn, the time of ignition was scheduled to occur one hour before landing.

Gunner had to make a decision. Based upon Artie's analysis, Vandenberg Air Force Base might not be safe for landing. He considered his alternatives. Back to Boca Chica? Kennedy? A cornfield in Nebraska? Hell, the Gulf of Mexico was a nice big landing zone, and it was close to home.

Yeah, *that's the ticket*, he said to himself, one of Heather's favorite phrases. He could hear her voice in his head, and for a change it didn't make him sad. In fact, it encouraged him, giving him a new source of strength.

"Artie, we're modifying our course for touchdown in the Gulf of Mexico."

"Major Fox, the Starhopper is designed for a land-based landing."

Gunner laughed. "Today, we're gonna have a change of plans."

The deorbit burn lasted almost four minutes, slowing the Starhopper enough to begin its descent. Gunner checked the straps on his seat.

"Major Fox, our speed and trajectory will not allow for a Gulf of Mexico landing."

"Why not?"

"Major Fox, I have detected a significant amount of man-made debris in the Starhopper's path. It will likely damage the spacecraft beyond repair."

"What's our next best option, Artie?"

"Major Fox, I suggest the Caribbean Sea."

Major studied the flight deck monitors. Then he looked ahead, as the Starhopper had completed its rotation back to where the nose faced Earth, and started the final glide to touchdown.

"I see it," he said as the sun began to rise and reflect on the shattered satellites. They twinkled in the dark sky like shards of glass floating in the air.

Gunner focused on his controls, navigating the Starhopper closer to Earth. The large body of water that had likely been created by an asteroid sixty-six million years ago revealed itself through the clouds. It was a big blue target surrounded by islands to its north and the jungles of South America just beyond it.

Suddenly, the Starhopper was knocked into a nose-over-tail tumble. Gunner barely caught a glimpse of the burning fireball that sped past, catching a piece of the nuclear missile supports as it flew by.

Bells, whistles, and Artie created a cacophony of warnings that screamed at Gunner from all directions. He tried desperately to correct the spacecraft as it tumbled toward Earth. He hoped that the atmosphere would provide him some *grip* so that he could take over the controls, similar to the way the space shuttle would land.

Like an airplane. Something he understood implicitly.

Gunner was becoming disoriented from the relentless rolling motion. The Starhopper was slow to respond to his fighting the controls. Outside the spacecraft, the sky view was changing. It was familiar. He'd been there before.

The stratosphere.

"I've got this," he muttered to himself.

You've got this, my love. Heather's voice joined in.

Gunner struggled, but the one-hundred-twenty-foot-long spacecraft finally began to respond. At this point, he didn't concern himself with where he was going to land. He simply wanted to guide the less-than-responsive bird to a landing that didn't body-slam him into the Earth.

"Terrain. Pull up! Terrain. Pull up!"

Artie's robotic voice warned Gunner that he was too close to the ground. He was coming in hot, but he couldn't slow down.

Then he felt it. The tops of trees were clipped by the missile supports. Two *streamers*, forty-foot-wide parachutes designed to increase drag on the spacecraft to aid in braking, were deployed and forced Gunner forward in his seat. They grabbed air, and trees, and then with a massive jolt, the Starhopper hit the ground and began to slide sideways, crashing through the jungle and hopping across a small river.

Then it rolled. Over and over, breaking foliage and throwing Gunner's arms and head around. Bits and pieces of the spacecraft were being torn apart with each roll, the trees taking a hefty toll on the machine that likely just saved them from being scorched.

Eventually, it was mercifully over. The Starhopper had found a final resting place. Its top was torn open like a can of sardines, leaving Gunner to look upward at the light show taking place in the mesosphere as the early meteors, the remnants of IM86, were burning up.

Gunner looked into the sky and mumbled the words every space shuttle pilot hoped to say when they lifted off into space. The words were more than symbolic of a successful mission. They were an indicator that the pilot had made it home alive, which was always Gunner's number one priority.

"Wheels stopped, Houston."

Then everything faded to darkness.

THANK YOU FOR READING
ASTEROID: DIVERSION!

If you enjoyed it, I'd be grateful if you'd take a moment to write a short review for each of the books in the series (just a few words are needed) and post it on Amazon. Amazon uses complicated algorithms to determine what books are recommended to readers. Sales are, of course, a factor, but so are the quantities of reviews my books get. By taking a few seconds to leave a review, you help me out and also help new readers learn about my work.

And before you go …

SIGN UP for Bobby Akart's mailing list to receive special offers, bonus content, and you'll be the first to receive news about new releases in the Asteroid series. Visit: www.BobbyAkart.com

VISIT Amazon.com/BobbyAkart for more information on the Asteroid series, the Doomsday series, the Yellowstone series, the Lone Star series, the Pandemic series, the Blackout series, the Boston Brahmin series and the Prepping for Tomorrow series totaling thirty-eight novels, including over thirty Amazon #1 Bestsellers in forty-plus fiction and nonfiction genres. Visit Bobby Akart's website for informative blog entries on preparedness, writing, and a behind-the-scenes look into his novels.

Made in the USA
Monee, IL
19 March 2021